The Forgotten Condition of Things

Robert Froese

Flat Bay Press

Flat Bay Press
P.O. Box 217
Harrington, Maine 04643

Copyright © 2001 by Robert Froese

All rights reserved

This is a work of fiction. All incidents, names, and characters are either imaginary or are used fictitiously, and any resemblance to actual persons, living or dead, is entirely coincidental.

Printed on recycled paper

Acknowledgements

Thanks to Michael Alpert and Bernie Vinzani for assistance with book design. Thanks also to Martin Ferrick, Jim Lehman, Cindy Speaker, Constance Hunting, John Burns, and especially my wife, Leonore, for answers, suggestions, criticism, and support during the writing of this novel.

ISBN 0-9715382-0-4

for Leonore

The Forgotten Condition of Things

~S~

THERE IS SOMEONE standing behind me. I can feel it. Or maybe she has made some noise—silk on wool, something like that—though I'm not aware of it.

I am glad it isn't Dr. Tarantula, or Dr. Sun.

In fact, I know exactly who it is who has moved this close. I don't turn around. I don't move a muscle. For awhile she stays—offering herself. It's plain. None of the others would do this.

Then, some time later, I realize she's gone.

Another time. Probably the same place.

A fly buzzes against the window, knowing nothing of glass. It falls to the sill and is up again, trailing a gown of dust. Over and over this happens. I've been watching for awhile now.

Something about it seems wrong.

The fly wants to get on with it. The real business of its life is cut off, frustrated by glass, a thing beyond its reckoning, a thing out of another dimension, as far as the fly is concerned. Why?

We are flung through this world like planets of divergent suns.

To my right, Mrs. Dibrizzi, an explosion of gray frizz in a housecoat, sits down on the sofa gradually. She ignores the magazine rack, as though at a terrific mental effort, and concentrates instead on the cup of tea she's carried with her to the sofa. She seems to wish the cup merely to remain resting in the palm of her hand, a simple equilibrium. She doesn't drink the tea.

Maybe — this is Rye's idea — Mrs. Dibrizzi is inching her way along a higher plane of existence. We know as much about what is really going on with her as the fly knows about the windowpane.

Every thought is like waking up, if you're really paying attention.

For awhile, June, they have me again. In the fluorescence and stale air, lemon wallpaper and tile. I think I must be back here for a reason.

The reason crouches somewhere overhead like an animal, waiting.

I don't know yet whether the animal is friendly.

This will sound nuts. You haven't spent time here.

Rye says that floor tile is the underlying justification for this place, and I believe he is on to something.

Never mind the carpet.

Floor tile delineates the spiritual dynamics of these rooms. People plant their shoe soles on it, their minds propelled in maverick orbits. And it doesn't yield an angstrom. Tile isn't just the skin for the floor, a covering for plywood and I-beams. It is the fundamental assumption, the very reason the floor exists.

Tile. Sure, you'll hear talk about its ugliness, but everyone comes under its influence. All day long they stride back and forth over it, as if it's the floor of the universe. Glossy and blank, unforgiving, it is the answer they've all been looking for.

Now it waits for Mrs. Dibrizzi to relinquish her hold on the teacup.

She does.

The plastic cup falls and bounces against the buffed surface, spilling a Rorschach of tea at her slippered feet. A moment later someone will mop this disturbance, this blemish. Things can happen here all of a sudden, and they don't alter a thing.

Mrs. Dibrizzi's watery eyes stare beyond her open hands, her hair a tortured enigma. Her expression hasn't changed. It never changes. It is as if she's been frozen in the moment of almost remembering.

Autumn 3

Wherein our heroine first hears of the Wild Child.

Now in the liqid half-light of dawn, Evelyn sits angling a spoon into her grapefruit. In this old farmhouse (still new to her) on the edge of the Maine North Woods, she feels—as she is—dressed for work: charcoal skirt and olive-grey sweater, a double droop of coral beads nearing the rim of the bowl as she leans a bit to meet the spoon.

Evelyn's thinking has just surfaced from a wordless perception that things appear not to be moving. It is the first week of October, and the window at the kitchen table is open. Birds twitter in the trees bordering the lawn. More than three weeks ago, summer was supposed to have ended with an abrupt cast-iron frost that browned all the gardens and started the maples turning. But since then there has been nothing except sun and haze and an interminable stillness in which, now and then, you can hear leaves dropping.

The papers are full of Columbus Day sales. Evelyn, here at the breakfast table, has almost nowhere else to look but at a full page trumpeting one of these sales in this morning's *Bangor Daily News*, held up two feet away from her like a sloping billboard. While finishing her grapefruit, she contemplates this, the rationale behind a Columbus Day sale. She does not get far with it.

The newspaper shudders. Evelyn slides her grapefruit dish aside, replacing it with the bowl of muesli, and from behind the paper she hears a grunt of bland astonishment.

Evelyn's husband, Richard, it's been said, has a handsome, angular face. But at the moment she can't see a thing of him except his fingers, a sprig of his hair, and a shoulder and elbow jutting from the Columbus Day ad. If he resembles anything, it is a personified newspaper, an impression she enjoys for its spine-tingling novelty, until something tells her to drop it. She goes back to digging at her oat flakes, nut meats, and yogurt, leaving him to pursue an existence she stops short of imagining on the other side of the newsprint partition. He won't eat until later, until after she is gone.

It isn't that she minds. In fact, she enjoys the solitude, especially at this hour, so soon after the unraveling of sleep. She plies her spoon and chews delicately, avoiding noise. She is waiting, counting on the aggregate of her being to reform, to recapture its familiar, indefinite substance.

"I tell you . . . ."

With the suddenness of his voice, the silence blares. Evelyn turns to the window, where the birds are keeping their distance, a swarm of blots, flitting and twitching among the branches.

" . . . the State of Maine keeps up the way it's going, you're not going to have a hospital to work in."

Richard's arm emerges, feels for his coffee cup, and is gone. It seems, as Evelyn thinks about it, that he has been on the same page for some time now. She hears him sip.

He peeks out from behind the paper, as if to confirm her presence.

"Here's something." There is a pause. "You remember last week, that assassination attempt?"

Evelyn holds her spoon suspended. She looks at him.

He says, "That girl, the one who tried to shoot the Governor."

She crosses her booted legs beneath the table, stares as if through the newspaper, as if focusing on the assassination attempt, as if on the edge of remembering. At last she shakes her head, goes back to her muesli.

"Don't tell me you didn't hear about it."

Evelyn's gaze veers to the tablecloth. Soon she will have to leave for work.

"I might have heard. I probably wasn't paying attention."

"It was all over the news."

After a pause, Evelyn says, "What about it?"

"Alright. The Governor was out at a groundbreaking, you know, Hardwood Hill, where that mammoth resort is going in? And right in the middle of the ceremony some girl sneaks out of the woods with a deer rifle and takes a shot at the guy."

"Where was this?"

"Aurora. About twenty miles north of here, on the Airline."

"But she didn't actually hit him."

Richard chuckles. "Be better if she had. The bullet ricocheted off a bulldozer, shattered the windshield in some parked car."

"A girl? How old was she?"

"Oh, and the other thing, she wasn't wearing shoes." His eyebrows jump. "Beginning of October in the Maine woods—a barefoot assassin."

Dank air, mingled with the agitation of the crickets and birds, seeps through the open window at her shoulder.

"You ought to see the pictures of her. Wild little thing."

"Why was she trying to shoot the governor?"

Richard shakes his head. "They've had her in jail a week now, she hasn't said a word. Either she won't . . . " He reaches again for his coffee. " . . . or she can't."

"What do you mean?"

"Really, Ev, you ought to read the papers, at least watch the news. The story is, it took five guys—construction workers *and* state troopers—to get her to the ground, in the process of which they knocked her senseless. She wound up in the hospital, unconscious over eight hours. And now she doesn't talk."

Something in this is bothering Evelyn. All this information rushing at her from the wrong angle—an aborted assassination, a brutal arrest, a wild child in the woods with a deer rifle, barely twenty miles from here. Where on this earth has she *been* the last few days?

Richard has turned back to the story. "Anyway, what I was getting to . . . says here she's scheduled for psychiatric evaluation. Maybe you'll be having a look at her."

Evelyn finds her coffee. She says, "Probably not. I think they handle forensic assessments in the jail." But she isn't sure about this. She has been at the hospital barely three weeks.

"Oh." Richard opens to a different page. "Couldn't you still be one of the . . . examiners, whatever they're called?" His voice is even. He is already losing interest.

She sips her coffee, her eyes trying out the pine cabinetry.

"Assessment team," she says finally, as though something has pulled the words out of her. She turns again to look out the window, where the birds now are motionless as if painted to a plaster sky.

It begins, as it has before, with ringing in the left ear. Then a rush, and the hearing in both ears goes cottony. And suddenly she is thrust right out of herself—how else to put it? Everything has become unthinkable. She can find no stillness. Her heart seems to have been torn from her, leaving her in a rupture between now and the next moment. There is the feeling that, for her, there may *be* no next moment.

Richard—somehow at the brink of her vision—looms forward, spreading the newspaper on the table.

"Hm!" he exclaims flatly.

The coffee cup in Evelyn's hands seems like the center of something. She holds on to it tightly, exerting disproportionate pressure on so small an article, but perhaps it helps. Her thumbs work back and forth over the porcelain, which feels to her like rubber.

She gets up from the table, finds herself in the linearity of movement: what is begun can carry one through a sequence of steps. Her bowl and spoon go into the sink, where also she dumps her coffee. She is reluctant to let go of the cup. Turning to leave, she takes it with her, passing by Richard shifting in his chair, absorbed in the paper. Out the door, she thinks it will be something for him to figure out, what has happened to the cup.

* * * * *

Jodie, their closest neighbor, lives about a quarter of a mile away. A woman of maybe thirty—shoulder-length, straight, honey-blonde hair—she's recently separated from her husband. Each morning, with two kids in the car, she pulls out of her driveway around the time Evelyn leaves. And when Evelyn returns, there she is too, sometimes a few minutes ahead, sometimes behind. Once in awhile on weekends, she sees Jody in her garden on the side lawn. Otherwise she seems to stick in that house—with or without the kids, Evelyn can't be sure. She never sees the kids outside.

One Sunday morning early, hearing a car drive off, they rise to find on their doorstep a cardboard box filled with zucchinis.

Richard brings the box in, sets it on spread-out newspaper on the kitchen table. The box bulges at the sides under the weight of the zuchinis, which are like great green, bloated marks of punctuation. Richard picks through them, persistently, as though hunting for something at the bottom of the box.

"Can you believe it?" he says.

His expression looks wounded.

~S~

IMAGINE, June, no warning at all. It's only my second or third day here. Everyone's run off to meet some new admit, leaving me finally alone. Plopped on the edge of the bed they call mine, I'm ready to close my eyes. Maybe I'll have a minute to myself, a chance to get some focus.

And all of a sudden there he is, his whiskered face inquiring, peering into mine, his breath ragged and sour. He smells as if he's slept in his clothes. I just keep staring straight ahead, but it's hard. There's something about his eyes, probing. A full minute, it must be. I'm thinking, I can't take much more of this.

"Ahh-haa?" I hear him muttering. Like it's a question. "Ahh-haa?"

He backs off then, bows at the waist, lifts my hand, and kisses it.

"His deepest apologies." His head bobs. "The name is Roland Rye. Dr. Roland Rye."

What now?

"Had the man a speech impediment, the name might be Dr. Why. Which, applied to him, would fit like Spandex. But, in any case, apologies . . . *mm* . . . It is only that this academy encourages certain expectations, or—should he say?—nonexpectations. It scarcely matters. What goes without saying is that he has been resident here far too long."

A brown suit, I'd say second-hand. No tie. Slippers. His crinkly, grayish hair could use combing, and the guy badly needs a shave. Dr. Rye.

What am I supposed to do?

The hallway is quiet. I've never had anyone kiss my hand before. I don't know why, but I look him straight in the eye and whisper, "You seem pretty damned sure of yourself."

"Ah." Finger in the air. "Sometimes yes, sometimes no. The trouble is . . . *mm* . . . in the Doctor's case, the self is equally sure of him. He'll never gain the upper hand where that beast is concerned. However. However. One thing is clear: the Doctor is quite, quite sure of you."

I just look at him. I don't say anything.

He shrugs, sways back to cock an ear at the hallway, then leans into me. "You go right ahead, by the way, with that enchanting performance of yours, meditating on antimatter or whatever it is you do. Dr. Rye, you will discover, practices a different subterfuge altogether: that is to say, to maintain at all costs an unfailingly gratuitous discourse, gushings upon gushings of words with all the appearance of meaning. Which goes to prove the cunning of the derelict mind. His meanderings can run on endlessly. And without consequence. It's all the same to him. It doesn't even begin to compensate for the color of these walls."

His posture sags. His eyes drift. I think the guy is really a lost soul.

But he bounces right back. "Here! What he has in mind—to give an example—something like the grandiloquent haywire in which he presently has you ensnared. Or does he? In your case, it is difficult to tell. He might as well be talking to the paper towel dispenser, not that that deters him in the least. No, not at all. Here in The House, in this macabre establishment, the Doctor speaks to everyone and anyone, even—he kids you not!—the staff. He actually takes pleasure inflicting this mischief, alternately boring these professionals to tears and amusing them. Only yesterday . . . *mm* . . . in full view of the nurse's station he held ardent discussion with the laundry cart. It is a fact! So, you see, should ever, ever the opportunity for genuine dialogue arise . . . ."

I feel him take my hand again, his hands trembling.

" . . . he can . . . *mm* . . . commune for hours without raising, by way of suspicion, so much as a nurse's eyebrow."

This is Dr. Rye, my first friend here. He goes on and on, his voice just above a whisper, his eyes favoring a space a little to my left. It's like he says, he might be talking to me or to something else in the room. His voice is beautiful, I think, except for that little *"mm"*, the high note of panic, like the voice of someone inside trying to get out. And, all the time, his hands flit from his pockets to his beard and, during the tangles of his longer sentences, stabbing the air between us with marks of punctuation. I like him. I have a good feeling about him.

But then the air turns electric. I know what's coming.

Androscoggin appears, like a sound made visible. She circles the doctor, showing a rare curiosity. She says, *This one is put together out of too many pieces. It's no wonder he's falling apart.*

I'm afraid Rye will see her, hear her, and in fact there is a jitter about the eyes. But it's the same when I speak, or even think about speaking. I see him shrink. His hands begin to stammer. His eyes dart for time. He likes more to talk than to listen.

But now all at once he stiffens. His head swivels.

I barely hear the cushiony squeak against the tile in the hall.

His hands dig into his pockets, and his voice booms as he heads for the door. "Please, please, don't bother with Question Twelve. It's a multiple choice. There are sources aplenty for that kind of information, here in The House. They keep files on just about everyone, as just about everyone knows. The place has all the virulence of a data bank, whatever that might be. He doesn't keep up with the changing times. But he'll be happy, in any event, to consider your case. Perhaps over lunch some day."

At the edge of my vision, the dark bulk of him disappears into the hall.

Then a different movement—a nurse poking her head around the jamb, checking on me.

Androscoggin hovers, as if studying the actuality of a doorway.

The House

In which Evelyn becomes acquainted with a number of the inhabitants.

THERE ARE MORNINGS when, emerging from her car, her hand still on the door metal, she is stopped cold. It may be just a matter of getting used to the place (or facing up to what it reminds her of). But there she stands, staring, and she can't help it. The edifice of the Hospital is so much to take in. Towering and grey, slate-roofed, a century old, it coils labyrinth-like along the crown of this hill among timeless palisades of pine and ledge. Merely the sight would have been enough to inspire the awe and calm of finality in anyone depositing a loved one for safekeeping here in the company of the clouds. Whatever was brought here, one could rest assured, would need go no further.

Who knows what was inspired in the patients themselves?—fretting out the back windows of the automobiles that brought them, then left without them. Evelyn can't judge from the patients she has seen, who refer to the Hospital as "here" or, sometimes, as "The House." They say, "I can't wait to get out of here." Or, "At least in The House nobody bothers me."

She can't quite decide for herself, either, what it means to be working in this hospital. Her three weeks so far have been a pressure and a blur, without even a moment to set up her office. She is supposed to have been devoting her days to

Admissions, where before long she expects permanent assignment. But mostly she has been filling in, relieving overloads for the D and E Ward psychologists. "It'll give you a broader picture," Gary Benjamin said, during the first-day tour through the corridors. It is one of the Chief Psychologist's duties, painting a reasonable face on things.

So here she is bending her attention beside her desk, booted legs crossed beneath her clipboard, familiarizing herself with the charts of patients she has not yet seen. From time to time she raises her eyes, as if seeking the relief of a window. But the window is at her back, and her eyes instead run over the stack of cardboard boxes, lettered in black-felt marker, containing her books. A hung tile ceiling, a dusty parquet floor, and a fireplace—this is the improbable configuration of her office. For furniture, she has a desk, the chair she sits in, and a wastebasket. Bookcase and filing cabinet, she has been told, are on order.

The very first week, she asked about the dust. The janitor—a small man, quick in his movements—stood stiff-armed. "Not a lot we can do," he said. He pointed to the grate in the floor, shielding a hole large enough to swallow her chair. "There's the dust of centuries down there."

She nodded, passing over the exaggeration, but asked, since the room had baseboard heating, whether it wouldn't make sense simply to put a cover over the grate.

The janitor shook his head. "Part of the ventilation system."

"The ventilation system."

"Cover it and the State'd be on us." He was bending now, getting on with his work, lining the wastebasket with clear plastic. "We're required to keep them open. By law."

"I see."

Backing out the doorway, he saluted her. "You have a good one."

She was on the verge of nodding, on the verge of some reply, but he was gone then, and her gaze instead was drawn down through the grate, into the murk of that cavity communicating with God-knows-what.

* * * * *

She is reading, her eyes running over the particulars of a woman rendered in print. Louise Dyer, a twenty-six-year-old waitress and single mother. Louise. Whose existence has assumed the consistency of glue. Who one day instead of waiting on tables, was discovered by a coworker to be standing in an alley behind the restaurant, in the rain, "soaked to the skin." Whose home life congealed to a mishmash of soiled clothes, unopened mail, and mouldering food. Who would no longer leave her third-floor apartment, even to buy groceries, for fear of not being able to make it back up the stairs. Finally her eight-year-old daughter, Amber, telephoned a neighbor to report that Louise would not get out of bed. "There was a fire here," she added. Something had ignited on the kitchen stove, blackening the ceiling.

Here in the arena of patient charts Evelyn is an attentive audience, turning pages, watching human figures, indistinctly formed, play out their disintegrations in words. She looks forward to this part of her work, which doesn't seem like work at all. She enjoys reading, apprehending, within the austere texture of print, these discrete bits of information. Louise's strict Roman Catholic father. Her uncle's electroconvulsive therapy. Her own attempt during a prior, manic episode to start her own church: "The Church of Colors." Louise Dyer.

But suddenly there is the actual Louise: no longer the human figure constructed of words. She sits impenetrable, stoop-shouldered, not five feet away, her unannounced red-rimmed eyes casting about the featurelessness of the office. A pilling powder-blue sweater and shiny mustard-gold slacks. Evelyn could lean right across, run her fingertips over the fibers of these clothes. That's how near the woman is, how actual.

"You're Louise, is that right?"

The patient flings a look at the wall.

"I'm Evelyn Moore. I expect Dr. Astor's told you, I'll be replacing him for a few days while he's away. I'll be working with Dr. Kilgallen."

Nothing. Nothing from Louise, except the activity of her hands in the hollow of her lap, scrambling over one another like newborn puppies.

The chart lies on Evelyn's desk. She scoops it up, scrutinizes it, though this is unnecessary. She remembers perfectly well what is in it. Louise has been diagnosed bipolar, moderate-to-severe, her treatment hindered by an extraordinary intolerance to medication. She has suffered severe side-effects — headache, nausea, arrhythmia, tardive dyskinesia — from a broad spectrum of drugs, including tricyclics, MAOIs, and second-generation antidepressants. John Kilgallen's frustration is recorded as well: "The unusually arduous search for an appropriate therapy for Louise has been considerably complicated by her own recalcitrance: specifically, by her repeated refusals of electroconvulsive therapy and by lapses in her compliance with the regimens of her various medications."

Evelyn flips back through the pages of the chart. Drugs, drugs, and more drugs. Has anyone even bothered to talk to the woman?

She sets the chart aside on the dusty gloss of her desk.

"Louise, can you tell me how you're feeling this morning?"

The patient's head veers and her eyes close, as if Evelyn's voice is inflicting pain.

Hinges squeal on the office door adjacent, belonging to Paul Sun. The patient's eyes crack open, and they remain fixed and oblique as the Vibram soles of the doctor chirp away down the hall.

"It's alright, Louise. Tell me what it is that's troubling you."

True, the right sort of knowledge about a patient's past gives a useful shape to the patient, a shape the therapist can begin to work with. But what sits before Evelyn is not a useful shape. If anything, it is something hostile to this, a perplexity of flesh and suffering with an evasive will of its own, a will running often contrary to the patient's own best interests.

The way Louise sits hunched over, Evelyn is seeing more of her hair than of her face. And when finally she looks up again, still it isn't at Evelyn. Anywhere but there.

"What is it, Louise?"

The patient responds with a toss of the head, indeterminate, perhaps involuntary. A hand flies from her lap to rake the strings of her hair.

"My . . . neck." The first word a whisper, the second breaking hoarsely from her throat. Eyes shut tight.

"Yes?"

The head droops, and the patient recedes like a tide. From beneath the wrack of hair, an eye blinks open and closed, open and closed, staring, perhaps at the fireplace.

Within Evelyn's own face and neck, there awaits a musculature, the miraculous chemistry of which somehow achieves her countenance, her expression. The particular mechanisms for this are veiled, precipitous, but at the moment relaxed and ready: a proportioning of acetylcholine, calcium ions, and certain enzymes. She does not have to think about it. It is part of the design of living: the less she thinks about it, the better. Quickly she says, "Louise, can you tell me how your neck feels?"

For the first time, the patient looks at her.

"How I feel is shitty!" She leans forward, a bony hand clamped like a starfish at the base of her skull. "The way they frig with my head . . . ." Her face retreats behind a weave of fingers, from which Evelyn hears a thin sound, like water running through pipe.

"Louise . . . ."

Now the patient is shaking her head, fingers riding up into her hair. "I'm not stupid, Doctor. I am not stupid. I can feel what's going on. You think I can't? Look here. Lookit." She flops forward, elbows jutting at the walls. Her fingertips ravage through her hair, exposing gashes of white scalp. "Lookit."

Evelyn, uncrossing her legs, leans forward. She feels through the thatch and rope of the patient's hair, dull orange-blonde ending in dun-colored roots. A mild rash, flaking of the scalp. Perhaps a temperature. And, in the air that seems to thicken, enveloping the patient, there is something more. A zone or an aura. Like radiant misery.

"And I know just how they're doing it." The patient, still bent forward, is talking into the floor. "Their meds. Damned little time capsules, they're not fooling anybody. You think I'm blind? They got things written on them."

"Louise." She lets her hand fall to the patient's shoulder, gives it a reassuring squeeze. "I see a slight rash there. And you may have a bit of a temperature. But I don't see anything else."

Hands gripping her knees, the patient rocks from side to side.

"However, I will talk to Dr. Kilgallen about your medication."

"I'm not talking to him. Not to anybody. Him and his pills, they're frigging killing me."

Beneath the mop of the patient's hair, her mustard-gold slacks are stained wet with tears. Her fingers wipe at them. "I'm not taking any more. I'm not. You tell them."

Evelyn is nodding. "If you're experiencing discomfort because of your medication, then Dr. Kilgallen needs to know about that."

"Discomfort."

Straightening up, then bending over again, the patient flashes a smile cut deep as a wound. It seems she can not sit still. It is as if she has an itch that needs every part of her body to quell.

"Discompert," she says, her voice cooling down, vacant.

"Alright, Louise, how about this."

The patient is rocking faintly, her gaze averted, seeming to scan again and again the recess of the fireplace.

"Suppose I were to speak right away to Dr. Kilgallen."

She sees no sign that the patient has heard.

"Juscompert," is what the patient says, shaking her head.

~S~

I WAS BROUGHT HERE out of a storm.
 The police hurried ahead, held open doors, urged me in. I was swallowed, washed down hallways with the rain. They moved me deceptively, in stages, but I could tell I was losing ground, sliding, cascading toward the belly of something hard, angular, and dark.
 Later I was paraded, exhibited in rooms with fluorescent lights. They forced me to sit. My eyes were wet. For something to do, I blinked them, turning the ring of probing, joking faces to crystal and then blur. The voices I heard seemed to come, not from these faces, but from another time. I could feel strands of myself unraveling, being drawn in different directions.
 It was then, as I sat there—my neck pinned back toward the ceiling while one of them fooled with my eyes—it was then I heard that other sound. I needed something to pay attention to, anything but what was happening to me in that room. So I listened. It droned on, like a ship's engine heard from somewhere inside the hull. An engine, propelling this place, with all of us in it, toward some destination none of us knew.
 Only the day before, I'd felt I was in for a change. I'd been in jail a week. The guard would talk, the words would spring from his mouth and click around the floor of my cell like grasshoppers. I sat at the edge of my mattress, less than a

ghost, the life of the place going on around me as though I weren't even a memory. Outside the bars of my window, the maples held onto their leaves.

Then they came for me. And by the time I got a look out of a window here, those leaves were a wet skin over the ground.

Word must have come down from somewhere: express delivery. So they shot me through that storm in a Blue-Silver Ford, state trooper deluxe. All the time hammering rain. I was hurried from one dry place to another, jail to the cruiser, cruiser to Admissions, handcuffed. There were moments I wanted to say something, compliment their efficiency, anything to nudge them a little. But I kept quiet. The cruiser cut like a shark through the traffic: bedraggled invisible souls stalled in the gray downpour, trying to imagine their way out of the stoplights and one-way streets, all that mini-mart and car-wash sadness. Then we hit the interstate and drove into the wind.

On a hill, through the rain, I saw the black stone roofs of this place, appearing and reappearing among the pines, nearer and nearer.

After the turn in through the gate, the cruiser slowed, and so did my blood. Blacktop wound ahead under trees, the great trunks rising out of the lawns like doorways through which we passed, unknowing, into the world of mists. We were losing momentum, rolling upward through a wet green room, a landscape without sky.

I was trying to take it in.

It wasn't the handcuffs I resented so much as the glass, sealing me off, closing me in with the upholstery and paralysis, the sullen breath of my three escorts. The one in front of me, next to the trooper driving, craned his neck completely around to stare at me. Then something crackled on the radio that they all had to listen to, the trooper's neck tense, his hands gnawing the wheel. We were passing a pond just then, which I don't think any of them saw. In the shadows there, a few ducks paddled tentatively, wary of Blue-Silver.

But there weren't any people out, I noticed. Not here on this hill. The rain had driven them all inside, deep into corners.

The police held a yellow slicker over me. Very polite. No chance for the rain to wet my skin or hair. Saving me for lethal injections, I guess. I remember, that was the day I took the vow of silence. Not so much a vow, really, as a recognition.

There wasn't any reason to talk anyway. They asked me questions as if they knew me. As if it had all been taken care of. I was already there on their pages, for them to thumb through. They'd delivered the real me on their clipboards only to verify against this mess bundled in from the October weather.

That was why I decided on silence. And why I ate the papers from that lawyer's briefcase. My own defense attorney. After that they looked at me differently.

If I'm going to say something, I like someone to be listening. Words weigh too much to throw them around like sand.

Locked Room

Feeling poised on the brink of some discovery, Evelyn is introduced to himself, Dr. Roland Rye.

J OHN KILGALLEN is busy with a patient.
 Returning, lingering just inside the doorway to her office, she glances from the empty fireplace to the wall over her desk, where her eyes find its single feature, a picture hook. Among the cardboard boxes to her left is one down low, larger than the others. She pulls this out, tears open the flaps. The print is right on top. Berthe Morisot's *La Lecture*, given to her by Richard, how many years ago? The child, reading amid the greenery of the terrace, at peace. On the mounting board it weighs next to nothing. She holds it at the edges with the fingertips of both hands, lifts it. The hook catches, pulling the print flat against the wall, where it hangs, gladdening already the sallowness of the day.

* * * * *

 Despite Richard's talent for argument, Evelyn feels it is understood between them that hers is the superior intellect. She isn't sure how the understanding came about—certain key victories of hers in the skirmishes by which minds try one another. In any event, she has preserved within herself a locked room, to which Richard has not found the key. She believes he has looked for it. But by now it is clear that he has given up, somehow content. It is inside this locked room that she hides away all the doubt her husband assumes he exorcised years ago. A storehouse of doubt. A virtual time bomb—that's the current phrase—a virtual time bomb of unbelief.

These days she takes in Richard's talk, his stories and his speculation during dinner and over drinks, as one might listen to a pleasant, mildly inventive music, say a well-executed cocktail piano, something that does not begin and end, but rather simply flows. She wonders at times just how he can keep it going. Surely, somewhere inside, he has his own locked room, where dwells a childlike vulnerability.

Or does he?

She has watched him hanging his shirts, waterproofing his moccasins, slipping on his socks. His preoccupation over his supply of socks. He seems at times, for all his muscle, too thinly constructed, as if he might at the slightest adversity fly apart, or move back to Connecticut. What is it that holds the man together? She realizes, of course, human beings are like this, their peculiar energies waxing and waning, and, if she is to trust in the forbearance of others when it comes to her own weaknesses, she must certainly exercise for him, her husband, a similar patience. And yet there are times she can't quite muster it. There are times, in fact, she would like to grab him by the hair and shake him. These waves of misgiving arise uninvited, during quiet moments that almost every day now blossom in the current of her routine. It is a devastating objectivity, she thinks, that allows such incisions into the marital trust.

She believes this.

* * * * *

"Well, well. And what brings you, might he ask?"

The patient's oiled-walnut voice catches her in the act of consulting his chart. She does not actually witness the movement of his lips, and by the time her eyes have taken him in, his eyes are elsewhere—the greeting and the man unconnected, yet to be put together.

She says, "I'm here to see you."

The patient's fingers worry the grizzly stubble along his jaw. Roland Rye, seated close by her desk, is supposed to be fifty-two. By his appearance, she would have guessed ten years older.

"Well..." He looks at her. "...now you see him." He looks away. "Now you do not."

She knows it from his chart. Still it takes her by surprise. "You prefer to refer to yourself as 'he'?"

Lighting up with what looks like eagerness, he moves to adjust his posture. "Oh, yes, prefer to refer...." Fingers ransacking gray, lionish hair. "Yes, certainly. Certainly he does."

"Can I ask why?"

"Oh. Oh." Taking a breath, he subsides, examining the backs of his hands, first one, then the other. He murmurs, "It is a question. It has been asked before . . . *mm* . . . many times. Certainly many times. He would speak the way ee cummings writes, without capitals or punctuation, but then who would notice? No, it appears unacceptable to them, that is to say, not the question, but this perplexing absence of the capital 'I.'" He draws the letter in the air between them. "In his talk, that is to say. It's absence."

"Well, I don't know that I'd call it unacceptable. Let's just say it can be confusing."

"Ah, well." He raises a forefinger. "You might consider . . . *mm* . . . ."

It is distractingly like another voice, this little high-pitched "*mm*," a single-syllable whimper, marking progress like the tap-tap of a cane through pauses in his speech.

"That is to say, it may be a random omission, merely a matter of chance, the lack of this ego-evocative pronoun whenever and wherever he opens his mouth. Though that would seem to promise, if not require. Would it not? That at some future moment, by way of compensation . . . *mm* . . . you may hear his speech lapse into a virtual blithering popcorn of the first person. Hm? It could happen."

It is not easy pinpointing the presence of this man. Aside from his speech and the little second voice, there are the fingers wriggling with energy, pointing, inflecting, drawing punctuation as he talks. His eyes meanwhile chase around the room, eluding her.

"Then again . . . *mm* . . . while you're trying out hypotheses, you might as well wonder whether he has the first idea what he's talking about. Either way—what is your name again?—you are left without a thing to go on. But then . . . *mm* . . . you would not be the first."

"Evelyn. Evelyn Moore."

"Ah? Oh yes. Well, you see . . . truth is, there have been others before you. But never . . . *mm* . . . never a woman. He wonders why that is."

His eyes, in one of their startled flights around the room, discover the print she has just hung. He leans away, holding immediately still, as if better to take it in.

"Do you like that painting?" she asks.

"That painting . . . *mm* . . . " His eyes return to his hands. "Oh. Oh. How he would love to discuss art! To discuss art . . . certainly. Yes. And to eat fresh fruit. To stride determined and assured, devote entire afternoons studying at wooden tables. To watch the sunlight levered across the wide-plank floors. But no, he is condemned to plastic tile. A form of penance, he suspects, for past sins, each little square roughly equivalent to a Hail Mary."

He shifts in his chair, leaning close to her. "What is it, after all? Don't you know this place? Where do you think you are, the University? No no, he tells you, those days are quite past. This is afterward. After . . . *mm* . . . anything you could care to think of. Into the post-post-modern. Beyond the final pages of any textbook. After the very last word. Nothing, as you are aware, makes sense anymore. The landscapes recede. The moments lead away. You appear, and immediately he is afraid."

The patient examines his hands again, the fingernails now, bringing them up close to his face.

"Can you tell me, Roland, what is it you're afraid of?"

The patient seems to give this some thought. He leans forward, motions her to do the same. In little more than a whisper, "Have you gotten a close look at that man Kilgallen? . . . calls himself a doctor. The fact of the matter is . . . *mm* . . . . He doesn't know quite how to say this . . . but, you see, out beyond these walls is a world—not the world you're familiar with, no—it feeds into here through subterranean vapors. And, oh! . . . there, right away . . . he can see your disbelief. You wait! Next time the opportunity presents itself—but don't let the fiend notice—you look at him. Observe him carefully. The man has an eye *exactly* in the top of his head."

* * * * *

Esther Boyle, the charge nurse in Admissions, appears a bully. Normally nurses don't interact much with the patients, leaving that to the mental health workers. But Esther has made herself an exception, keeping a suspicious eye on things, maintaining tight control. She is a large woman with an expansive forehead and a face that seems by nature to verge on a smirk, though she never, ever smiles. She wears her daily rotation of polyester suits like badges. She calls them "outfits." In this hospital, almost nobody wears a uniform.

To Evelyn, whenever they pass in the hall, Esther presents a fixed expression. And something more, a sly regard from somewhere about those eyes.

* * * * *

"Who have you seen today?" Walter Rafferty asks, breaking what has seemed a prolonged silence.

The lunch crowd around them has dwindled to a solitary few, left behind like crumbs. Without looking at these people, she is nonetheless aware of them at their tables, deliberate, wiping their mouths, perhaps listening.

"Four..." she surprises herself with the softness of her own voice, "four patients." She lays her sandwich down. "The most challenging, I thought, was Louise."

He nods.

Her sole preparation for Walter Rafferty, the dark and rangy psychologist from E-Ward, has been the remark of Chief Psychologist Gary Benjamin, who said, "He's a Jungian, though if you ask him, he'll tell you he isn't." Evelyn hasn't asked him, not yet anyway. It hasn't been half an hour since this apparently shy man ducked through the doorway to her office, introduced himself, and then, half-turning as if he'd forgotten something, muttered a string of syllables she simply failed to comprehend. Nonetheless, as his face swept back in her direction—a face suggesting a bewilderment equal to her own—it was clear: she'd received an invitation.

He drove the two of them in his car (the aging Volvo with dog hair on the upholstery making her feel somehow peripherally altered) to this luncheonette in some out-of-the-way shopping center. House of Sandwich, the place is called, an unremarkable deployment of tables and chairs among rubber plants and philodendrons. Here she sits opposite him now in too-warm semi-brightness, looking out through venetian blinds onto asphalt while nibbling whole-wheat-breaded triangles of tuna salad, crunchy with celery. The sandwiches aren't bad.

"Bipolar?" He nods again, as if answering his own question. "I remember Louise."

"I noticed in her file, she used to be your patient."

"For awhile, yeah. But she was scared to death of me. She might do better with a woman."

"She was afraid of you?"

Walter Rafferty, the long wolf of a man who is somehow folded into the chair across from her, shrugs. "Accused me of practicing black magic."

"Seriously?"

He raises a wild eyebrow. "Inscribing incantations on her amoxapine capsules."

"She seems to have developed," Evelyn observes, "a fairly prolific anxiety."

"Then came the low blow. She accused me of being in league with John Kilgallen."

She smiles, turns to the window. But there remains the feel of the man across the table, like a residual pressure against the side of her face.

"What do you think," she says, "about her medication problem? If you don't mind my asking."

Walter Rafferty shakes his head, and the chewing motion of his jaw slows. "I don't mind, but . . . you've read the chart."

"I'm thinking of Wellbutrin, in particular."

"Are you asking me if I think it's good for her?"

"I was just wondering, given her history, whether at this point it might not be more harmful than beneficial."

Walter Rafferty takes a moment before he says, "I imagine that would be worth wondering."

Her next question (she can feel it coming) is about John Kilgallen. But somehow the opportunity seems to pass.

Another lunch customer gets up to leave.

"Roland Rye said this morning that he'd never seen another woman therapist."

"Oh you've met Roland."

"Yes. Gary Benjamin said he'd be a good introduction to the institution."

Walter Rafferty is amused. "Rye's been wearing Gary out. Nobody else will take the guy."

"He seems a little manipulative."

"Gary? He's alright."

"I mean Roland."

His eyes slide from her out to the smoky light of early afternoon. "I've done a few sessions with him. I calculated the guy's had more years of college than I have, and at better schools."

"Do you think he belongs here?"

Walter Rafferty, finished eating, drops his napkin on the table. "The story goes, he was out wandering around the Bangor Mall, smelling like a urinal, lecturing to the shoppers. Police were called in, they found him in the wishing pond playing with the pennies. He'd fallen off the foot-bridge, nearly cracked his head open. Couldn't give the judge a coherent answer. They brought him here."

"The date of admission was seven years ago."

He shrugs. "You get people like this in any institution. The army. Prison. College. They hang on, the years go by, they just don't want to leave. He's got a refuge here. And maybe society owes him that. Last time they found him in the wishing pond. Next it could be the river."

All the other tables are empty.

She nudges her plate aside.

Walter Rafferty stares off into the dull sun of the parking lot. "Roland's right," he says, as though this is a new thought. "You're the only woman on professional staff. As far as I know, you're the very first. Congratulations." He smiles, then stands. He seems even taller than she remembered.

On the way back to the hospital, Evelyn passes through a moment of disconcertingly simplistic clarity. She has her new job, her new patients, her new house. In Walter Rafferty maybe a new friend. And she has Richard, her not-so-new husband. But what else? She knows there is something else.

~S~

I MOVE in the company of spirits—exactly how many, I don't know.

They appear and disappear with hesitations in my thinking, using my mental life as a gateway into the world. Their words break free of quicksilvery auras: they have things to say to me. And I listen. But afterward I am left wondering, do they speak from outside or inside my head?

I've given them names—Aroostook, Penobscot, Passadumkeag, Androscoggin—though sometimes I have trouble telling them apart. Their true names are unpronounceable: long, mournful syllables with consonants like cut glass.

The spirits offer advice on just about anything. They cling to my shoulders and speak an English so refined I have to concentrate to understand what they're talking about. Their words seem always exactly right, but—some of them, I have to ask—are they words? Words maybe I've used only in dreams. Words maybe forgotten long ago, or never known. I hunt them in dictionaries. Finding one is a revelation. I sit with the page open and feel, like a paleontologist, the breath of a distant energy.

But, though I like the attention of these spirits and I respect their wisdom, I wind up arguing with them. They have a precious view of things, I tell them, not knowing what it is to be human. I might as well argue with the rain.

Not to know, says Penobscot, *is to know.* The air rumples, the equivalent of heads nodding in mist, and I get a single look from their many eyes—which aren't eyes at all, but more like the knowledge that you're being seen. It's a little frightening when they all agree. I don't understand them, but I know I'm not supposed to. I have my own way to go. I have my body.

The spirits came into my life both all at once and gradually, introducing themselves one or two at a time, between the new and the full moon, three Februaries ago. They appeared at unlikely hours of the night while I was out prowling around Black Woods. They say *I* surprised *them.* They'd never seen anything like me.

That first night was dark. I was out on snowshoes, listening my way among conifers at the head of Upper Sand Brook. Shapeless black against shapeless charcoal gray, where in order to see a thing I'd look not directly at it, but off to the side. I was almost getting used to it when I realized something felt different, not right. I stopped. I waited. I felt the passing of time by the flecks of melt on my face, telling me that the clouds closing over the ridge were spitting snow.

Then the voice. Turning the dark to bronze.

You have immaculate form, it said.

Where? Behind me? I stood dead still.

"I have my rifle," I said, half whispering. It was a lie.

There were no sounds, not the brook, not even the wind on the ridge, until a frozen maple cracked from the cold. Then nothing.

And a virgin, I see.

I said, "Look, you've got the wrong person."

Another sound then, maybe laughter, definitely from behind me.

I slipped off a mitten, felt for the limb of a cedar, glanced back and saw him: the only light in the woods. Like billowings of sleet backlit by the moon. Except there was no moon, no sleet.

He asked if I liked the way he looked. Leaning back against the tree, I took a breath. I answered that he was beautiful. He said anytime I wanted him to change he could.

That was how it started.

All my life I'd heard voices. I'd more or less gotten used to them. But this was something else. As if pieces of the world were stirring, opening their eyes.

The other spirits came to me pretty much the same way, their arrivals spaced four days apart. It's the way they do things, by celestial clockwork. As if they can't help themselves.

"Doesn't it bore you?" I asked Passadumkeag the night he came. "Having everything decided for you?" He only laughed. I think it was a laugh.

"And anyway, why are you all men?"

There was silence.

You would prefer not? We can be women if you like. The voice already modulating.

"No, that's alright."

Four nights later, Androscoggin arrived eagerly in the timbre of a woman. I tried asking her about the boredom, and the blackness around us went taut.

The Kingdom of Boredom is within you, she said. The air slackened. *But then you knew that.*

"Right. It was a stupid question."

Almost three years now, and the spirits haven't left me. They're here now, several of them—even in this place. They say they've grown attached to me, though I wonder what this means. They say I'm something special. I say everything has its price.

Periodic Table

Evelyn learns of a gruesome incident and senses certain battle lines beginning to be drawn.

Not every day, but whenever her irregular schedule allows, she brings her lunch to the Conference Room, where for half an hour Gary Benjamin, Paul Sun, Jeremy Teresco, and Joy Cahill, the Admissions secretary, sit eating at the vast table in assorted postures of recuperation. All except for Paul Sun, that is, who may be said to need no recuperation. The psychiatrist for A and D Wards is not seen in this institution without his white lab coat. Even here, eating lunch, he's wearing it. Once in awhile Mark Zieglitz joins them, as he has today. Mark Zieglitz, it is generally known, did his internship in a hospital in Massachusetts, and he seems to like to talk about this.

Today the talk is about the hazards of working in a mental hospital. Evelyn, having finished her brie-and-endive sandwich, is trying to make her celery sticks last. She likes the feel of something to hold onto.

"Compared to Danvers," Mark Zieglitz says even while tearing into his sandwich, "this place is a daycare center." His last few words come out a little fuzzy. He chews before continuing. "A certain clientele there the staff were forbidden to go near. You had to slip the food in on a retractable tray."

Paul Sun, smiling, looks as if he's about to comment. But he doesn't say anything.

Joy, nibbling the first of three Oreos, shakes her head.

"Like Forensics," Jeremy says.

"Worse," Mark says. He has interrupted his eating to give his sandwich some scrutiny. But he can still talk while he does this. "At Danvers, there were always incidents. One patient, her specialty was pulling off people's fingers. Anyone dealing with her had to put mittens on. You think I'm joking? The nurses giving her injections were wearing mittens."

Gary Benjamin, laughing softly over his own sandwich, dismisses this with a wave of his hand.

But Jeremy, moved perhaps by institutional loyalty, doesn't give up so easily. "I don't know," he says. "Wasn't there a doctor here, a few years back, thrown out a window or something?"

"Einhorn," Joy says. "Gee, I forgot about him."

Evelyn, around whom the violence of this world seems to swirl always out of sight, is curious enough to ask, "Who?"

"Marcus Einhorn," Gary Benjamin says. "Psychiatrist here."

"When was this?"

"What . . ." Jeremy turns to Paul Sun. " . . . five, six years ago?"

Paul Sun doesn't say anything.

Evelyn is filled with questions. "How could anyone be thrown out a window? Aren't the windows here all screened?"

"Yeah, well this doctor went right through one."

"It wasn't good," Gary Benjamin mutters, shaking his head. "It wasn't good."

For a moment, the talk falls silent.

Paul Sun stands then. "Seven years ago," he says. "October, 1990." He neatly crumples his trash into a ball, brushes the crumbs from the table into his hand, and exits the Conference Room.

The sheer abruptness of his performance is startling, as though it might be meant as a statement. But with Paul Sun, it's difficult to say. The man is so expertly composed, he could be roiling with some suppressed emotion, or he could be headed back to his office for a quick nap.

※ ※ ※ ※

Late afternoon. Her resolution dribbling away, she goes anyway. She pokes her head into John Kilgallen's office, raps with her knuckles on the jamb, wondering as she does so whether this is the way to approach him.

"John, are you busy?"

The psychiatrist, fingers wrapped around his chin, is staring into the screen of a computer on a table beside his remarkably clean desk. There is a surprised moment between his looking up and his smiling. He has sharp, handsome features—blue eyes behind his glasses, close-cut grey hair, and pink skin. For some reason, she thinks he looks Australian.

"Come in," he says. "No, no, come in." He rises, then glances once again at his computer screen. "Evelyn. Have a seat. Please." His arm juts toward a cushioned chair by his desk. It is the chair, she guesses, ordinarily for his patients.

She would rather avoid a sit-down meeting. As if by some gravity, she finds herself drawn to the other side of the room, to the window, looking out on things that are not John Kilgallen's.

"Oh, this is a nice view," she says.

"Have you been finding your way around alright?"

"Oh, yes. It seems . . . almost like home."

John Kilgallen's laugh is quick and sharp, like the features of his face. There is not a lot wasted on that laugh.

She turns from the window.

"The reason I've come by . . . I don't mean to take up your time."

"Oh, not at all."

"This morning I had a session with Louise Dyer."

"Louise." The psychiatrist pushes his glasses up into his thinning little-boy haircut, his expression gnawing on this information.

She says, "It was the first time I'd met with her."

"That's right." He is shaking his head. "Astor's gone. I forgot you were taking her on." Still standing, he steals a look at his computer screen, then strikes a key on the keyboard. Then another key. And one more before he faces her and smiles. "How did it go?"

There is first of all the terrible, focused clutterlessness of John Kilgallen's office, which she feels as a tangible distraction, over and above that other distraction that she also feels but cannot name.

She says, "Louise seems pretty severely distressed."

"Yes." He settles back into his chair, which squeaks singularly, like a stroke of punctuation. His sitting down clears her view of "Synaptic Transmission and Mood Disorders"—a pharmaceutical-company poster fixed centrally on the wall behind him. Her eyes run down axons and dendrites diagrammed in pink, lavender, and yellow.

"She's complaining about her neck."

Kilgallen's expression suggests the attention of someone listening to a joke.

"What bothers me," Evelyn continues, "is that it seems to go beyond merely a physical complaint. I don't know, I may have missed it in her chart, but I didn't notice in prior episodes any mention of psychotic symptoms."

The psychiatrist cocks his head. "And you're seeing them now?"

She has no need to think about the question. And yet the answer seems to merit a pause.

"She's under the impression that we've put something in her head, something to monitor her thoughts."

"Oh!" The short laugh. "God forbid!"

The computer screen falls black, but he seems not to notice. His eyes resort to the tile ceiling. "Imipramine . . . doxepin . . . phenelzine . . . amoxapine."

She stares at him.

"Her medications," he says, "have not been kind to her, poor thing. Nausea, tachycardia, rash, Parkinsonism, you name it. She's been through the gamut."

John Kilgallen directs a hand to pluck the glasses out of his hair. He sets them precisely on another, ghostly pair arising in the sheen that is the surface of his desk.

"So now . . . ." He sighs. " . . . she is suspicious of the Wellbutrin."

"It may be she's developing a reaction to that, too."

"Well, I'd be willing to consider that possibility if she were in fact taking it. But it appears now that she has not been. I got word this morning from Esther Boyle: she's been cheeking it." John Kilgallen's hand is up again, smoothing over his hair where his glasses used to be, worrying the little glint of scalp. "There's been a pattern of that behavior. She has, on the whole, been uncooperative."

"Considering what she's been through . . . ."

He nods.

And, aside from his taut smile then, what else is there in this room for her to look at? On the wall over the bookcase hangs a grand scroll of the Periodic Table, the elements arrayed like building blocks in some interrupted construction, or in some ruin. The blocks recall Louise's pills, with "things written on them." The entire Table gleams with signification. It is as if, it occurs to Evelyn, she has stepped directly into this man's science, which is where she is now standing. It is as if his science has these walls, this forbidding cleanliness.

"I appreciate your input, Evelyn." He nods again. "Certainly we'll take another look. But offhand, I would think it imprudent at this point to retreat on medication. In her case, the dopamine route seems to have been the most effectual. Of course, we shouldn't rule anything out."

John Kilgallen's words make a sensible enough impression at the same time that they provoke her blood to the point of throbbing in her temples. For the moment, she must defer. It is late in the afternoon. And now—standing here in the presence of this man—she is visited by a fleeting image of her husband. She wonders what, at this very instant, he might be up to.

※ ※ ※ ※ ※

What are neuroses anyway, if not exaggerated forms of behavior we all exhibit? Richard said that. She assumed it went without saying. What disturbs her is this phrase, "we all." He is forever sprinkling it into his commonsense analyses of her feelings, smiling, as if only this morning he encountered precisely the nuance of emotion she has just now ventured to confide.

Inwardly she has less and less patience with this kind of talk. What kind of a life is it in which one's feelings are everyone else's? Outwardly, well, she keeps quiet about it.

※ ※ ※ ※ ※

Walking through the weakening light to her car, she can hear the clip of her bootheels over the pavement, the scuff of leaves. They are everywhere, the leaves, muddling the parking lot and lawn.

She can feel it coming as her fingers coax the latch. The door pops open and swings wide. She does not get in. Her hand spreads needfully, moving along the white-enameled surface of the machine that each day brings her, each day takes her away. Her heart races, her vision swarms with teasing points of light, and then once again she is staring through the moment. As if the leaves might speak. As if time could break apart this way, yielding gaps of thundering clarity, into which one might easily vanish.

Then she is somehow in the car, turning the key in the ignition, glancing up through the windshield. And as the engine comes to life, her eyes catch the shape of someone over among the pines, against the grey wall of ledge. Even at this distance and in this light, she recognizes Walter Rafferty, standing tall, treelike, unaccountable against the folds of weathered rock.

Facing obliquely away from her, he looks at first exactly as though he is urinating against the ledge. But no, as her car moves out of the lot and onto the winding drive, she gains the angle to see that his hands are in his pockets. He is merely looking down, staring at rock the texture of elephant skin, as if contemplating a climb.

Driving, she turns her head, watching him as she can, the blacktop curving away and descending, until the moment comes when it is no longer possible for her to see him.

* * * * *

On weekends she ventures early in the morning beyond the maples that shade the house out into the overgrown yard. There in the wet sunlight, roaming in rubber boots, she recognizes lilac, apple, rhubarb, what looks like forsythia, and a sloping bed overrun with tiger lilies. The thick lawn pulls at her feet. Despite the crickets and fuss of the sparrows, there is, in the way it all hangs together, a ready stillness.

At first there seems no way to begin. But little by little she applies herself, hunting in the tangle for the outlines of shapes that please her. She discovers in a slumping shed a wheelbarrow, several spades, some shears. She attacks what remains of the gardens, choked with goldenrod and grasses. She clears spaces around the trees. Over the weeks, she creates out of the relocation of vegetable matter, a compost pile almost as tall as she is.

She shows Richard the results of her work.

"Great," he says. "Great. Looks good."

From time to time, as she kneels, weeding, she pauses to gaze over the tips of the meadow grasses toward the edge of the forest, as though she might be expecting some change there.

~S~

I'M BECOMING one of the patients. I didn't think I would. I've turned my face to plaster, my mind to a fluorescent hum. I've just about embedded myself in the walls, but the eyes of these people right away pick up anything that doesn't belong here. So now I'm theirs. A glance in passing, the pressure of an elbow, one way or another they let me know. The men are first. They swing in like ground hornets attracted to something on the wind. Then the word, traded in whispers.

"That one there . . . . The *assassin*."

The stares run over me like hands. I'm becoming part of the fiction I've climbed into. I wonder if I'll be able to get out.

I tried ignoring them at first, which was pointless. They knew. Maybe Rye told them. Or maybe they figured it out for themselves, that I'm holed up in here, inside myself, pretending not to be. Anyway, these people, these fellow inmates, they love the idea. They come around, orbiting my vow of silence like naughty, conspiratorial moons. They talk to me, standing guard, pretending to chat with one another, acting as if I were a piece of the furniture. Eddie even taped a sign to me, which nurse Boil removed fast. It read "Out of Order."

They want to hear all about the assassination. What's there to tell? Who is this governor anyway?

Patients. Eddie's the aggressive one. He talks blistering outrage with his gravel voice, lets everyone know he's a victim of "the system"—not to mention bad drugs. Always on the make, he leans into the soda machine, looks me up and down and invites me to step into his Lincoln Town Car.

"Get away from the House for awhile."

"No thanks," I say, "my mother used to drive one of those."

"Nah." He laughs. "Mine, you ought to see sometime. Under Chamberlain Bridge. Bangor side."

William, standing beside him, nods. "It's nice."

Eddie turns to him. "What the fuck do you know about it?"

"I've seen it. It's . . . like shorefront. Suburban almost."

"Suburban." Eddie shakes his head. "Shit."

Eddie, forty-two years old—reactive schizophrenic, or so he claims. He's holding on somehow, yet I doubt, as I look at him, whether anyone has ever loved this man. He needs to get back to his Town Car by the river. He shrugs it off, but the fact is he no longer knows his own life. Something has been entering him, hurling him into these sudden zones of shadow and explosive movement. But, he'll tell you, he isn't crazy. Another couple of weeks and he's out of here.

William isn't so sure, about much of anything. Pliable, accommodating, he drifts along the walls, angling in on things. You turn, and there he is, hand never far away from his mouth, as if holding the ghost of a Chesterfield. He has dark hair and eyes to break a woman's heart. When I first talked to him, I felt a little dizzy. His head is always in motion. It's subtle—you might not notice. Weaving as if to some rhythm, the lilt of some music only he can hear. A flower-scented music, with a drum beat. Music the night before the eruption of a volcano.

William is thirty-four. He's worked a good part of his life at the IGA, in produce. I asked him about his Chesterfields, but he says he never smokes around the fruit and vegetables. I believe him. His skin smells of citrus and coffee grounds. I picture him in a red apron, conscientious, snapping open boxes of pineapple and melons, knowing how to judge the ripe, the overripe. I wouldn't know this.

William doesn't say a lot, but it's clear he listens from the heart. I speak to him, and he doesn't take his eyes from me, doesn't interrupt, doesn't rearrange his face. I ask him what he's doing here. And then he does look away, the hand, without its cigarette, going for the mouth. That inner, distant music has him now.

But where, in all of this, are the eyes of the women?

Fay and Louise situate themselves like posts. As if our coming together is only the smallest interval between something and something else. We've made our little hellos, but we don't find the way to go further, and so we stand stiff, facing in directions where we expect no doors to open. Fay is hard and livid—we can't know what her problem is. Off in a corner with her blouse half-buttoned, she looks as though any minute she might take a bite out of the wallpaper. Louise is all unravelled, living in fear of her own skull. Mrs. Dibrizzi meanwhile attends to locomotion, standing up, sitting down, contemplating these maneuvers, quavering, open-mouthed.

The new admit yesterday was somebody named Morgan, who I don't like the look of one bit. His hands are used to violence. No one else seems to notice. He hikes his pants and keeps his shirt—the same yellow as these walls—buttoned up tight. I remember him, or somebody just like him, showing up years ago at my mother's front door, handing out bibles. He had a scary little smile then. But that's gone now.

Morgan's face looks older than the rest of him. It's a face impossible to read. His eyes go nowhere, they are shields of gun-metal. There are times when he stops, like a dog with its nose on the wind, and I imagine him seeing in some spooky way, picking up traces of radiation here and there. Whenever Morgan enters the dayroom, Mrs. Dibrizzi suddenly quivers with urgency. She rises then and gropes her way out.

The two of them, I have the feeling, understand this.

Angels of Death

Bringing Evelyn and the Wild Child, unexpectedly, into the same room.

SATURDAY, close to noon. Richard, returning slowly from the mailbox, pushes his way past the storm and front doors without looking at either of them. He is studying the mail, the *Bangor Daily News Weekend Edition* in plastic tucked under one arm.

He says, "There's a letter from your mother."

He keeps a couple of the envelopes, slaps the remainder on the hall table.

"Why does she bother writing when she calls you twice a week?"

Evelyn, comfortable on the sofa, glances up from the book open on her lap. Her eyes return to the page before she answers. "Mother? She's always having second thoughts about our phone conversations. She uses the letters to make them right."

"Second thoughts. Why not just stop hounding you in the first place?"

She twiddles a lock of her hair, her elbow resting on the back of the sofa. "She doesn't hound me." There is something held back in her tone, which is casual, emollient.

She goes back to the book, but before she has quite found her place, she breaks off again to look up at her husband, who has opened one of the envelopes and is lingering, regarding its contents.

He shakes his head. "Goddamned Reichland's churning the account."

She waits, her gaze withheld to the window at a point equidistant from Richard and her reading, an attitude that could be construed as receptive, but not encouraging. This meditative pose likewise helps quiet the thought that her husband—now tearing into his second envelope—is unemployed, a condition traceable through an intricate and somehow irksome history.

Richard as a matter of fact is seeking, not a job, but rather—as he puts it—"a situation." Over the last several years, as she has looked on, he has transformed professionally into something he refuses to name. "Scavenger" might be a word for it, recognizing market potential in things under other people's noses, especially worn-out real estate. "I play with property is all," he says.

It's clear to her what he is. What isn't clear is how she feels about it. She's been striving for an open mind. Two years ago Richard was an investment counselor, self-taught, and before that a grant writer. But, as she is not about to forget, the thing that he was first, when she met him, was a graduate student in anthropology—ABD, perhaps a year away from his doctorate. Evelyn was just out of the hospital then, and, as her mother observed, meeting this sparkling "young idealist" seemed to do more for her than all that therapy. The word "idealist" was Richard's own, which, Evelyn supposes, should have indicated something. Her fiancé and later new husband promoted himself so well under the term that for years, long after he'd given up on the Ph.D., long after it should have been obvious that his real interests lay elsewhere, Evelyn continued to think of him as an anthropologist—perhaps one with a rebellious streak. Even now, at times, she can lapse into wondering.

Out of the corner of her eye, she sees Richard glance up from the contents of the second envelope to look at her.

Then he's back to frowning at whatever's in his hand. He says, "What are you reading?"

"'A White Heron.'"

He shakes his head. "You and your novels."

Lacking the energy to set him straight, she stares at him. The envelope in his hand is brown. This means nothing to her, but at the moment it seems like a gift, this entirely neutral fact.

"Hm!" he exclaims, frowning.

What does it amount to, living with a person whose words appear directed into the ether?

It's not as if the man can't talk.

* * * * *

Why have they come here?

What has drawn or driven them, smack up against the edge of the forest in eastern Maine?

Richard thinks he knows: it was that visitation by the Angels of Death. That black Connecticut night. It has become one of his favorite stories. Now that he can laugh about it.

He'd worked late and was driving the Bavaria home along Interstate 86, the highway virtually empty. All at once he noticed a cluster of headlights moving up in his rearview mirror. They seemed to come out of nowhere. Two dark, heavy automobiles—Cadillacs or Lincolns—slid by, one right after the other. The first drifted into the lane ahead of him, and the other pulled abreast of it, while a third came up to fill the space on his left, and a fourth closed in behind. For the speed they were traveling, they had him packed in pretty tight. It felt like he was doing seventy in a parking lot. The recklessness of it irritated him, until he realized what was happening. Together, they all began to slow. Richard glanced to his left, through the two layers of glass, into the dark interior of the car next to him and saw what looked like a mirror image, a shadowy face looking back at him, smiling teeth glinting from the light of the dash.

A huge green sign rushed by on his right—the Vernon exit. By the time he'd made his move, Richard barely had room to cut across the grass and catch the ramp, knocking his muffler off. The rest of the way home, he took the back roads. He kept his eyes on the rearview mirror, his hands wringing the steering wheel.

It was after midnight when he switched on the light in the bedroom, waking her. He paced at the foot of the bed and told her the story.

"I don't need this," he said.

"Who were they?" she wanted to know.

Richard was shaking his head, pacing. "I can see it. I could be lying, right now, on the median strip, with a bullet in my skull."

"Would you like me to fix you something?" she said.

"Fuck this. I'm out of here. I can make money just as well someplace else." He stopped his pacing but continued shaking his head, staring, whether into his past or into his future, he wasn't telling her.

He headed downstairs then, for the Glenfiddich, hanging on to the neck of the bottle that night, not even bothering with a glass. Eventually he calmed down. But he never worked late again after that.

In any event, they are here now, "someplace else." And, Richard's drama notwithstanding, Evelyn can't help wondering why.

She feels the move may have had more to do with her.

* * * * *

Tuesday, before daylight, Evelyn awakens to the drone of wind in the maples by the road. She rises ahead of Richard.

On her way to work the rain begins to fall in wild, sporadic sprays against the windshield.

At the hospital, she can hear the storm swelling outside. Rain is thrown in diagonal waves, each one a sustained frenzy against her window. Occasionally in the intervals, it is quiet enough for her to hear the hum of the computer on her desk.

The morning is like a wall to get around. She is seeing a patient, then alone, then seeing the next. She is in and out, in and out of her office, where the damp in the air today intensifies the odor of dust.

* * * * *

She has a meeting with Eddie Magaro, an abuser of numerous and undetermined psychoactive substances. Eddie doesn't know, himself, all of what it is he's taken.

Eddie is the recognized alpha male of the ward, whose presence normally rings out in the dayroom and in the halls above all others, except perhaps for Roland Rye's. Eddie's voice prickles the skin. It is a voice to straddle motorcycles and lurk around street corners, a voice to penetrate the flash and blur of a mugging. Eddie wields his voice like a weapon.

He sits right across from her, his hair thoroughly combed and oiled, his shirt tucked in. He's quiet enough now.

"How are you today, Eddie?"

His gray eyes drift from her face to her hands. He shifts in his chair. His shoulders half-shrug at the same time his neck twitches. It is as if Eddie's skin isn't fitting quite right this morning.

"Yeah, fff . . . . complain I guess."

She can barely hear him.

His eyes move from her boots to her blouse.

"Is there anything in particular you'd like to talk about?"

He shifts and shrugs.

He shakes his head, mutters, "Naw, I fff . . . ."

Eddie may be having difficulty with his sentences, but certainly not with his eyes. They've been all over her. And when his gaze finally connects with hers, he seems startled.

He shrugs, flustered.

"Hey . . . mean . . . you're the doctor."

* * * * *

On her way to retrieve a chart from the Admissions Office, she runs into a crowd in the entrance hallway. Immediately, she can smell and hear the rain. The smell comes from the clothes of those bodies blocking her way, the sound from the rain itself, outside. The bodies are silent. There is something in the air. Joy, the Admissions secretary, stands with Paul Sun and Jeremy Teresco huddled on the maroon all-weather carpet with two men in dark suits, one blue, one brown. The men's shoes and the bottoms of their trousers have been stained damp.

Seated at one end of the bench behind the men, a young woman is draped in a yellow slicker. Above her, a little apart from the group on the carpet, looms a state trooper in full rain gear, his hands clasped behind his back.

And now Joy hurries off to a filing cabinet, without noticing Evelyn. As she waits to get the secretary's attention, she can feel the trooper glance her way. In the hollow of the entrance hallway, the storm's howl seems magnified. The outer surfaces of the glass front doors, even under the shelter of the portico, are spattered all over with droplets, wet leaves, and dirt driven by the wind.

"We need her back on the twelfth," one of the men says.

Paul Sun, paging through documents the man has thrust at him, nods.

The dark eyes of the woman on the bench—who appears little more than a girl—gaze, not down, but straight ahead into the back of the brown-suited man. Her wrists lie handcuffed together on her slickered lap. Water drips and drips from the trooper's raingear, and from hers, into the carpet stained wet under her feet. She is barefoot.

"She hasn't spoken at all since her arrest?" Paul Sun seems to be asking no one in particular. He is still turning pages of documents.

"No." The taller of the men, the one wearing blue, talks at the woman on the bench, as if addressing her. "Cat's got her tongue, I guess. Oh . . ." He remembers now. "She did say one thing."

Sun glances up from the file.

"While she was in the hospital, unconscious." He turns to the shorter man in brown. "What was it again?"

The shorter man looks at him. "She said, 'The spirits are on the other side of the swamp.'"

"Right. That's it."

"That was all she said?" Paul Sun wants to know.

"Yeah, I was there when she said it," the man in brown says. "That was it. Not another word."

Paul Sun looks over at the woman, who, as far as Evelyn can see, has not even blinked.

But now Joy has noticed Evelyn and apologizes. The chart, she says, shaking her head, was misfiled under the patient's first name.

A moment later, the folder in her hand, Evelyn turns to leave. She tries for a last look at the girl on the bench, but they have her up now and are removing her slicker, preparing to lead her through Admissions.

On her way back from the front entrance, Evelyn realizes she no longer hears the rain. She muses over this, wondering after the rounding of what corner or the closing of what door the sound left her, or whether here in the corridor some trace of it survives, too faint for hearing, spiritlike. A question of threshholds, probably. In any case, by the time she reaches her office, she is sure to pick it up again.

    Later that afternoon, it is as if she senses something at the window. She turns and is confused by the complexity of movement. Focusing, she sees the wind-tossed pines distorted by the smear of rain down the glass. And something else?
    What is it?

~S~

EVELYN MOORE.

The first time I saw her, I was stuck on the bench in the entrance corridor. They had me waiting while, thread by numbing thread, this place attached itself to me.

Time had run on ahead, leaving me in a vacuum of clarity. I could see that the building was drawing me in out of the rain on a slow breath, deliberately. In the brightness I could hear the staff rustling from doorways, converging to get a look at what the police had brought in.

I could easily have lost myself to the knowledge that I was inside here again. That might have been the effect they were after. What I saw on the way up those stone steps seemed final. The outer walls—grey-block masonry, eye-socket windows covered with mesh, the quiver of dull-red ivy in the wind. Then I felt the corridor slipping over me. There was no mistaking the wallpaper and tile, the rectangular thinking and taut mouths of those emerging to claim my paperwork. These people had been leaking away for years, their movements engineered now by remote powers. From the inner recesses of that hallway and those intersecting it, I began to make out the drift of intention, something like a plan at work.

Waiting on that bench, I felt the cold advancing down my wrists and over my skin, separating me from my clothes, sucking me into that flickering space where there is the danger of vanishing. Could I hold on?

And then I saw her.

She appeared softly, all at once, out of nowhere. As if brought by a melancholy music. I did not have the impression that she'd entered the corridor by walking. She stood a few feet apart from the others, as though she was some form of accident. I wondered why she seemed so familiar. She might have been a memory risen from my childhood—somebody's young mother maybe. Not mine.

June, she had the sweetest face of resignation, and quiet autumn clothes. Silk. Wool. A skirt, a blouse, a scarf.
And boots. Right away I was afraid for her. I tried picturing her at home. A moment of hesitation, maybe at a window. I tried imagining her strolling through autumn. Kicking fallen leaves, in those boots.

I wondered who she dressed for. A simple question, filling me over with a sadness that made the corridor feel more like a church.

Amazing, I thought, that there could be such a woman, so funny and strange, and yet so known to me. I felt inseparable from her. I felt that her attempts at living were attempts that I had made. I felt that, just this morning, I was the one who'd put on her stockings and gone down to her breakfast to face her day. How can people stay so apart?

This was where my thinking was. This was what first delivered me from the leering brightness of that corridor, where the staff circled around, efficient as spiders, joining certain connections to me, severing certain others. All in readiness, I supposed, for the big Master Spider, waiting somewhere deeper in that building. As far as they knew, I was submissive, stunned, oblivious on that bench. They hadn't even started with me yet. I had my eyes open, but I wasn't supposed to be seeing anything.

I could see *her*, though.

Certain things were clear: that she was lost, missing pieces of herself. I could see that she was slipping—as I was sure she could also—toward the time when she would no longer be possible. She was running out of exhaustion, and there was nothing to take its place. A few days, a few weeks. The corridors would be eating her alive.

Rain slanted, hammering at the door glass, the noise like a dilemma washing over all of us. Water squirted between the doors and hurried in a stream into the carpet. I could feel it underneath my feet. I could see it under all their shoes, these people in a clot together, grinding their teeth around a clipboard. Aroostook passed over their heads silently, like an inquisitive fog, examining them as though they were something up for auction. Finally his vision connected with mine. For once, he didn't have anything to say.

Once, twice, I could feel it. Evelyn Moore's eyes moved my way. I wasn't working any spells. I wasn't doing a thing. It was all just coming together on its own.

I wondered if she had a daughter.

And then someone handed her some papers, like the others had, and she seemed to lose her justification for standing there. She turned and disappeared from that space. But it had begun. From then on, we were connected.

Autumn 2

After her second glimpse of the Wild Child, Evelyn hears about a race of insect people.

HER MANY INERT MOMENTS bleed into one another. She looks ahead always into nothing. Two nights in succession, she dreams she is living in a glacier—or no, that her life *is* a glacier, a slow, frozen movement triggering ominous reverberations, and all around the edges the continual trickle of erosion.

    As a little girl, she once took a ride in a cable car up a mountainside with her father. Her grandmother, in the car ahead, lost her straw hat suddenly to a gust of wind. Little Evelyn, seeing the hat tumbling among the trees and rocks below, cried. Her father tried to comfort her. "It's O.K. Gramma can get another one. We can can get her another one." But she could not think of the hat as something replaceable—rather what she felt was the force of loss: the hat was gone.

* * * * *

    Thinking back, she supposes she should have known. But in one's life, one must play things out, not simply jump to conclusions. Otherwise there would be no life, only the protracted and sterile contemplation of folly.

"Director of Student Mental Health Services." She hadn't been there a year when the words, coming from her mouth, had the consistency of glue.

It had, initially, all been so seductive. The carpeted seclusion of her own office, its entrance buffered by a capable secretary. Now and then a student dropped in—beaming, breathless, arms loaded with books, eyes rolling at a too-ambitious courseload—just to say hi, then had to run. The students seemed bright. The secretary knew them by name. Evelyn experienced in those first few weeks a rubbery kind of elation over the lucidity and promise of professional life.

Often, leaving the Center, she would find herself as in a dream, walking across a New England campus in the blaze of autumn, fulfilling some cherished and easy expectation of what college campuses ought to be. The grounds were aflame with sugar maple, the buildings feathered in woodbine the color of cabernet. Through the sweet, smoky, heavy days, the crickets trilled so that the blood swooned. Then, bang, the air would clear and the wind move in, colliding with the leaves. Oh, she remembers. Several times on her way to meetings, she gave in to urges to cut across the grass.

Weekends Richard took her in the Bavaria along roads with frequent bridges, aiming vaguely for the Berkshires. It was for Evelyn the appropriate distance. From the bedrooms and breakfast tables of country inns, she mulled over fragments of her weeks as if they were scenes from a book she'd been reading. Some of these she ventured to share with Richard in the interstices of his own reports about this or that parcel of real estate. Her husband accepted the interruptions with a raised eyebrow, an amused "hm!", a sip of his St.-Emilion. At the time, it seemed like conversation.

One evening at home he caught her smiling so broadly he asked her what was up.

"I'll tell you what," she announced. "I really like what I'm doing."

"Good," he said, and he smiled too. "Good."

But even then, in the midst of that glorious and sunlit autumn, there rained traces of something else, like brown scale. The austere knowledge and wariness of purpose that so characterized her thinking was still with her. The following January, Richard troubled to ask her how the job was going. Bending, rummaging through a briefcase at the kitchen table, she replied, "A lot of the time it's like playing office."

Spring semester dragged on, and those bright students came to her morose, homesick, hating their fathers, their overweight bodies, or their amphetamine habits, unable to sleep or to get out of bed — "soft" cases, most of them, the fallout of material well-being. Evelyn, living comfortably, felt herself flirting with something like contagion. (Above and beyond her father's estate, Richard was making good money then.) She hadn't trained in clinical psychology in order to play nanny.

Then late one night, sudden as a thunderbolt, it happened. The bedroom light switched on, and Richard appeared with his mouth flung open, his suit soaked with perspiration, to tell her the story of his run-in with the Angels of Death. Two months later he had found the farmhouse in Hancock, and she the opening in Bangor.

She could say she's made a career decision, but that isn't the way it feels. Rather, reflecting now in the dust-infused climate of this office, she can imagine herself the focus of intentions not her own. Something has brought her here. The idea sounds silly, but it also intrigues her. Already, every one of her days seems less familiar than the one before. Sitting with her back to the window, she tries forming a picture beyond the aberration of these bright rooms. What she sees is forest and, beyond that, the gradual and final prospect of winter.

* * * * *

Amy, young and cheerful in the glassed-in booth of the nurse's station, checks through the med log.

"Let's see," she says, "Louise, Louise, Louise." She sucks on a lollipop, playing with the white stem, running the red jewel of sugar back and forth over her lips as her other hand drags a finger down the column of entries.

Evelyn, outside the open window of the partition, can see Louise plainly in the dayroom, one of a constellation of patients on the overstuffed furniture, aiming themselves at the television. Dennis Finn. Faye Morse. Blanche Dibrizzi, with the walker. And Louise, a fist against one eye. Two or three other faces, without names.

"Yup." Amy nods. "Her schedule's been pretty regular." Peering over into the dayroom, she grimaces sweetly. "She doesn't look so great though, does she?"

"No, she doesn't. Has she resisted?"

"Taking her medication? Last week she had a couple of difficult days. Till Esther threatened to get Dr. Kilgallen."

"Her dosage is the same?"

Amy's finger goes back to the log. She nods. "Seventy-five milligrams."

Out in the dayroom, the patients remain in equilibrium, staring at the t.v. screen. All except one. Just to the right of the window overlooking the courtyard, a woman stands with her back to the t.v. and the nurse's station.

"That patient," Evelyn says. "Who is she?"

Amy sucks on her lollipop, and her eyes flare. "That's the Davenport girl," she says. "Tried to shoot the governor? The police brought her yesterday."

"I'll need to get a look at her chart."

"Oh. You'll probably have to go to Forensics for that. She's officially theirs, but at the moment they're not equipped for female patients. So they're keeping her here, seeing as we're the only other secure ward. Look. She's even got her own watch dog." Amy bobs her head at the mental health worker stationed across the hall from the dayroom. She lowers her voice. "Name's Frank."

Frank has his metal chair tipped back against the wall, his arms folded. He is staring at the television.

Amy makes a face. "Frank from Forensics."

The Davenport girl hasn't moved. She is standing, facing a row of chairs against the wall, as though, in trying to decide where to sit, she has blown a circuit.

"How long has she been like that?"

"I don't know. Twenty minutes. Whatever position you put her in, she stays that way. Then, maybe an hour later you look and she'll be different." The nurse's eyebrows form two arches of amazement.

"So, for her chart, I'd see Dr. Griswold then?"

"Yeah, I guess so." Amy's voice falls to a whisper. "Lots of luck."

* * * * *

Midway through the session, the patient interrupted to say he needed a smoke. He asked whether they could go out on the steps. So that's where they are now: Evelyn, arms folded, leaning a shoulder against the building, her jacket draped against the chill of late afternoon, the patient in his shirtsleeves, perched on the aluminum railing, cigarette stuck in the crotch of his fingers.

Last week's storm hasn't changed the weather. Two of the grounds crew are out flicking rakes against the leaves lying wet, matted on the lawns. But the air hasn't turned. Autumn is hanging on.

While the patient talks, the setting sun at Evelyn's back gives the scene in front of her the look of an ascension in thickening amber: the patient's white shirt, the shrubbery bristling beyond the steps, the parking lot and shadow-marbled lawns, and finally, in place of distance, the rising wall of pine. Perhaps because of the sun, the patient faces away while speaking, giving her his profile. But now and then he turns to her against the wash of golden light, squinting.

"Yeah," he says. He is looking at his cigarette. "I guess you could say I never finish things. I mean, I don't know if it matters. But . . . I feel like I'm not really solid that way."

"What sorts of things don't you finish, William? Can you give me an example?"

"Well, college. I never finished college."

He shows her the cigarette. "And . . . I was going to quit smoking. So I didn't finish that either."

"It's not an easy thing to stop smoking."

"Yeah, I know. But . . . . like I started to wax my car. You know, this little Subaru—red and kind of junky, but I decided to wax it. I thought, maybe it would look . . . more like an actual car. And what I did, I only waxed half of it. I only had enough shade—you know you're not supposed to wax in the sun—well, in front of my apartment, I only had shade for half the car. So I got half of it done, and then I never finished it. I never finished it. The front half is shiny, and the back half is dull. And . . . I left it that way."

He smiles, shakes his head. "My car is stuck somewhere now between how it used to be and how it was going to be. And, see, with me, that's the way everything is. My whole life has like . . . fallen into the crack between what I have in mind and what I actually do."

She laughs.

"Can you tell me," she says, "why you didn't finish college?"

"Yeah, well, actually . . . I mean, I probably shouldn't include that. I think I really decided; in the case of college, that it was a dangerous place for me. I think I really made a conscious decision there."

"You say college seemed dangerous. What do you mean by that?"

"I think . . . yeah, in college, see, there's too much potential. That's what I think. Like . . . voltage. There's too much. The place is too open . . . to possibilities. It would be different, say, if I had a specific goal. I could just go and learn and get out. But in college, *I* think, what they're really trying to teach you . . . is to question everything. I think that's true. And, see, I just don't need that kind of stimulation. I don't need any more questions. My life is a hurricane of questions, you know what I mean?"

She nods.

At first, inside, she wasn't sure: the motion was so subtle. But here in the outdoor light, there is no mistaking it. William's head is never still.

She says, "So you feel more comfortable working in the supermarket."

"It's a safer environment, yeah. Definitely. I mean, the store is a place you can't really question. People have to eat, they have to do their laundry. I'm not hurting anything working produce. The customers . . . they need their fruit and vegetables. Potatoes, they're real. Onions are real. It's not the sort of place . . . where you can wander very far off base. I mean, there's not a lot of room to have exaggerated thoughts in produce. Beauty Care, something like that, might be a different story. But I feel . . . pretty secure, really, handling things that come out of the ground."

Suddenly she hears the door open and turns to see Warren Griswold, his black hair combed straight back, emerging from the building with his briefcase. The forensic psychiatrist stands, his pallid face wrinkling into the setting sun. He grins fleetingly at nobody, and, after checking his wristwatch, descends the steps between them.

William holds still, unobtrusive as the shrubbery while Warren Griswold's short legs carry him unhurriedly across the asphalt to a blood-red Buick, the glint of a key in his hand. Evelyn's attention is split now between William's silence and the psychiatrist as he opens the door to the Buick, deposits his briefcase on the rear seat, ducks inside himself, and pulls the door shut. It is nearing five o'clock, the session almost over.

William says, "See, in college, all the time, I was having trouble . . . socializing. Interacting with people."

He speaks in this way, in bursts, rising rapidly to the crests of his sentences and then hanging, as he squints at her, as if it might really be too much to express all at once.

"People were like . . . on a television screen—they were there, but I couldn't get through to them."

Griswold's Buick, a bright alarm at the edge of her vision, recedes down the long drive.

"Did you talk to anyone about these experiences?"

William shakes his head. "I couldn't get near anyone. See, it got worse. I began noticing . . . especially a few of the students, there on campus. There were maybe three or four of them. They'd stick out in situations. You know, in the bookstore, I'd see them, and in the dining hall. And once I started noticing, just everything about them began to attract my attention. They'd hang out together and they'd use certain signals."

"What sort of signals?"

"Like . . . hand signals. And certain facial expressions. And tongue clicks. I know what you're thinking: that maybe they were deaf. But it wasn't like that. It was much, much weirder. It was like . . . whatever they were doing, they were only pretending to do, while always something else was going on under the surface. I mean, what I'm trying to tell you . . . is basically indescribable. That's how weird it was. You know? I'd watch them. Time would slow down. There'd be this . . . silence, over everything. A dining hall full of people, and all I'd hear would be their tongue clicks. And once in awhile, one of them would look at me. See, they knew. I think they played with it, maybe, the fact that I was watching them. I don't know. But at some point it hit me . . . that these weren't really people. They were more like . . . another species. Like a race of . . . insect people."

William looks at the end of his cigarette, then away into the distance. He seems agitated. "See, the thing was, I knew this. I knew it. It wasn't just a feeling. I could see . . . right through their human disguises, to . . . what they really were. See, it's impossible. I can't describe it. It was just . . . the most intense reality. Even when I think about it now. It's there in my memory, like a trip I'd taken, to . . . Jerusalem or someplace. You know, it stands out, over ordinary experience."

"And this intense reality, William. This has begun to reappear? This is why you've checked yourself in here?"

William, staring off into the pines, nods. "There's been . . . a certain odor. In the morning, the air feels . . . a certain way. I can tell."

He looks at her, shading his eyes, then moving his face into her shadow. "You know, the funny thing is . . . I think I'm a little in love with it too. I think, maybe, that's the real reason I'm here. To guard against that."

~S~

SOME DAYS filled up with people, making the air nervous, like just before lightning. You and I, June, we ran off to the woods.

We held ourselves breathless among the insects. We perfected our walking, moving over land without a ripple of violence. Twigs wouldn't snap. The ground was like a slow ocean, our steps meeting the waves. (I showed you. And then you showed me.) Again and again, we stopped and listened, watching for the moment when everything would be there, ignoring us.

Far above us, where new leaves fluttered, collecting light, crow sentries looked down and saw us: two startling blotches of wrong colors sliding below, foreshortened, arms and legs extending, retracting, amoeba-like.

I knew a guy, an English teacher, who spent a lot of his time trying to write books. Then nights and weekends, he'd head off to some tavern to drink with lawyers. Leaving me sitting in his apartment, which I think was supposed to be some kind of roadmap to his mind. He liked the idea of my being there, I think, while he was gone. But I wouldn't stay. I'd slip away to our woods. Later I'd tell him. I asked if sometime he'd like to come along.

He laughed and shook his head. "Nah. Nymph in the glade, it's O.K. for you. I think it's good that you do that. Me, it's impossible."

"I think that's good too," I said. But he could tell my voice had gone through a change.

"See . . . " He wasn't going to leave it alone. "I'd never be able to get around the fact that the whole pretty business is just an aesthetic fabrication. Because, really, there's nothing out there but a lot of goddamned plant matter. A lot of cells churning away, photosynthesizing, rotting—that's all it is. Until you come along and see something in it. Without you, without someone to appreciate it, the forest is insignificant. It might as well not even be there. That, my dear, is the unlovely truth about the natural world."

Before he'd even finished talking, he was back at his typewriter. I thanked him for letting me into the secrets of my mind, which I guessed I'd been underestimating. As for his mind, I suggested a laundering, a good hanging out. From what I could see, his description of the woods would better apply to himself.

"I'm not plant matter," he said, clicking away at the keys. "I'm animal matter."

"You're doesn't matter," I said, wanting the last word.

He stopped typing then, but only laughed and poured another drink.

Later under pine, I took off the clothes I'd worn in his apartment and buried them. I scratched the guy's name there in the soft dirt.

Aubrey I think it was.

A Virulent State of Mind

Evelyn initiates contact with Dr. Tarantula.

DAY BY DAY she learns things. About Warren Griswold, for example, who seems to prefer the monitored security of the Forensic Ward, repository for the criminally insane, where women may not routinely venture. Out in the open, she rarely sees him—an acerbic figure no taller than she, with too-black hair and an old, old face. His deep-set eyes, bushy at the fringes, harbor each a lozenge of reflection at the center. Here and there in the corridors, he makes his way dartingly, spiderlike, on business. He has been here, Walter Rafferty says, as long as anyone can remember. Except for Warren himself, the longest serving employee is Ethel Foster, who has been at the Hospital twenty-seven years. Warren Griswold was hired three years before Ethel.

The patients understand who he is. Dr. Tarantula, they call him—some of them. Others, when his name comes up, act as though it hasn't, staring fixedly away until the subject evaporates. In this shut-away world, Warren Griswold is keeper of the innermost chamber. Who can know how deep it goes?

Evelyn maintains her own doubts about the man. Despite the fact that, since the day of introductions, the forensic psychiatrist has never so much as nodded a greeting, has little more than glanced her way, she has accumulated the impression of being seen, even watched, by him.

This doesn't stop her, however, from picking up the phone and punching his extension.

"Griswold."

His voice is instantaneous, there and gone while she is staring at her blank computer screen.

"Hello." She turns in her chair, her eyes roving the yellow walls. "This is Evelyn Moore, from Admissions."

"Yeah?" Just that burst of a syllable, barely recognizable, then nothing.

She goes ahead. "I find we're housing a new admit here from your ward. Sophie Davenport? I'm calling to see if I could get a look at her chart."

A pause. Then, "She assigned to you?"

Some quality of the voice nags at her attention, as if it is a voice that needs oiling.

"Well, not exactly. But as long as she's here, I've taken an interest."

Another pause. "Sorry," he says. "I can't help you there."

"I'd be happy to share observations with you."

She hears now from Warren Griswold an indeterminate sound, what could be an acknowledgement or a groan.

Then simply, "How long do you want it for?"

"No more than, say, an hour or two. If you'd like, I could stop by and pick it up. Whenever's convenient."

As she glances toward the window, the phone is silent.

She wonders if he is still on the line. And then suddenly her office seems changed, as though someone has moved into the doorway. She turns, but there is no one. Only the computer screen has popped on again.

"Alright," Warren Griswold's voice says. "Tomorrow. Between three and four, I'm tied up anyway."

Evelyn thanks him. She sets down the receiver, both bewildered and more than a little pleased with herself.

It will be something to tell Richard.

* * * * *

Gary Benjamin has remarked that in the corridors, where there are no windows, it could be any time of day, you'd never know the difference. She finds this isn't true. Every afternoon she can see it—the light, a little at a time, goes gray. How this can be she doesn't know.

She is thinking about this when, rounding a corner, she runs straight into Walter Rafferty. She knows him, before seeing him, from the odor of his sweater, the scrub of its wool against her knuckles.

His hand is there to steady her shoulder. He is as tall as a father, and as familiar. And, for some reason it occurs to her, perhaps as dangerous.

But she is telling him anyway of her success with Warren Griswold.

His eyebrows jump. "Sophie Davenport? The shooter? I'm amazed he'd give her up so easily."

"Did I say it was easy? Besides, he isn't giving up anything. He's just letting me have a peek at her chart."

Walter gives her a quizzical look.

"What?" she says.

He shakes his head.

"Bevare . . ." he says in mock Bela Lugosi, " . . . de Spider."

* * * * *

Looking up from her desk, she asks, "Roland, how are you today?" She is in a mood to make headway.

Roland Rye, studying the wall from the patient's armchair, tenders a smile that might as well be radiating from beyond the room. His grey stubble has advanced to beard.

He tips his chin up. "Debilitated," he says.

"And what would you like to talk about?"

Roland Rye's smile flutters and is gone. Shifting in his chair, he squints at the fluorescent tubes overhead.

"Ah, you see, decision-making is decidedly not his talent. The mere thought . . . *mm* . . . sends him into a panic."

"Why is that, Roland?"

"Why." He examines the backs of his hands. "Yes, of course. Why. Not. . . . *mm* . . . The point is that his expertise lies elsewhere." He leans forward, whispers, "You might ask him where."

"Where, then, does your expertise lie?"

"Ah, precisely here, in this . . . this . . . where you . . ." He waves a hand, a substitute for the word he isn't finding.

"You mean this hospital," she offers, "where I'm employed?"

"Ah. Ah. Here, indeed, you may be employed, but to call this a hospital, he believes, would be to blur a useful distinction. By which he means the distinction . . . *mm* . . . between a certain operative edifice and a virulent state of mind."

Roland's eyes squeeze shut, as if in bright light. "However. Yes. Here in this . . . *mm* . . . whatever you wish to call it, he knows the terrain well. He observes, perhaps, what you do not. Your 'newness' here, your . . . *extrinsicality*, if you will. It discomforts you—he can see that. Despite those semesters of training in the famous rigors of your discipline, which—rumor has it—enable you professionals, in the face of stupifying derangements, to remain, shall he say, objective?"

She must be careful with her words. Therapy must not center on the therapist.

"Well, Roland. Would you prefer to see someone who has been here longer? A therapist more familiar to you?"

"Good God, no. He is merely recommending a particular vigilance."

"Vigilance about what?"

"Oh, well. For example. That little goddess of wisdom, brought in the day before whenever it was."

"Do you mean the Davenport woman? Sophie Davenport?"

Roland raises his palms, one at a time, from the arms of his chair, peering under them. "The one whose documentation you've arranged to have a look at."

This information stops her cold. "How do you know that?"

His head swivels toward the door.

"Roland, how do you know that?"

His voice lowers. "Hm? You wouldn't want her to end up like the others."

* * * * *

That evening, on the way home, there is a slowdown in the traffic. She inches forward and eventually sees, luminous in the dusk, the golden fleet trucks and yellow-helmeted workers of Bangor Hydro. They have been cutting a swath through the trees on the side of the road, moving the edge of the woods back. They may be intending to erect new poles, or perhaps widen the highway. She can't tell.

Then the traffic moves again.

* * * * *

Richard possesses superior peripheral vision, enabling him to observe people's expressions without their knowing. While he can appear distracted, lost in his own world, he is in fact very well tuned-in to what is going on around him. She knows this because he told her.

Now at the dinner table, he says, without looking at her, "I signed us up today at the Fitness Club in Ellsworth. I thought maybe Saturday we could play a little racquetball."

With a carefully blank face, she accepts this offer as a well-intentioned gesture, although she detests racquetball. The combination of sweat and hard angles gives her the impression it is actually unhealthy.

Then she opens her mouth to tell him about Sophie Davenport's chart. But something stops her, and instead she stirs her salad. When she looks up again, her husband does too, tossing her a little flip of the eyebrows along with that smile of his, which seems to come from nowhere and always stays right where it is.

That night she has a dream from which the only thing she can remember is a sound. Awake, she realizes it is a sound like rain on leaves. She gets up then and goes to the window. But outside there is an almost perfect quiet, and the sky is full of stars.

~S~

EARLY THIS MORNING I saw a raven sailing through these walls, as though searching for something. It wasn't an ordinary raven. Its feathers reflected no light and removed even the color from the rooms, so that for a time all the yellow and gleam of this place became impossible. Every thought led to the blank window of its eye. The raven flew without a sound, passing from room to room, its wings beating like someone's idea of a heart.

I told Androscoggin, and the air tightened, the way it does whenever I make a mistake.

That was no raven, she said *It was a ghost. More and more, the world is knocking them loose. You'll see.*

A grip on my elbow, and I'm whisked to a room—an office, a lounge—delivered by Esther or Ethel. There the Doctors are waiting. One of them maybe looks up as I enter. The rest stand around, perch on the arms of chairs. One paging through my chart. Two others having a conversation. As if my unruly silence is a natural part of their day. Which it is. Then something switches on, and it all turns quiet. They look my way with something like forgiveness. It raises the hair on my arms. The one with my chart closes it, runs a finger along the edge. They're ready to get to work.

June, if you could see them. Hanging in my face like dentists, two or three at a time—poking, speaking in flat voices, recording their suspicions on tape. I want to faint, or break somebody's nose. The minutes pass without any boundaries, oozing one into another. I keep them that way, not wanting this to make sense. Not wanting anything later to be angry about.

Then my name. Spoken softly, like a disappointment. They are seated now, trying not to be in a hurry. I'm supposed to take my time. One looks at his watch.

It isn't long before the silence is too much. They weaken, give up and go away, and I am yanked back to PW3. I feel all that doctor anger in the pinch of the nurse's fingers on my elbow.

In the woods, even now, there are pale shapes running. They leap and melt among tree trunks before you're sure you've seen them. You might have thought they were deer, if they hadn't moved so soundlessly, if their eyes hadn't turned and caught yours so dolefully and exactly, seeing entirely through you.

They disappear, as if sucked out of sight. As if drawn by the threads of another world. They leave you behind wondering if you'll be on the wrong path, always.

Walls

Recalling a discovery regarding the architecture of her life, Evelyn then listens to Holy Scripture.

Late afternoon, she pulls her eyes away from the computer screen. As if to see the memory more clearly. Not one she's been looking for. But there it is just the same, like a forgotten photograph in a drawer.

It was at the Connecticut house, in the deep of a windy night in November. She had lifted her face from the pillow, vaguely surprised from sleep by the perception that her life had walls and a ceiling. She lay there, her head propped on one arm, trying to formulate contour in the dark.

Her vision seemed muffled, chasing after dusky impressions, murk so thick that whatever she looked at directly she could not see. Anyway she knew where she was: within the containment of the bedroom. Beyond which were the hallway and stairs, leading down to the foyer. The front door straight ahead. And, on opening it? Then you were outside.

What did that mean, to be "outside"? The idea seemed utterly flat to her.

* * * * *

Sometime later. Beneath the blanched fluorescence of this midweek afternoon, the minutes seem bounded only by memory and dream. She is walking with Paul Sun, Jeremy Teresco, and Mark Zieglitz, rounding one bright corner after another, zig-zagging with the corridors on their way to the conference room at the front entrance. They are scheduled for an admission interview. The idea of it touches her heart with the same fingers of dread she has felt before each of these interviews. As she walks, she wonders what it is like for Paul Sun, whose stride through the hall seems capable of drawing her own along with it. The man has been at this, after all, for twelve years.

Moments later, they are all seated in the conference room, the four of them facing the man they are to interview. He is what's called a Title XV—one bound by a court-ordered psychiatric evaluation. Local media has described him as a "disgruntled employee". Morgan Fontaine, accused of attempted arson, was apprehended in a stairwell at the University of Maine physics lab wielding a can of gasoline.

Paul Sun's voice is agreeable. "How would you prefer to be called, Mr. Fontaine?"

Tight-lipped Morgan Fontaine draws his lips even a little tighter. A smile.

This man on the brink of becoming a patient has pressed himself forward as far as he can in his straightbacked chair. His arms rest on the conference table, hands over his elbows. He gives Evelyn the impression of someone yanked out of his own century, which perhaps he is. Employed as a technician at the lab he is charged with trying to burn down, Morgan claimed to have invented a device to generate electricity from woodstoves. Mass production, according to Morgan, would eliminate the need for power plants. Failing to impress his superiors with his invention, he later accused them of trying to steal it and threatened retaliation, publicly. Testimony from coworkers indicated antisocial proclivities. Morgan kept himself apart, refused to touch a telephone, and—it was discovered—in order to go to the bathroom, would walk across campus to a men's room in another building. In what little communication he offered his peers, he readily quoted the Bible.

Now he sits in this room, against his will. Pasty-skinned, slight of build, he keeps his shirt buttoned to the neck. His first response to every statement, every inquiry is that smile. But one can easily imagine that, under the taut surface, there boils something else.

Sitting directly across from this apparently tormented man, Evelyn finds it more comfortable to turn her head toward the level stare of Paul Sun, in whom, at this moment, the spirit of the conference room seems to have assumed flesh. The psychiatrist has chosen to sit to the left of the patient, perhaps eighteen inches back from the table, in a swivel chair that remains silent even as he moves. Yes, Morgan Fontaine might at first think him soulless, predatory in his white lab coat—someone from whom the truth ought to be concealed. But Paul Sun has a way of seeming larger than this. Paul Sun possesses a talent for evolving into the moment. Just one or two things are troubling him, getting in the way of his understanding. He's looking for clarification. And so on. For awhile, he goes on like this. Then all of a sudden he stops. Seconds pass.

An abrupt wiggle of posture and Morgan Fontaine begins talking, at first matter-of-factly. There has been a mistake. The can of gasoline—he will say it one more time—was intended for refueling his truck, parked right around the corner. "Go on and check, they towed it to the station. The gage is still on empty. Unless they filled it themselves. Which I wouldn't be surprised."

Paul Sun nods, revealing nothing.

"The only reason I went into the physics building was for a drink of water."

Paul Sun stares, without nodding.

Morgan Fontaine rubs his nose with a knuckle.

"Do I look like the sort of person who sets fire to buildings?"

The psychiatrist's face shines with impassivity. Paul Sun asks questions. He doesn't answer them.

Morgan Fontaine's eyes shift to Evelyn. "I want you to see what's happening here." He leans over the table, counting off items on the fingers of one hand. "A man's had a hard day, he's trying to get his truck started, he's thirsty . . . and for this, he winds up in an insane asylum. Do you see what kind of a world this is?"

In the diagnostic interview, the interviewer is an informed observer, but at the same time also a stimulus. In basic terms, the purpose of the interview is to stimulate the interviewee so that he or she is revealed in the light of informed observation. This distinguishes it from therapy, the added purpose of which is interventive: that is, to effect change.

But which stimulus to apply? And precisely how? Suppose Evelyn were to ask the questions? Or Jeremy? Or suppose Paul Sun were to ask different questions? What then would be revealed about the buttoned-up presence sitting before them who goes by the name of Morgan Fontaine? Is it part of Paul Sun's expertise that he knows of wrong questions, questions to be avoided, questions that might induce Mr. Fontaine to reveal himself other than as he is?

What, in fact, is he?

At some point, during a lull, Evelyn opens the file folder on the table before her. "Mr. Fontaine," she says, causing Paul Sun to half-turn in her direction, "we know very little of your background. Could you tell us about your family?"

Morgan Fontaine folds his arms and snickers. "Why? You think maybe they're from another planet?"

Evelyn then is distracted by the accentuated motion of Paul Sun as he removes a black felt pen from his shirt pocket, uncaps it, and sets it on the conference table.

Morgan Fontaine stares at the pen, the point of which is aimed his way.

For a moment, the entire conference room is still.

"Mr. Fontaine," Paul Sun says, "this invention of yours—could you explain it for us?"

Morgan Fontaine sits as though transfixed. Perhaps he hasn't heard the question. Then the smile. Tonelessly, he says, "I know how it looks. I don't stand a chance. You think you have it all wrapped in a nutshell. Dealing with some poor dope here, stealing the fruit of his labor. But you're on a collision course here. That's one thing you haven't calculated into the equation. You're on a battleground."

"Ah." Paul Sun is animated. "What sort of battleground?"

Morgan Fontaine's eyes flare, but he remains rigid as steel. It's a wonder that a voice could come from anyone so immobile. Though it is not quite the same voice as a few seconds ago. "Neither repented they of their murders," it says, "nor of their sorceries, nor of their fornications, nor of their thefts."

Paul Sun tilts slightly forward, like a tree just before falling.

"And in those days," the voice says, "shall men seek death and shall not find it."

It all happens with such explosive suddenness that she will later have difficulty reconstructing a sequence. A shriek is torn from one of the upper floors, prolonged, rebounding between the granite ledge and the stone walls of the Hospital and reentering, like a deja vu, through the window. Morgan Fontaine is up and against the wall, holding his chair out with one thin arm, as though Evelyn, Paul Sun, Jeremy Teresco, and Mark Zieglitz might be converging lions.

Later, on the way back through the corridor, Mark Zieglitz chuckles. "All wrapped in a nutshell," he says.

Paul Sun glances at his watch.

Evelyn wonders, "He won't be staying in Admissions, will he?"

"He'll have to," Paul Sun says, "until Warren finds space for him."

Mark Zieglitz says, "You keep him away from chairs, he'll be alright."

~S~

THIS IS what it's like.
    I'm looking out a car window. Not far off, a train is speeding in the same direction—open fields then slices of woods between. I see her, then lose sight of her again. Everything a blur, streaming. But it's a little like slow motion, too, because of the way we are fixed, aware of each other. Guard rails, the trunks of birches spinning by. Toward what?
    What we both want to know is what's up ahead. Somewhere, there's a connection. And then what will she say?

    Meanwhile, on moderate seas off the coast, banks of clouds are soundlessly forming, gathering. This has been going on for weeks, the clouds merging, building, rolling, swelling. Already they are hundreds of feet high, and thick, pressing right down to the water. Conspiring fog.
    The gulls lilting in the waves nearby do not act threatened. They stare and hold their distance, turning first one eye and then the other, as if the edge of the clouds may be an opportunity. They do not enter.
    Here in the lounge I look around at the others. I think, they're not seeing any of this.
    What's most interesting, Penobscot says, *is what you can't quite understand.*

The doctors will not give up.

Every other day now, the Chief Psychologist scoops me up from the dayroom, steers me on private strolls. He thinks he can trick me into talking. First he offers me a cigarette, then a bite of his Hershey bar. Would I like to walk out on the lawn today? How about here by the edge of the woods? Hard to believe, autumn's almost over. He's shaking his head. I encourage him, acting as if I might be on the verge. We walk, kicking through the burgundy and gold leaves covering the grass. He asks me, do I like autumn? *He* does, it's his favorite season. He looks at me, then away again. But I can see he's uncomfortable walking in the leaves. Maybe the soles of his shoes are slippery. He keeps his fingers vice-gripped to my arm, in the manner of the mental health professional. It's the way they move me from place to place. The second he lets go and turns his head, I veer into a tree.

Outside on a day like this, life floods in all at once. I want to cry.

Documentation

The Wild Child is brought to Evelyn on many sheets of paper.

DAILY it occurs to her: she is working at last in a hospital. Mostly in the corridors she notices the force of the change. It is like being shipwrecked. It is like going alone on a long journey, for no reason.

One evening, across the dinner table, Richard catches her staring. He smiles. But at this moment she makes a face and turns, as though directing her hearing to something outside, in the black beyond the window. "What?" he asks. She shakes her head. She isn't sure. Perhaps there was something. Richard grins again. He is awfully good at grinning his way around. One minute a grin, the next he's nowhere to be seen.

Her days at the hospital accumulate, without recognizable order. It is as if she is feeling her way. It is as if—despite the fluorescence and the cheerful walls, recently papered childish yellows and pinks—her overall impression is one of darkness. It's hard to pinpoint. The staff appear, if not outright friendly, at least not overly grim. And the patients?—how appropriate that word seems. Entirely without hurry, destinationless, they move, pause, congregate, aim themselves into corners, as if waiting for the next minute to slide into place. And the next. And the next. They seem to prefer the halls, dayroom, and canteen, shunning the austere beauty of the grounds, except to duck out a door now and again to smoke a cigarette. Their eyes—slack, out of kilter—don't often connect with hers. If the patients notice anything about her in particular, they're not saying.

There are moments, however, when Evelyn cannot escape the feeling that there is something else about the institution, something she ought to understand. Something that, each time she tries pursuing it, slips further from conscious grasp.

Meanwhile, she has her panic attacks not to think about—three of them so far. She knows enough about positive feedback loops. It's clear, at least immediately, what needs to be done. In the realm of mental health metaphor, panic attacks are like hastily constructed walls, on the other side of which awaits the real terror. Perhaps if one just keeps moving.

* * * * *

Three o'clock. Evelyn has one hour.

Sophie Davenport's "chart" isn't a chart. It is more like a dissertation, an inch-thick packet of paper. Besides the report of origin by Detective Roland Davis, there are the statements of the Medical Center ER physicians, the report of primary investigator Detective Carl Freeman, the transcription of an interview with a Mrs. Elizabeth Farnsworth, the preliminary assessment (conducted in Penobscot County Jail) of State Forensic Psychiatrist Warren Griswold, various court documents, previous police records, and a chart remaining from an earlier involuntary admission to this hospital. There are forms, face sheets, transmittal letters. The latest dated yesterday.

This haphazard aggregate, this squander of information—what is it for? Its pieces appear to have converged from great distances, coincidentally, like luggage in an airport. One could stare all day and make nothing of them. But she flips through the pages, anyway, her eyes chasing a feeling.

First, the report by Detective Davis, assigned to executive security at the golf-course groundbreaking. During a demonstration of the tree harvestor, according to Davis, a gunshot was heard, apparently from the woods to the east. Witnesses, including Davis, observed the round "deflect off the tree-harvestor, raising a puff of dust near the Governor's feet." They then saw the subject, Sophie Davenport, several hundred feet away to the east, running, carrying what looked like a rifle. Three site workers, arriving on the scene at that instant, "directly in the subject's line of escape to the woods," assisted Detective Davis and another officer in overtaking and apprehending her. After Davis placed her under arrest, she continued resisting forcefully and attempting to flee, throwing one of the site workers to the ground and injuring him. Eventually, she was herself thrown to the ground, and her head struck a rock. She lay then without moving, apparently unconscious. Transported by ambulance to Eastern Maine Medical Center, she was diagnosed as having suffered a concussion. After over eight hours, she seemed to regain consciousness in her hospital bed. Attending officer Adam Willey reported she looked about the room but did not speak to him. Nor, apparently, has she spoken to anyone else since.

At the time she was apprehended, Sophie was wearing jeans, a heavy woolen hunting jacket, but no shoes. She carried no carkeys or identification. Her pockets contained "matches, some form of biscuit or bread, and seven spare rounds of .270-caliber ammunition." Remarkably, during the struggle accompanying her arrest, Davis reported, "the suspect was observed to be laughing." As if she were having a good time.

Three days after the arrest, an aunt living in Franklin recognized the photograph in the newspaper. Elizabeth Farnsworth came forward with a name and a bit of background. Evelyn absorbs what she can. The name, Sophie Davenport, attaches to a dusky shape, from which stray particulars stand out as if under the flash and tremble of lightning. The girl's mother, for example. Who, on being told of her daughter's arrest, declined to cut short a vacation in Spain. Asked whether she would be providing legal counsel, Mother replied, "Are you offering me a choice?"

Sophie, twenty-six years old, has had prior arrests. Once in Princeton for public nudity, and another time in Ellsworth for shooting out floodlights in a car dealership lot with a .22-caliber rifle. Both, during her teens, treated as juvenile offences. And then State Police, responding to a disturbance at the Bangor Mall, arrived at the scene to find the girl impaling cupcakes on the fingers of store-window mannequins. She taunted the police, then resisted arrest, and spent the night in jail before her aunt posted bond the following morning. The presiding District Court judge ordered her psychiatric evaluation at the state mental hospital.

And before that? There must have been a child. What of the little Sophie? Lizzie Farnsworth recalled her as "lively, inquisitive, brassbound. Not exactly friendly." She was an only child who carried on conversations with animals. She took long walks, even at the age of five. Her parents put up fences to keep her in. She climbed over them. At night she was visited by wild dreams from which she could not be awakened, even sitting up in bed with her eyes wide open. She would not shut her bedroom window any time of year, using it often to get in and out of the house.

When she was ten years old, her father, an architect, bought land on Window Lake, outside of Franklin, and built a camp on it. He named it Sophie's Grotto.

But she and her mother were effectively spirits at war.

And then, when the girl was fourteen . . .

(Afterward it will seem to Evelyn that she knew what was coming.)

. . . her father's automobile skidded off the road and submerged itself upside down in the Merrimac River.

Though Evelyn has, from these pages, no picture of the automobile, she knows the moment already. The domain of velocity, of steel and glass revolving. The quickened recognition, the looming wall, then slipping through . . . to nothing.

What then?

Weeks after the funeral, the girl appeared at her aunt's back door, "like a wraith. Her eyes only half in this world. I sat her down and made her eat a sandwich. She didn't say a word. The light seemed to pass right through her."

For awhile Sophie tried living at home with her mother, an arrangement that did not last. The girl refused to wash, smudged herself in thick vegetable smokes, withdrew to her room with books on witchcraft. Her disappearances, a week at a time, so embarrassed her mother that she gave up reporting them to the police. After a third suspension, Sophie left school permanently and moved in with her aunt in Maine. Over the next several years she worked briefly as a waitress and took up seasonal employment making wreaths, raking blueberries, digging sandworms. She lived for a period in the camp on Window Lake. And at times, for months at a stretch, she dropped out of sight.

Evelyn pages ahead to the hospital admission form. The Xerox copy of the blue paper has come out dark and smudgy. Her eyes run down the form to Diagnosis on Admission:

SCHIZOTYPAL PERSONALITY—MOD. TO SEVERE

The bloated, back-leaning capitals crowd the box near the bottom of the page. And then the slash of a signature: Dr. Marcus B. Einhorn. Evelyn finds her head shaking involuntarily, neither at the doctor nor at the diagnosis, though she has not quite fathomed either of these, but rather at what it is she feels: the terrible actuality behind what is seen. She looks at the date: October 21, 1990. Almost exactly seven years ago.

The girl was held in Admissions for a week but never released. Rather, she "disappeared" from the hospital. Apparently she escaped.

At some point, Evelyn decides she'll never have enough time with the chart, and what she's looking for isn't in it anyway. So she returns it to Griswold's blankfaced security guard at the outermost door of the Forensic Ward. Ahead of schedule. Faced with the indifference of the guard, his jaw working at something, she allows the slab of documents in her hand to indent the bulge of his stomach. "Here," she thinks of saying, "chew on this for awhile." But she keeps silent, watching his eyes roll from the chart, now in his hand, up to her face. His chewing produces a clicking sound as he pulls himself back into the echo and dinge of the chambers behind him. He has to push the steel door hard, twice, before it clanks shut.

At least they aren't keeping her there.

* * * * *

On the way home, it occurs to her that she is always driving away from the sun. Every morning west to Bangor, and in the evening east again to Hancock. The drives take her over the same terrain, but the look and feel are different. Mornings draw her into these days at the hospital that rain now with such bewildering blankness, while evenings return her, senseless, to nights that slip over her like sleep. And as she moves each way with the traffic, winding among the wooded hills that obscure the horizon, she belongs to neither one world nor the other, neither the hospital nor her home. Somehow, she is not becoming used to this. She believes it cannot last. Day follows night follows day follows night, without one instant of reassurance. Only the tension between them seems real.

Brake lights of the cars ahead pop on. The traffic light at Holden brings the line of cars to a standstill. Evelyn looks at her gas gauge, near empty. Rather than wait at the light, she pulls into the Mobil station, the full-service island. While the tank is filling, the attendant cleaning the glass, she strays from the car, out across the asphalt to the border of weeds around the station. Somewhere between thoughts, she turns on her boot-heel and stands, surveying things. The traffic light changes, and the lines of cars begin moving again. Headlights switch on against the increasing dusk. Alongside the pumps sits her white Corolla, its stationary profile of gleams and reflections awash in the noise of accelerating traffic. The faces in the moving cars stare ahead into their separate worlds — so many worlds, streaming by her like a meteor shower. One could never guess from the expressions on those faces that Evelyn is standing here, contemplating them. Nothing could be more removed from those stares than the substance of her thinking. She is, to these passing lives, not even part of the background. How easy it would be not to exist.

She wanders on into the Quick-Mart at the station, looking at the items that might be purchased by simply bringing them to the register. But she brings nothing. She pays for the gas and is out the door. Moments later, without it having entered the chain of her thinking, she is back in the stream of traffic. It's true, consciousness can sometimes get in its own way. Then one had better move automatically, or else be left behind.

The road ahead is darker now, defined by the lights of automobiles. Every so often she glances off into the shadow of the roadside, as if detecting something.

~S~

WILLIAM HAS a foot in more than one world. Maybe, too, he has particular thoughts about me: the way he acts as though he's on two strings, one drawing him near, the other yanking him away. He moves in, as if with some intention, and then he's gone.

I wonder, does he watch me when I'm myself? Does he think I'm too wild?

This morning I think, maybe he's holding something back, some powerful secret he's keeping in reserve. Maybe he's waiting for the right moment, or for me to bring it up. So I do. Before he has a chance to slip away, I put my foot right down on his.

I whisper, "Is there something you want me to ask you?"

It stops him alright. He stands there, wrestling with that on-and-off smile, and nods as though a thing has finally come to him that he's known all along was inevitable. His cigarette hand appears between us, like a third party. He looks at it, turning it over. We are standing by the coke machine, where generally talk runs better than anyplace else. And all at once it comes pouring out of him.

"O.K." he says. "Like . . . right now . . . I have this scene in my head." His hands burrow into his pockets. He squints ahead past the coke machine.

"See, I'm standing on this beach, where it's windy and cold. The sky . . . the sky is like . . . wool. Surf, pounding the jetties. One wave after the other. The wind . . . " his arm sails out "is blowing spray all the way back to the road, where . . . maybe, there's a car parked. I don't know. I don't know whether . . . I should worry about the car being there, maybe getting wet, or . . . about it not being there. Because, then, what am I doing there? How did I get there?"

A hand emerges to rove his thick hair. "The way it is, I begin asking these questions, and what I get are like pictures. Like photographs from . . . another time. A picture of me driving some large dark car. The car is larger than the picture. I can't quite see it all. The interior and slow motion of the car suggest . . . I don't know . . . opulence. Then there's a picture of me walking, I think it's along the edge of a golf course. Sunny lawn in the background. A place I've never been. My white shirt glows in the shadows. The pictures, they seem, you know, like possible answers. But contradictory. Contradictory. And the longer I look, the more the pictures become like one another. The more they become . . . like echoes. Till after awhile, it's just me again back on that beach under the clouds, the sand in my shoes, like I belong there. Like I could never be anyplace else."

William is shaking his head. "The place is . . . so friggin' empty. And I know . . . I know . . . there won't be any resolution. Nothing's going to be decided, by my standing there. But I do anyway. As if . . . the lunacy of it has some kind of power. As if . . . if I wait long enough, if I satisfy some requirement, you know, of stamina or . . . desperation, then maybe something will open up. It will lead somewhere. Maybe somewhere in my life."

His eyes stir, and I feel his foot pull away. He doesn't say any more. And then I hear the clang of Frank's metal chair. Nomadic Frank, staking out the territory behind my back.

William's hand makes a pass at the coke machine, as though to choose a button. But it's only a suggestion. The hand covers his mouth, and the next second he is gone. So all-at-once, I can almost forget he was there.

Behind me, the chair squeaks. Frank clears his throat.

On Into the Silence

Including Evelyn's encounters with two pairs of eyes: one that will not look at her and one that will not look away.

WHERE IS the center of consciousness? Somehow behind the eyes, it seems. Consciousness doesn't equate that way with any of the other senses. The ears, the nose, the mouth, the skin—all of these report to consciousness. But if she were asked where her own active self is located, she would say that it is there, like a passenger, behind the windshield of her eyes.

* * * * *

There is not enough room on her desk, so she smooths the road map across her knees, her eyes trying its crinkled geography. Every day she has seen the sign for the turn-off. Twenty, thirty minutes from home.
Beside her, the computer hums.
There.
Window Lake.
Her finger stops beneath the blue shape. Not like a window. Like the footprint of something. Like an eyesocket. Mrs. Dibrizzi's.

* * * * *

Well, she must admit, she has asked for it. And now the girl is straight across from her. At the little table in the tiny lounge. They have been sitting here for several minutes. Esther Boyle's exit down the corridor is only just subsiding, Evelyn's gaze still hanging in that direction, her smile fading, a smile that now seems pointless. It is not the right beginning.

Except for the hum of the soda machine, the hall is quiet. Evelyn shifts in her chair, refers to her lined yellow pad, on which nothing is written, and then looks into the girl's face. It is, of course, the face she remembers from that morning on the day of the admission. Dark hair cut short. Still darker eyes.

"You're Sophie, aren't you?"

Sophie is situated perhaps five feet away, across the table. This is about the optimum distance for interviewing. But, it's obvious, the table is wrong. Its planar surface cuts the girl off below the pocket of her white flannel shirt, leaving Evelyn with something like the view in a passport photo. And Sophie is holding herself inappropriately, as if she has never encountered a table before, arms plummeting straight at her sides, the table edge jammed against her ribcage. It was Esther Boyle who created this position with a summary thrust of her biceps when first sitting the girl down, the nurse's anger over who-knows-what spilling even now into Evelyn's efforts, contaminating them.

"I'm Evelyn Moore."

She finds it easy, even pleasant, looking into Sophie's face. Certainly, there is intensity in the eyes, in the flare of the nostrils. But she can not readily imagine this soul shooting out lights with a rifle, knocking over policemen.

Evelyn hears the softening in her own voice, as though it were the voice of someone else. "Is it that you can't speak? Or are you choosing not to?"

But there is no response from Sophie, who is looking not quite at her, not quite at anything.

"You will, soon, be undergoing some tests, to see if your silence is due to a physical condition. But I thought you might prefer to tell me yourself."

Sophie holds herself as though waiting for an injection.

"When you were arrested by the police officers at the construction site, you were knocked down." Describing the scene now in front of the girl, she can almost see it. "For a long time you were unconscious."

The hum of the soda machine switches off. And Evelyn's fingers, playing with her black fiber pen, stop. Her sentences have been falling with a certain cadence, at intervals in the silence, like waves collapsing on a breathless beach.

"I wasn't there to see what actually happened, what was done to you. But the police report says that when you finally awoke in the hospital, you weren't speaking. Can you tell me anything about that? Anything at all."

Because of the table, the girl's hands and feet are blocked from view. The staff can not keep shoes on her. Evelyn imagines the feet crescented together, blue-veined against the tile.

She lays her pen down on the lined yellow pad. "You may write it if you'd rather." She slides the pad to the middle of the table.

Some distance down the corridor, a metal chair rings, unfolding. Frank takes his time sitting down, his back to the wall. But once he crosses his legs, he settles in quickly, applying his gaze to the wall opposite as though reading something there, as though picking up where he'd left off at his last watch station. He seems content to be doing this.

It is because of Frank that they are meeting in this lounge. When he saw Evelyn's office, he shook his head. He didn't like the window, and he didn't like the proximity to the entrance. Better if they'd meet somewhere off the main corridor. So here they sit.

"Sophie." Evelyn lowers her voice to barely a whisper. "I'd like to help you."

If Sophie has heard any of this, she gives no sign. She is a head-and-shoulders snapshot at an ambiguous moment, a frozen stare open to rapt interpretation.

Evelyn's eyes turn skittish. She keeps finding other things to look at, as if this may alter her chances.

Perhaps minutes pass. Possibly for the sake of making something happen, she has taken back the yellow pad. Its blue lines repeat in parallel, defining many narrow, interchangeable, barren spaces. Inches away, her fingers hold her pen at the ready. She has no idea what for.

Heels click along the tile floor. A mental health worker, not Frank, approaches from the hall, glancing at them as he stops at the soda machine. He stands, poring over his palmful of change, and Evelyn faces what she has to show for her being here: a conspicuous silence. The coins fall through the works of the machinery, snapping switches, triggering decisions. The paper cup rattles into place, fills.

Well, what about the silence?

The worker brings the cup to his mouth, sips, and stares at the two of them facing one another like parties in an interrupted argument. Then, just when Evelyn expects some remark, he turns. His heels click away back down the hall, withdrawing from this silence, which is after all perhaps not so much conspicuous as intrinsic and full. It is a silence no one could enter.

Evelyn's thoughts ascend like balloons. Her eyes run at Sophie, and then away. "Can you tell me, is there someone you'd like to see?"

She understands she would be happier if there were no one.

Even Frank seems to have disappeared. The stillness across the table seems the center of something. It is like discovering how to breath underwater.

At intervals, she is not afraid to stir the air with a question.

"Is there anything, anything at all, you'd like to say to me?"

There are questions she doesn't ask. What if those eyes were to turn her way? And if they were to see her, what would they see?

Anyway, there are no answers. Evelyn sets her pen on the yellow pad, takes another breath, rides on into the silence. It seems, for the time being, enough.

* * * * *

That evening in the parking lot, over the low-slung roofs of cars, she catches sight of Warren Griswold, his head cocked in her direction. With that fire-red Buick at his back, he seems expectant. But he doesn't greet her. He only flexes his shoulders, rising onto the balls of his feet like a chauffeur, like a jockey. A short man ready to drive something.

She waves, quickly ducks into her car. As she backs out and pulls away, she can see he's still there. He is standing, watching. A pair of eyes receding in her rear-view mirror.

~S~

STANDING AT THE WINDOW and standing at the window, I feel the morning come and go, not slowly. The light slams in. My body aches. The air in here is dead as glass. Memories want to visit, but today they don't get far. I see them outside, disappointed, crowding against the iron fence. The world isn't allowed in here. We have lemon walls and chemicals that take on the appearance of rooms, atomizing soft-brightness. The place is one big medicated straitjacket. All there is left is to calm down.

Nurse Boil enters and looks straight at me, as though on the verge of saying something. Instead she draws the curtain, watching me. But it's no good. Her eyes miss what is real. Cut off from my memories, I can accept the gift of the curtain.

"If you want it open," she says, "you let me know."

* * * * *

Evening—a thing to look forward to. The sudden eruption. Voices pipe up. Doors pull closed—decisively, from elbows. Somewhere outside, cars are starting. A final flurry, then quiet.

Lone nurses, here and there a worker, blink and stare, settle into their stations: everyone else has left. The place is emptier than if they'd never been here. The rooms look surprised, then dead as architecture. Time slows, congeals in the stillness. The corridors darken, semi-illuminated, to become a long series of traveling shots and sharp angles, on many levels, without significance. Without expectation. I wouldn't know whether to measure them in miles, or in years. I have tried them, these corridors. They are irresistible. They go on and on, until it is hard for me to take anything else seriously, until all of meaning seems to return me here into this one baffling simplicity: there is no stopping and no way of knowing which way is forward, which way is back.

Eventually, when all of this is past the point of remembering, I hear car doors thump, keys probing locks, the first tentative birdsong of voices. Only this way do I recognize it's morning. And these same people have returned, washed, sheepish, heads fluttering as if from some discrepancy in their thinking. But after all, they're the staff. They know how to walk straight into the day. They've done it so often, they've gotten used to making it out of here alive. Today, tomorrow, they will enter and leave, enter and leave, free or bound, depending on how you look at it.

We're the ones, Rye proclaims, running the place for *them*.

Louise turns her head to the wall. She doesn't think so.

The Canning Plant

Wherein her husband, Richard, reveals his Grand Plan and is thus himself revealed.

Evening in Richard's blue kitchen. The same blue he brought into the Connecticut house, now here. Federal blue, he told her once. A color somehow out of Richard's past, a past impossibly hidden from Evelyn on the other side of what she has forgotten. A Federal blue past, still capable of engendering circumstances like this kitchen, in which, for the past fifteen minutes, she has been ordered to sit, absorbing Satie from the livingroom CD player, while her husband prepares dinner.

The occasion smells of garlic, coriander, and butter. Richard is stooping over the range in concentration, affording her the nape of his neck above his shirt collar. He is sautéing something—a shellfish, she thinks, though he won't tell her. Only his elbow moves as he works the pan with a wooden spatula. On the counter, a bottle of Champaigne in an ice bucket sits close by the range—perhaps too close, because Richard's hand, still holding the spatula, now shoves the bucket aside to where the angle of the bottleneck exactly opposes the rake of the cutlery handles from the knifeblock, though she can't imagine that he can see these angles from where he stands. Regarding the Champaigne, she is suspending curiosity. Richard often resorts to it as a way of celebration—a little too often, she feels. Surely something is in the wind.

"We set a new record this morning," he announces. "Seven catalogs in the mail."

"Seven?"

"Not counting duplicates." He reaches for the white pepper. "Christmas is how many weeks away?"

"We should stop buying things from them."

He shrugs. Bending, he adjusts the flame. "I see it as a sign. The economy's rebounding." He looks at her.

But Evelyn has nothing to say about the economy.

The conversation goes on like this, gratuitous and sporadic. Richard has taken care of the Bronco—turns out it was the sending unit, which is lucky, because the fan would have been a lot more money. She wonders whether Richard actually knows what the sending unit is. She certainly doesn't.

As a matter of fact, she is barely listening. Her mind is, well, not exactly anywhere. Against Richard's patter, she chooses the remedy of disengagement, neither dwelling on her meeting this afternoon nor quite letting it go, but rather holding still, contemplating this perfect and charged neutrality, knowing all along that what she wants isn't far off, like a highway in the night, running parallel always to her thoughts.

But even through her distraction, she can tell that all this talk of Richard's is preliminary, merely an hors d'oeuvre. He has something to present to her, something that will come out only later, when the time is right. She thinks she can guess what it is.

Richard removes the sauté from the flame.

"You hungry?" he asks. He raises the lids from a couple of saucepans, peers into the steam.

"Very. What's the occasion?"

And suddenly he turns, and he is gazing at her as if he has nothing else to do, as if, ripe with appreciation, he is formulating his next sentence to communicate this. But then he lifts a forefinger and is off, now into the livingroom, where she hears him eject the CD in favor of another.

Outside it is dark. The panes of the window by the table are fogged over from the cooking. Evelyn wishes they were not fogged, though she thinks this absurd, this wish to see the darkness more clearly.

In a moment, her husband is back, removing the salad from the fridge.

"So how did things go with you today?" he says.

She looks into his face as he looks into the salad he is putting in front of her. She takes up her fork. "Gee, I'm not sure what to say."

Richard, installed across from her, is half-filling their goblets with a white Bordeaux. "Really!" he says, his eye on the rise of liquid in the glass.

"The woman who was arrested for shooting at the governor? I met with her this afternoon. I tried to interview her."

"Tried?" He is up again, opening the fridge. "Oh, right. She doesn't talk."

Jars clatter. Evelyn turns to watch her husband rummaging along bright shelves.

"Hm!" The tone in his voice now is not light, but solidly perplexed. "We seem to be out of olives."

She returns to her salad, a cooler air moving through the kitchen, as though pouring out of the fridge.

Then he is back at the table. "So this woman. What's she like?"

It takes her a moment. "Well . . ." Her eyes move to the window, its steamed-over darkness. "On the surface, catatonic."

"So what do you think, she's faking?" Richard is wasting no time with his salad, his fork methodically stabbing greens.

"I don't know."

"What I don't understand," he says, "is how anyone can be that clumsy. I mean a step of that magnitude, assassinating the governor, it's not like, say, running to the store for chips and salsa. You don't just wing it."

Evelyn is slowly chewing salad, her teeth denting stems of parsley, tearing into leaves of endive, releasing their juices into the vinaigrette. The sensation is marvelous.

Richard has risen and withdrawn with his empty salad dish. Through the rising organ tones of Albinoni's Adagio, Evelyn can hear the clinking of utensils. Without quite seeing him, she knows him to be forking pasta onto dinner plates. And now spooning out the sauté. And now, in the fridge again, clattering jars. At some point will come the pop of the Champaigne stopper. But not quite yet.

The plates are set on the table, steaming. Richard sits down, pours a little more wine.

And as she looks away, his voice says at last, "I've made a decision."

She turns, studies the corners of his mouth.

"The time is right," he says. ". . . as they say." He may be close to smiling, but he isn't taking his eyes away from his pasta. "There's no getting around it. It's going to be a hell of a lot of work."

Rooms in time. From somewhere the phrase comes to her. And that is what she feels approaching, rooms she may be forced to enter and not allowed to leave. An entire gallery of rooms in time, in which Richard will no longer be cooking pasta, but instead attempting to revive his dissertation. It is a move she has long favored. And now the prospect startles her.

"But I've already done a lot of the research."

It all seems thrown together. She isn't seeing herself as a part of the picture.

"The one big question," he says, "is the liquor license." He flutters his palm over the table. "Which could be tricky."

Liquor license.

"What are you talking about?"

He leans over his plate, fork in hand. "The Canning Plant," he says in a breath of enthusiasm.

It is as if the world, in eclipse beyond the walls of this room, has spun half around. And at last she sees it. Several weeks ago, a drive along the coast. She doesn't remember town names. But the factory, yes. They stopped so he could poke around, peer in windows. He was always looking at property.

"The sardine factory?" she says.

"In a couple of weeks, it'll be on the market."

"You never mentioned anything about this."

"I had to be sure. It's is part of an estate. Eight years in probate, they're up to their earlobes in legal fees—Christ, I should have been a lawyer. But eight years, and the whole mess gets straightened out just last week. I tell you, Ev . . ." Requiring emphasis, Richard taps the tines of his fork against his plate. "this is ripe. Everyone I've talked to thinks the place is junk."

"Gee. It sounds really attractive."

"They're not in a position to evaluate." Richard is back at his linguine, twirling his fork against his knife.

"But you are."

"Is this, or is this not my specialty?"

She doesn't answer this. "What do you propose to do with the place?"

Richard actually stops eating. He puts his fork down.

"The Canning Plant," he says, his voice little more than a whisper.

He repeats it. The Canning Plant. This dark, archaic structure hanging over the water on piles is an incredible find. Exactly what he's been looking for. Abandoned, neglected for fifteen years. No one wants it. He, Richard, will pick it up for a song, and turn it into a restaurant. The timing couldn't be better. Real estate is in a slump. Tourism in the area hasn't begun a comeback. It is only a matter of months before the place is discovered by some sharp-eyed orthodontist from New Jersey with half a million to invest.

"A restaurant?" Evelyn says.

"Ev." His hand, extending across the table, finds hers. "The Canning Plant. Did you get a good look at it? Aged wood, the old equipment, the place is magical. You sit people down in a scene like that, serve an onion soup, prime rib, lobster—fundamental American fare—couple of French sauces. Yorkshire pudding. Put in a bakery. Yeast breads, heavy on the grain. Everything nicely done, they'll think they're dining in a Herman Melville novel. I tell you, even the locals'd love it. It's a captive audience here. There's nothing else in a fifty-mile radius."

Evelyn is dumbfounded. "But is that something you want to get into?"

"It doesn't matter. The place is up and running—three, four years—then if you want, you sell." Richard rises, moves to the counter. "Investment, it's like the chain letter concept. You jump in, the earlier the better: that's where the money is. By the time everyone else finds out, eager to get in, it's ready to die. You make your exit."

Evelyn finds the energy to spear a Brussels sprout. She shakes her head. But her husband is facing in the other direction.

"Do you have any idea," he says, "of the money there is in a thriving restaurant?"

At the pop of the Champaigne stopper, Evelyn jumps.

"Five years," he says. "Five years. We'd be in a position, Ev, we could do anything we want. Hah!" Amidst the glug and effervescence of pouring, he discovers a thought. "I could even go back for my degree. Who knows?"

* * * * *

Staring out the windshield into the broad thickness of morning rushing at her, she is at the same time aware of her hands on the steering wheel.

It is remarkable, she thinks, the intensity with which one can feel nothing. Of course, it isn't nothing that she feels, but more like a virtual paralysis. It is as if she has fallen into the cracks between emotions. It brings her to the point of wondering about her own neurochemistry, whether this dreamlike immersion in an inertia without boundaries might not better be understood as a matter of serotonin reuptake. On the other hand, there is the firmness, the actuality of that steering wheel.

~S~

LATE AFTERNOON, I'm wandering in my thoughts, which are a torn landscape.

A flip in my pulse. Suddenly she's there in the doorway.

The suddenness is mine, not hers. I never see her arrive. It is as though she has been there always. It is as though she *is* the doorway.

Tonight Nurse Boil is on duty. She has locked me in my room. And Aroostook says she's watching the door. So probably I'm here till morning, compressed between these walls and the ceiling, all at right angles to myself. I could spend the night, it wouldn't have to be a problem. The trouble is that night isn't allowed here. They need to keep the lights on, always. Inside and out.

People do this, I've noticed. They leave things lit up, televisions running in their bedrooms. The silver-blue flicker of the screens sets unhealthy dreams in motion. It adds up. People are losing themselves. Their memories are leaking into circuitboards, and the other way around. Pretty soon they won't know who they are. Standing in front of full-length mirrors, already they're having doubts.

So am I, lying here, deprived of night.

Outside my cell window, down on Hamburger Avenue, a million pinpoints of candy-color neurosis shimmer above cold pavement. And on the other side of my cell door, the corridor excretes its steady glow like some waiting intestine, with red scissors of light spelling EXIT in contradictory directions. I am trapped. I lie here, understanding now how it happens. One day at a time, I am dissolving.

At last dawn comes like an outlived promise, a cold, slow flare to the east. The air goes gray, bleeding a stain of visibility over the valley floor. Streetlights fade and, in case I've forgotten, I can begin to see the world again for what it's become.

No Horizon at All

Evelyn hears another ghost story and feels Dr. Tarantula closing in.

T HERE ARE voices.
    She can't remember exactly the first time she heard them. But it doesn't matter. They aren't the kind of voices that need worrying about, arising as they do out of the actual if veiled realm of what the janitor calls the ventilation system.
    For awhile, in fact, she isn't even sure they are voices. She could imagine the murmur of aging machinery, the groanings of swivel chairs, sounding like that.
    Soon, though, it's clear. There are two men speaking. At times she believes she can nearly make out words, especially this morning—some change in the air, perhaps, teasing the voices nearer consonants and vowels. She holds herself perfectly still as the shapes of these sounds percolate through the grate in the floor of her office. She listens.
    One of the voices is laughing.
    Then she recognizes words.
    "No, she's not," the laughing voice says, repeatedly. "No, no, she's not." The other voice simply drones on.
    Bent over in her chair, her ear toward the grate, she feels the dizzying, warm rush of humiliation.

* * * * *

"If you'll forgive his asking," Roland says, "how is it for you? Things never transpire, of course, quite the way one expects, but by now you have . . . *mm* . . . perhaps begun to wonder whether you've made the sensible move, coming all the way as you have from California . . . ."

"Connecticut."

"Hm? Beg your pardon?"

"I've come from Connecticut."

"Can this be true? Oh-ho!—well, there you go. That would make some difference, wouldn't it. Connecticut, of course. You'd be better prepared then, emerging out of that ravaged and kindred geography. Connect - i - cut, yes, sister to the very terrain over which you and he now converse on waxed planar surfaces that will one day crash in on themselves."

He blinks his eyes at her.

His voice slides into a whisper, heavy with enthusiasm. "Imagine, below and around you. The stunned remnants of Transition Forest. Through which once traveled luminous and tawny beings. Now the corner of Hogan Road and Stillwater Avenue, it is madness. What are left of their spirits these days have taken flight, haunting the architecture of the invaders. At this precise moment, these shadows are waging guerrilla cannibalism inside shopping malls. Black-winged, they patrol even these corridors. Invisibly." He raises a finger to his lips, apparently gleeful. "It is not suspected."

His finger stabs the arm of his chair, and his voice emerges from whisper. "Listen. Listen. Do you suppose? That, seven centuries ago . . . *mm* . . . you and he, occupying this same space would have found yourselves boxed inside this glorified antfarm? Hah! Certainly. Not. You might instead have held conference—picture this!—from the pendulous boughs of the White Pine. Your turpentine voices shot full of the calls of Uncommon Crows. Your legs, unbooted—imagine them!—dangling."

With his feet he pushes off first one slipper and then the other. His toes wiggle in his socks.

"What then?" He leans forward. "What then? Might not the winds have annulled your sufferings? Might you not thus comfortably have entertained darker thoughts? More animate possibilities?"

Roland appears, by the force of his sunblown gaze, almost to rise out of his chair.

"Listen. It has been delivered into his ear in palpable, anonomous whispers. That the Forest survives. And somewhere waits. Not even so far removed, who knows? Perhaps just over the horizon. In that direction."

His hand, taking flight, collides with the bookcase.

"Ah, but of course. It all comes back now. From where he sits, there is no horizon. No horizon at all."

Roland glances at the wastebasket. "And, for God's sake, forget about that window, it's perfectly useless. Given the parasitic nature of this organism. Its subtle methods of attachment." His fingers flick lightly over his jacket sleeves. "He needn't tell you what it feeds on. Good Lord, do you think this is a building you are in?"

* * * * *

Over lunch she asks Walter Rafferty about Dr. Marcus Einhorn.

Walter says, "Einhorn? Chief Psychiatrist. You've heard the horror story?"

"I heard he was thrown out a window."

"Fell three stories, onto the pavement."

"How did it happen?"

"No one could figure it out. He went right through a Chamberlain screen." Walter glances toward the corridor beyond the canteen. "It was awful. The last time this place had seen anything that gruesome was in the late fifties."

"What, someone else was killed?"

"Some doctor hanged himself. Up on level four."

"When was this?"

"I don't know, fifty-seven, fifty-eight. I don't know. It used to be the big ghost story here. Now it's Einhorn." Walter shrugs. "But a place like this. From time to time, some ugly things are bound to happen."

"So that's it?"

"Why? You think there's more?"

* * * * *

Corridors are rooms with many possibilities but with no fulfillment. They are fundamentally linear. Although they, just like other rooms, have a spatial dimension, we tend to experience corridors more in time. To be in a corridor, generally, is to be in transit.

In this hospital the corridors appear perversely numerous and long. Again and again, she finds herself drawn into them, until they begin to feel somehow essential.

* * * * *

At shortly after noon, lunch time, all the patients have left the dayroom. There is only the lone figure of Sophie, standing as if abandoned, vaguely facing the window.

Evelyn, seeing the nurses' station empty, moves quietly, slowly up behind the girl. A few feet away, she stops. From here she can see the texture and detail of Sophie's clothing, the rise and fall of her breathing. Evelyn doesn't say anything. In fact, standing here, she isn't exactly sure of her intentions. Perhaps she has approached this close only out of simple curiosity. But by the time, a few minutes later, she tiptoes away, the visit seems to have become something more. Like an offering.

Returning through the corridor, she finds her thoughts, dreamlike, coalescing on Walter Rafferty's sweaters, the fuzzy, doggy smell of them. He lives alone, she is pretty sure. With Airedales.

And all of a sudden, there is Warren Griswold!

He seems to spring wholly out of nowhere. And then quickly, as though regardless of all rules of engagement, he is touching her arm.

"Oh!" She jumps, reacting to everything at once.

"Well," he says, "what do you think of her?"

"I'm sorry."

"The Davenport girl."

This psychiatrist, phantom of the hospital's inner recesses, until recently had barely penetrated her thinking. Now it seems there's no getting free of him.

"Oh . . . I've only had one session with her." She takes a step back.

But he steps closer. What alarms her most is his skin, which has the white, shriveled look of something soaked overnight in cold water. Then the black black hair, the musk cologne. And that other odor.

"Session," he says, blank-faced. Then mumbling, "You probably want more." As if the idea hadn't occurred to him. His eyes stray to her shoulders, her hair. "We were going to meet," he says. It isn't a question.

Here in the corridor, confronting the prospect of meeting with this man, she can't think of a reply.

"Maybe in a week or so?" she says at last.

The lenses of his eyes appear to contract, recede—as if, without moving, he has pulled away from her.

Afterward, at her desk, she still feels the place on her arm where his cold, white fingers made their contact.

~S~

THERE IS a fourth floor here. It occupies this place like a cavity inside a skull. You think cavities are empty. Actually they are full of what is not seen.

The fourth floor is closed off. We're not supposed to go there. We're not even supposed to know about it. We might be tempted. Officially they call it storage, but I've had a look at it. The only thing stored up there is bad energy.

I mentioned it to Eddie.

He was standing, pumped as a rooster, in his bathrobe and bluejeans with Rye and the pudgy one they call Redtop. Eddie had talked both of them into the corner between the window and the soda machine. I was maybe two feet away, faking stupefaction over the venetian blind cord.

"Oh yeah yeah, sure," he said, slapping Rye in the stomach with the back of his hand. "We all been up there, right?"

"A fourth floor?" Rye gazed ceilingward. "Ah, of course, one takes the escalator!"

Redtop kept shifting his weight from one foot to the other, as though he maybe had to pee.

Eddie leaned my way with a conspiratorial voice. "Bitchin' spot for brewskies. There's holes in the wall where you drop the cans."

I was surprised they knew about it. I thought I'd been clever in finding a way, just the right wrist action on the stairwell doorknob.

"Shit, you ask me," Eddie went on, "I'd sooner they keep us up there than down here. That's a real cuckoo house, *that* is. Not like here, all this yellow paint and bullshit."

Rye raised a finger as if to speak, but Eddie cut him off. "Place down here is a fucking joke. And who's laughing? You see the smiles on all them bug doctors? Casing us from behind one-way mirrors, they're holding conferences back there. I feel like a fucking ballgame."

I thought Eddie was going to spit on the floor.

Then something changed, vaporizing the conversation. Rye turned toward the corner, and Eddie quit his talking. Someone was close.

"The gentleman has a point," Rye said, bending, peering behind the soda machine. "Somewhere here."

Eddie, standing his ground for eye contact, lifted his paper cup to whoever was passing.

A door opened and then closed.

"Arachnophobia." Eddie chuckled. "I ain't afraid of spiders."

The blind cord hung alongside its shadow. I was contemplating the two of them, trying to make myself forget which was which. Out of the corner of my eye, I could see Redtop, lumbering from side to side like a pachyderm with a chain around its leg.

Wounded Women

Proving that Evelyn and the Wild Child have something in common, and presenting certain animal noises.

S HE RECEIVES a message on e-mail concerning the replacement of windows. All offices on the north side of the east wing, first and second floors, have been scheduled for the next two weeks. The new windows and related repairs should result in a more comfortable working environment and help to conserve energy.

She glances at the list of addressees, the first initials and last names of those slated for this upheaval. The seventh one down is emoore. The array seems fundamentally cockeyed, like an alphabetized list, by first initial, of people destined to catch colds in the coming month.

* * * * *

Next thing Tuesday morning, she finds her eleven o'clock appointment with Sophie cancelled—no apology, no explanation. Warren Griswold, she learns only from Amy, says he needs the time for a Halstead Battery. "If she's not speaking," Evelyn asks, "how is he going to administer it?" Amy shakes her head. What is worse, the forensic psychiatrist has penciled Sophie in all morning for the remainder of her stay in the hospital. Whether he will actually use this time or merely intends to shut Evelyn out isn't clear. She decides to talk to Gary Benjamin.

At the sound of his name, the Chief Psychologist hits one or two keys more before spiraling around from his computer terminal to look up at Evelyn standing in his doorway. When he asks her how things are going, his fingers are still poised over the keyboard.

"Well . . . " she says, a little fearful of her own momentum, "I seem to have run into a scheduling dilemma."

Gary's eyebrows jump. "Oh?" His arm wraps over the back of his chair, his bearded face striving for brightness.

"I had my appointment with Sophie Davenport this morning cancelled out from under me."

"Warren?" Gary frowns thoughtfully. "You can't reschedule?"

"Well that's just it. He's blocked in her mornings now entirely. And my afternoons are pretty well booked."

"No time at all?"

She purses her mouth, feeling the pressure here of too many considerations unspoken. Of course she could rework her schedule, but it would be awkward. If the forensic psychiatrist wishes to engage her in a chess match over time slots, Evelyn knows, it is a game she can not win. And if it boils down to a matter of territory—as of course it does—Sophie Davenport is after all Warren Griswold's responsibility.

But Evelyn isn't prepared to say any of this. Gary Benjamin, twisted around in his chair, drops his gaze to the floor, as if the answer might be written there. "You know," he says, looking up, his voice softening almost to a different voice, a different Gary Benjamin, "Warren is tied up late afternoons, I think four to five, with the Accreditation Committee. Why don't you try then."

Evelyn nods but, for the moment, can't come up with anything to say, such is the force of her gratitude.

Finally, she says simply, "Thanks."

Gary Benjamin gives her a quick smile, turns back to his keyboard.

Returning along the corridor, she is watchful, though—it occurs to her—not very observant. The difference is between readiness for what is not there and recognition of what is. Arriving at her office, she feels as if she has been walking anxiously through fog.

* * * * *

"I told you Gary was alright." Walter Rafferty is shelling peanuts from a small paper bag, dropping them into his mouth. Though it is long after lunch, the man's office smells like a delicatessen.

She nods. Standing by the window, she can look either at Walter or down at the rear courtyard, simply with a shift of her eyes.

She says, with what sounds to her immediately like petulance, "Though I won't know till tomorrow whether this will work out."

Walter regards her in silence.

He says, "You're really taken with this girl."

The courtyard below is bounded by asphalt. The lawn, a thinning, darkening green, has been raked clean of leaves. Her eyes wander over this shady patch of ground as she measures what has just been said.

Walter peers into his paper bag. "I got a glimpse of her yesterday. A wounded woman—that was my first impression."

"What?" She stares at him.

"I'll bet she lost a father."

Evelyn turns back to that lawn, which seems to have a new depth.

"*I* lost a father," she says.

Walter, chewing a peanut, stops. "Oh." He sits up. "Oh."

Her eyes are at the window again, but stopping there, not seeing beyond. "What's that second 'Oh' for? You think that's why I'm interested in her?"

"You mean I was right?"

She nods.

"How?"

"An automobile accident. When she was fourteen." She turns to Walter. "The same way my father died. Except that I was twenty."

"Jesus."

"Anyway, it isn't just that. I don't know why I'm so drawn to her. I really don't think she belongs here."

"It may be better than where she's headed."

"Prison?"

"No, upstairs."

"The Forensic Ward? For the criminally insane?"

Walter shrugs. "I hear that's the way Griswold's leaning."

"By virtue of what diagnosis? Sociopathic personality? Paranoid schizophrenic? On what evidence? Suppose she's just a mildly mixed up kid in the wrong place at the wrong time."

"'Mildly mixed up?' Let's see, where does that fit into DSM-III-R?"

"Oh, come on, Walter."

"The trouble is, the privilege of supposition at this point is not yours. It's Warren Griswold's."

"Then it may be up to me to write the dissenting opinion."

"Which is probably why Griswold's locked you out of it. A dissenting opinion from outside the assessment team isn't going to carry a lot of weight."

"So what am I supposed to do, sit back and watch this man steamroll her?"

Walter appears to think about that.

But her attention now is taken by something she hears beyond the room.

"Listen," she says, turning toward the door. "That sound."

Walter looks at her blankly. "What sound?"

"There. It just came on. From somewhere in the building."

He listens. "I don't know. The furnace?" He looks into his peanut bag and, finding it empty, crumples it into a ball.

She strains to identify the sound, which more and more now seems a part of the background. "I keep hearing it," she says.

Walter says, "It's an old building." Then he is quiet.

Her eyes return to the window. She feels his dark contemplation.

"I'm obsessed about this patient. Is that what you're thinking?"

"No, that hadn't occurred to me. But it seems you're in a precarious position here."

She sees, below in the courtyard, a door open and a figure half-emerge only to draw back and close the door again. She waits, wondering what else Walter Rafferty might say to her. But he doesn't say anything.

Any minute now, a patient is to appear at the door to his office. Walter stands, his long fingers whisking peanut debris from his sweater.

Evelyn brings herself away from the window. She gives Walter a long look, then an attempt at a smile. But, as she leaves his office, it is through her skin that she recognizes, as if by a light pressure, a different kind of attention from his eyes.

* * * * *

She is in session with Morgan Fontaine, who has hardly said a word to anyone since his biblical outpouring the other afternoon. Maybe twenty minutes ago, Esther Bolye, that tow-truck of a woman, somehow managed to deliver him here to her office. For awhile Morgan sat, flushed and mute in the fires of his own private rage. And though he seems gradually to have cooled down, still he will not look at her. She has been forbearing, trying to draw him out, trying to get to the real Morgan Fontaine.

She turns aside to her desk for just an instant, and then hears—how can she describe it?—a low growl, like the sound that a dog makes when its hair stands, just before it breaks into a bark.

And this is how she reacts: she turns back to Morgan, but with feigned preoccupation, as if her turning to face him has nothing to do with that sound. As if she may not even have heard it. As if there may not even have been a sound.

Morgan hasn't moved. But he is looking at her.

* * * * *

Roland Rye, having taken his time seating himself like a man settling into a dentist's chair, now looks at her, expectantly. "So?" he says. "Isn't she wonderful?"

She cocks her head at him. She releases the question without a thought, straightening her skirt.

"Isn't who wonderful, Roland?"

And that is all it takes for his expectancy to loosen, dissolve.

"Who," he says, staring. His eyes slide away.

She watches him.

He holds up a tentative finger. "A moment ago—did you notice?—there was a thing he was prepared to say. He had, on his way here in fact, prepared to say it. This thing." He shakes his head, muttering, "But now... *mm* ... it seems to have escaped him."

Roland turns suddenly.

Following his eyes, she sees that the door is open a crack.

"Would you like that door closed, Roland?"

He shrugs, his fingers knotting, then nods.

Before shutting the door, she pokes her head out into the hall. It is empty except, distantly, some dark movement around a corner.

Returning to her chair, she waits for Roland to speak first.

He does not look at her. He appears agitated. His hands brush now at his jacket, now at his trousers.

"He is afraid," he says.

"Afraid of what, Roland?"

"Afraid . . . *mm* . . . of all these diagnostic positivists, if you want the truth. You've perhaps caught glimpses of them? — driving with their noggins denting the roofs of their automobiles. By method of brute force they would reduce him to grape jelly. He has been. . . *mm* . . . spied upon, derided, and — oh, the humiliation! — subjected to what passes for therapy in this correctional facility: those niggardly-scheduled interviews for which he regularly neglects to part his hair or clip his toenails, hoping thus to distract them with *symptoms*. But no, they persist, hounding him with methodologies that have all the efficacy of bumper cars: Interventive Behavioral Schlitzflasche. Neo-Rational-Emotive Gesundheit. God save him. Someone the other day was trying to raise his Hope Quotient. He is supposed to infer, you see, that these numbskulls know what in tarnation they're doing. You never saw such competence. It's absolutely frightening. He won't even mention shock therapy — unless, thereby, he already has."

She laughs. "This sounds more like anger than fear, Roland."

His head lolls. He scratches at his thinning hair. "It is gone, you see, a part of the endlessly evaporating present. It was there. It was. But another thing, and then another thing intervened, and the way split. And split again. And each time he thought about it... *mm*... he found himself in that space where thinking skips too lightly and can't quite get a hold, his every thought leading to a thought about itself, and *that* thought to a thought about *it*self, and so on until, in hardly any time at all...."

Roland has stopped with his mouth open, his wide stare fixed somewhere behind her. She hears the noise then, a paper-thin, undulating whine. She turns and sees, just outside the six inches of open window, a fly stuck in a web. The spider there, automatic, its quick legs wrapping, wrapping the fly, until the whine is silenced.

Hearing Roland's chair creak, she turns back to him. His eyes fall closed.

"There," he says. "There."

She tries to get him to say more, but he won't. It is as if he has simply shut down.

~S~

Science claims the forest comes from sunlight, air, and water. And the knowledge possessed by seeds. But go out and stand there. Enter the vegetable incomprehension of it. The intolerable swarming stillness. Try to find a space for yourself. Try—in that ripening, mouldering, vertical world—not to feel instantly stupid. And even if you stand for a long time, until your dullness falls away, until it seems you begin to know something. Then what? "Trees are arteries of sapwood," you decide, "sheathing the bones of old growth. The forest is its own history." Ask yourself, then, what are you doing there? You, who carry around thoughts like these. Your kind of knowledge—what is it anyway?

* * * * *

In the little room now, Evelyn Moore and I are facing one another. We have constructed this room out of expectations. It is up to us to tear it down.

She gets up, walks vaguely around the carpet, as if she has lost what comes next. I feel a hand on my shoulder. Her voice is so wonderful, I miss what it is she's saying—something, I think, to hold herself together. She returns to her chair.

She concentrates, trying to really look at me, while I stare off through the wallpaper. I am near tears over her.

Near the ceiling on one wall there is a vent. I wouldn't have noticed it, except for Penobscot, who specializes in ways in and out of places. He enjoyed coming through the door along with the rest of us, but even before Nurse Boil was stuffing me into the chair I saw him disappear into the vent like smoke. Now, minutes later, Nurse is gone and he is back, reporting.

This is no place to speak, he says. And if a spirit can be out of breath, that is the way he sounds. *This hole is entrance to a terrible complexity—more chambers than this house is said to contain. It is a malignant design. The way twists and separates. Along with fumes of combustion and sorrow are particles of predatory thinking. In one of those chambers, someone is listening.*

Evelyn Moore crosses her legs. The toe of her boot describes little circles of frustration in the air. "I have no intention," she says, "of sitting through another forty minutes of silence with you."

I almost look into her eyes. I would run away with her in a minute.

I ask Penobscot, "Who is listening?"

You know him. He is the one who holds your papers. The man is all darkness. In his head he carries pictures of you and this woman, in cages.

Slam

In which Evelyn commits a small act of violence.

WHEN SHE LEFT the hospital parking lot at five minutes past five, she believed she was headed home, but something must have shifted in her thinking for her to find herself here, at five-thirty, in the Bangor Public Library, scrolling through reels of microfilm. *The Bangor Daily News*, October 27, 1990. And there it is, crowded down to the bottom of the front page by coverage of the build-up of U.S. forces in the Persian Gulf. Column 3: "Psychiatrist plummets from third story: Death under investigation." She scans the text, continued briefly on page 4. Dr. Marcus B. Einhorn, Clinical Director, had worked at the hospital for seventeen years. He had been on his way to see a patient when the incident occurred. The window he fell from looked off a third-floor stairwell landing. There were no witnesses.

Minutes pass. Evelyn twiddles the crank on the microfilm reader, communicating tremors into the newsprint image, which swims as if under Brownian motion. What is she looking for? Staring at the text of the story, scrutinizing the spaces at its borders, she might be watching for something more to shake out of it.

* * * * *

While driving home, she experiences a sudden and uncharacteristic rush of longing for winter. The cold, the snow. The advancing dark.

There is one image in particular. It must have been close to twenty years ago. She and her father, on top of the Taconic Ridge on cross-country skis, though they'd hardly been able to tell they were on top of anything, the air was such a whirl of snow. Twilight was coming on. Heading down, losing the trail, they broke out of the stands of beech into hummocky meadow, their ski-tips cutting the powder like shark fins. Dusk was falling granular as the snow, and there was only the sound of their skis. She felt as if she were in a moment that could not have been reached from anywhere. They kept moving, carrying it along with them, racing darkness to the bottom.

Outside. There it was. Though it was so long ago. How much is embellished memory she can't tell. In fact, the more she strains for the feel of that moment, the further it seems to draw away, behind the gauze of her thinking about it.

* * * * *

The house they've moved into in Hancock is in many ways not very different from the one they left in Connecticut. She thinks of them as Richard's houses. Never mind that they were paid for largely by her inheritance. When it comes to real estate, her husband seems forever in front, obstructing her view. Choices evolve, and she finds herself walking through rooms, nodding acknowledgement — wide-pine floors, central stair, conversion to baseboard heating, porch entrance off the kitchen, spacious yard, each house about a hundred years old, well-constructed but in need of repair, a live-in investment.

So resonant are these connections that now just for an instant, crossing the murmur of twilight between her car and the porch door, she forgets which house it is standing before her. The house and the ghost of a house are one.

Beyond the yard, meadow runs to the wall of woods already blending with the dark. There are more woods, she knows, on the other side of the road, and still more filling up the fleeting, unpeopled miles over which she drives each day. She stops before the porch steps, her bootsoles teetering on the uneven flagstone of the walk. It is as if she has passed through something. The air is fluid with the trill of crickets. An owl hoots from the edge of the wood. After a while, it hoots again.

Here. Outside. This, it occurs to her, is where she truly has come: alone and tentative in the lowering evening, surrounded by forest about which she knows nothing. The house and the ghost of a house, by comparison, seem hardly real enough to step into.

Yet a minute later, there she is inside, closing the door. Down the hallway leading to the den, she sees Richard at his desk, on the telephone, the instrument tucked into his shoulder as he talks and works the computer at the same time. His finished dinner plate with fork sits atop the flickering monitor like a rakishly feathered hat. Richard must hear the door click shut, for now he turns, tosses her a two-fingered wave, without quite offering her his eyes.

In the kitchen, her place is set for dinner. She climbs the stairs, takes her time changing before descending to eat. One event flows into the next. At the kitchen table, she addresses the casserole and salad meticulously, remarking—it seems—every flower of broccoli, every disk of leek. She sips at her Beaujolais and turns occasionally to regard her own reflection in the black of the kitchen window. Once, for no reason, she tilts her head and catches a vision of herself like none she has ever seen. The world seems to have narrowed down to the surfaces of her fingers on the wine glass, to these few visible inches in front of her face.

After dinner, she does the dishes, then prepares for her husband a decaf and a brandy and sets one of these at each of his elbows while he is muttering, "Right . . . Right . . . Right . . ." into the telephone. He glances up at her then, mouthing "Ah!" in gratitude, eyes wide. "Right . . . " he says. "Right."

She reads for awhile then, upstairs in bed because Richard's interminable phone dealings are a distraction. Out of the scatter of his talk, particular phrases cling to her attention: variable rate, liquor license, effluent discharge, points up front. It is from just such puzzle pieces over the years that she has put together her impression of Richard's mind. But mostly now in this telephone talk there are respectful lulls. It's clear he is seeking advice, probably from one of the school chums in Boston.

At twenty minutes past ten, Evelyn Moore rises from the bed, switches off the light, and pauses at the bedroom door. From there, near the top of the stairs she can hear his voice below, muffled now, perhaps weary, meager as the reflected glow from his desklight in a house otherwise dark. Standing, holding the door at arm's length, her feet bare on the cold floorboards of a night without dimension, she feels ready. She steps back away from the light and, with all her strength, slams the door closed.

The explosion of sound propels her blood.

Afterward the silence is like a ship. She makes her way to the bed, slips under the covers, and sets her eyes in the dark, sailing.

* * * * *

She dreams of moving within an endless network of corridors. She is alone. Earlier there had been others with her, but somewhere along the line she has lost track of them. Again she has the feeling of something nearer to being remembered, something mushrooming just beneath her consciousness, like an erasure, a space where once there were impressions that now are gone. The corridors are long, and always, at the end of one, another begins. She tries to recall what it was in the past, what it is supposed to be, simply to walk as she intended from one room to the next. She is losing herself, she understands, because of this void, this ballooning nothingness from within. The corridors lie like forgotten ambitions, the tile floors shimmering always just ahead of her.

~S~

*T*HIS AREA *once belonged to ravens,* Aroostook says. The swooping tones of his voice spread in a broad gesture, taking in the buildings and the grounds of this institution. Aroostook knows a lot. I pay attention to him, even though without me he wouldn't be here. He and the others are local spirits. By attaching themselves to me, they've come to places impossible for them otherwise. The hospital fascinates him.

The work of devils, he tells me. *This enclosure takes away everything you need all at once and then gives it back a little at a time. Light, air, water, even the knowledge of where you are—all given back in mean portions.*

Windows, he says, are the worst liars, giving the impression you are seeing real pieces of the world, when in fact no such pieces exist. Whenever you look out a window, think of deprivation. Otherwise you may be tricked into believing in the life that in fact has been stolen from you.

It makes sense to me, but I wonder privately. Devils?

His voice answers. *You haven't seen them?*

That's the trouble with spirits. You've always got conversation, whether you want it or not.

* * * *

Frank is not as good as he's cracked up to be. He thinks he's a tough cookie, but he likes to watch television. He positions his chair just down the hall where he can see my door, but he's awfully interested in that television.

Then there is his boss, Dr. Tarantula—I'm coming to know *him* in ways I'd rather not. Last time I was here, seven years ago, I got away from him. He's not about to let that happen again.

He has Nurse plop me in G-23, a kind of decompression chamber somewhere at the edge of his Ward. He comes in then, looks me over, and closes the door. He knows and I know, the Ward is on his keychain, something for me to worry about.

I am crumpled on a chair in the middle of this room, which he knows and I know contains chemicals. First he's busy at the counter. Then he's standing over me. The heels of his shoes come together on the tile with a little sliding sound, like he's formally presenting himself. Close enough that I smell the canned meat on his breath. Then closer.

He smirks into my face. He says, "We've got a place upstairs for you."

I know he's up to something, but I can only guess what. The worst I can imagine is that he really likes me. It is a possibility.

"The carpenters are up there now."

Each sentence hits after a long pause. It's like water torture.

"They're making it nice."

He grabs my leg just above the knee, then squeezes. I'm supposed to imagine now he may be something other than a doctor. Actually, I wonder what a doctor is.

"No more running off now," he says.

Then he is back at the counter. I hear the clink of glass and other little nearly-silent noises. He wants me to look, wants me to give in to curiosity.

What will he do to me? I'm supposed to wonder. It sounds as though he's preparing an injection. Truth serum maybe. Or Spanish fly. I think he won't do that, not here. But I'm not really sure. It's a war of nerves.

Analysis and Discussion

Reporting a very one-sided conversation with the Wild Child and, later, a drive to Window Lake.

Quarter to three in the afternoon, heading out of her office, she catches sight of him just down the corridor. His back is to her as he stands with Paul Sun, conferring over something. She ducks back and softly eases the door closed.

This morning there was Esther Boyle's voice in the hall, calling, "Oh, Dr. Griswold!" her nurse's shoes padding by. Then silence. Why silence? And after that, all day long it seems, Evelyn was lifting her eyes from the computer screen to the door, alarmed by what seemed to be traces of his cologne.

Now she stands at her office window, well away from the door, never having felt so isolated, never having felt so hemmed-in as by this man on whom she can pin not a single blame. Her blood whirls with the confusion, the weediness of her thinking.

* * * * *

In the Admissions Visitor's Room—which is tiny, windowless—three upholstered chairs more or less face one another across a coffee table on pea-green carpeting. Other than this there is nothing, except bad air. She cannot avoid breathing, cannot avoid taking in the miasma of tobacco smoke and body odor from the previous uneasy meeting—between Scott, the young rehabilitation therapist, and dire-eyed Morgan Fontaine, who burned past her on his way out. The mix of those two minds in "conference" produced, if nothing else, a cup stuffed with soda-swollen, illicit cigarette butts at one corner of the table. Esther Boyle, today outfitted in maroon, had been headed out the door anyway when Evelyn asked, pleasantly enough, if she would mind taking the cup with her. The ballpoint pen between Esther Boyle's fingers wiggled as she stopped and glanced at the cup. "I'll get someone," she said.

So much for pleasantness. Evelyn removed the cup herself to the trash container in the hall, sidestepping for the second time the little yellow sign cautioning 'Wet Floor,' though the floor appeared perfectly dry. Frank, setting up his folding chair against the wall, paused long enough to follow her with his eyes.

Some residue of the nurse's venom shows also in the patient's posture. The rag-doll limbs and rigid back seem at odds with the cushioned furniture—as if to submit to those hands so acquainted with the ballpoint pen was to leave one's body behind. Sophie Davenport stares brightly off-kilter, as though unavailable to the hopelessness of this room.

Evelyn, not yet seated, lays a hand on her shoulder. "Could you try, just a little, to relax?"

There is no response, but with gentle pressure she is able to rearrange the woman, easing her into the chair.

"I mean to help you," she says, "if I can."

Sophie Davenport's eyes stare.

Evelyn reaches back, pushes the door with her fingertips until it clicks closed, and there appears to be nothing then but the containment of the room. She waits, looks again. The impression is not well-formed, but it comes to her that there may be something else, something skirting the range of her own thinking. The vacant affect of this patient is draining, leaving the room so depleted that she imagines she can feel it. Something else.

But then it's impossible. Four walls, a ceiling and floor—a box enclosing two people and furniture. A door. On one wall, a vent near the ceiling. Where is there space for something else?

Peering over her shoulder through the observation window, the little face-high square of glass on the door, she adjusts her view of the corridor to include a pair of dark shoes and trousers, legs crossed. There Frank is waiting, without magazine or book or anything else to speed the time, thinking God-knows-what in his steel folding chair, not four feet from the door.

During the more than two days since her first meeting with Sophie, she has depended upon the perception that it went well. They sat together apparently without guile, she doesn't know how long. She opened herself, really opened herself, to the woman's silence. She was sure of this, by the sort of instinct that does not encourage afterthought but in itself is enough. But now what? At this moment she stands, arms folded, grinding the heel of her boot into the carpet, while Sophie sits blank-faced. Not a suggestion of movement, not a flicker of acceptance. Only collapse. They will have to begin all over again. She doesn't see a beginning, but she will make one.

On a sudden urge, she decides on the coffee table, not exactly kicking it but sliding it over the carpet with her boot, entirely to one side. At least this time there won't be physical barriers. Then she crosses to the chair opposite Sophie and sits.

"Sophie," she says to the carpet, her head resting on her fingertips. "Sophie Davenport. I don't know where you are exactly." She looks up into the woman's astonishing face. Certain faces we encounter—has she read this somewhere?— exert unusual power over us, as though they contain elements of profound memories.

"I want to tell you honestly, I enjoyed our session on Monday. Even though you said nothing. I believe . . . something of value came from it. But I have to say, Sophie . . . ."

There are accepted behaviors regarding faces, she is of course aware, subtle balances of looking and looking away, muscular demeanor of the mouth and brow.

" . . . I have no intention of sitting through another forty minutes of silence with you."

These, Richard might say, are elements of the contracts to which we all subscribe.

"There isn't time."

But she now sits far, far from Richard, in a room accustomed to the crunch and obliteration of personalities, a room intimate with the liquefaction of social contracts, a room that seems even peculiarly malicious.

"If you won't talk," she says, "then I will."

So she is staring, as if this woman's face is the first she has ever seen.

Though perhaps it isn't so much the face as the moment that is remarkable, allowing all that sleeping history of recognition to awaken somehow in a particular contour of flesh—the slope around the nose, the swerve of the nearly-parted lips. The hair, coffee-black, combed perhaps with the fingers, doesn't curl but flops against the neck. Wisps flare up around the face like remarkable events. The volatile eyes don't acknowledge her but don't avoid her either. They are fixed like two little storms, stirring up fires that—she could imagine—have to do with love.

Evelyn lets go the pressure of her amazement, slowly, as with a long exhaled breath. But she has promised to speak.

"I thought I would begin," she begins, "by telling you what's on my mind, what it is I'm thinking about you."

And now an odd thing. She sees, or thinks she sees, the dart of urgency in that expression—something like movement under the stillness.

"Sophie?" she says. But her voice seems to go nowhere. Her words, released like arrows of cotton, crash the air and stall. They litter her thinking. The world shrinks to this, the envelope of her frustration.

Evelyn stands, leaves her chair, and knows that by this simple choice she is wrenching free of routine, moving toward the edge of something she hasn't quite glimpsed yet. She will make it up as she goes. Her speech comes out as in a game of redlight-greenlight, in thrilling, anxious little rushes and stops.

What does she say?

First: "Normally, Sophie, I wouldn't begin this way, divulging strategy without any input. But I've decided in your case to make an exception. I believe you're an intelligent and an unusual woman, and I'd like during these meetings to consult you. If we're to make headway here, it will be the two of us together."

There. It seems not a bad opening. Whatever in it she may find later to regret, it stems from the heart. And it doesn't hurt, surely, that emotion is more persuasive in the shape of reason.

So then: "The first question is whether you've elected silence. Or whether somehow you're lost in it. Your test results may determine this. But I'll tell you what, Sophie. I'm going to assume that you've opted not to speak. It gives me something to do—I can try to persuade you to change your mind."

Always these veins of pragmatism run through her sincerity.

Next, adagio: "Of course, there's the question of motivation. I wonder. Are you faking mutism to avoid punishment?—which seems the prevailing view here. Or are you refusing communication for some other reason? Say, a profound lack of trust." After a beat: "I suspect, having read your history, that you may have suffered abuse as a child. Certainly, with the death of your father, you suffered trauma."

The phrase "thinking aloud" occurs to her. For that is honestly what it feels like.

Continuing: "Without trust, Sophie, there cannot be communication. Without trust we are, each of us, locked inside ourselves. The truth is, in the end, it is ourselves we need to trust."

There can be a peculiar resonance to unedited thoughts, spoken aloud.

And: "Sophie, be careful. Your isolation may serve you well outside this institution. But in here it may be disastrous. Persist in silence, and they may keep you here, locked away, for a very long time."

They.

And: "You could end up wasting your life here. This would be a tragedy, I think, entirely unnecessary."

It hasn't escaped her attention, this invocation of 'they'. It feels somehow significant. But, for the moment, she prefers letting go, absorbing it gradually, to the quiet delight of her skin.

Finally: "Take your time deciding, Sophie. But understand, we don't have forever: eight or ten days, perhaps, not much more. Meanwhile, Dr. Griswold and others will be visiting you as well. You may talk to whomever you choose. But if you do not talk to someone, if you persist alone, then I'm afraid you may have little hope of a life beyond these walls."

A life beyond these walls.

And what else? Aside from what is said and what is thought about what is said, what else is there? All the while Evelyn is speaking, she is watching and listening also.

She feels pulled in different ways, launching sentences into a room she suspects is not entirely disinterested. These suspicions add to the distance of her own voice. Over and over, her gaze tries the walls, the ceiling, the carpet. Other than this, there is the observation window, its view implying the pressurized homogeneity of the corridor. Or admitting, suddenly, a face looking in.

Sophie's stare is itself a kind of room, locked to the outside. Her lips pause in the act of readiness to release the unbegun sentence, the one that might be said, but won't be.

Evelyn notices this: on inhaled breaths, her eyes prefer Sophie.

At some point it is clear. Something has crept into the reach of her hearing: from outside the door, perhaps even beyond the corridor, the whine of some machine.

She looks long at the hands and at the bare feet against the carpet, studies the clothing for the rise and fall of breathing. The woman seems embedded in glass, the eyes set in an accidental stare at a point a little to Evelyn's left. Surely those eyes are looking into something. Distant greening breezes, eruptions of birdwing on sloping meadows? Musty, angular horrors behind doors? There is no way of knowing.

The whine of the machine steadily increases. Evelyn rises from her chair, moves to the observation window and peers out to the corridor, where a janitor is advancing intently along the tile in incremental swaths with a buffing machine. The janitor's expression is as firm as his grasp of the controls. He never looks up from the floor. And when at last he nudges aside the yellow caution sign, it is with a looping, backward stroke of the machine itself.

She returns to her chair and sits. Rather than shout over the squeal of the buffer, she waits for it to pass. And when she does resume, it is with a muted voice, as if the effect of the janitor's labors has been to replenish the afternoon with an effluvium of anesthesia. She hears herself, remotely, mouth a warning about the wages of stubbornness, the need for cooperation. As far as she can tell, it's all the same to Sophie.

But Evelyn has other things to contemplate. Just what she means by "they," for instance.

* * * * *

She leaves right away, locking her office even a little before five o'clock, and maneuvers through traffic as though it isn't there, as though relying on the feel of the steering wheel in her hands. Just before Ellsworth, she turns left at the sign. The road snakes, splits, splits again. Consulting more than necessary the map on the passenger seat, she makes no mistakes. Finally, water is visible through the trees, and then she sees the turn-off for Window Lake.

How easily she has come here!

The woods turn by on either side unapproachably, as if on film. The lake flashes in and out of view. The old winding road around the lake sprouts many private drives, none with the name Davenport.

The sun just past setting, she pulls the car to a stop at what looks like a boat launch. The parking area is vacant. There are no boats or people.

For a moment she sits. Then, without her deciding anything, her hand reaches. The door swings open, and she steps out into a flood of colorful leaves. With her boots submerged to the ankles in rustling, she looks around and breathes deeply. She feels under the protection of a bright band of heedlessness.

The closing of the car door is not so much a sound as an abrupt flattening in the resonance of her hearing. She must move. Hands slung in the pockets of her jacket, she walks slowly, experimentally, succumbing to extravagant changes in direction. Cricket song pours around her. She keeps her eyes down, scanning the brilliant ground. For now, she'll refuse to name her thoughts, relying rather on a fascination with her boot tips, lunging and swishing one after the other like prows through the froth of foliage. Eventually her steps sink her into sand, and she trudges.

At the water's edge she stops.

Overhead, she hears a rattle of leaves. Several fall, one grazing her shoulder. But she does not look up. The breeze ripples the shallows into which she is fixing her attention, trying to gather the identity of this lake before lifting her gaze across it.

There are no sounds of cars on the road behind her.

She looks up then over the surface of the lake. The opposite shore seems painted to the evergreen distance, like a pause rendered in color. Like a recognition that between the fires of autumn and the final white wall of winter is this flecked, faded valley of gray, copper, and wine. Where a felt of leaves covers the ground.

Amid the general darkening, light clings to the far shore on a single yellow slope, as if the departed sun has found one translucent hill to shine through. She watches this, and after a while there is nothing to get in the way of her crying.

~S~

EVENINGS she heads home. Across the distance of the parking lot and through these dense stone walls, I feel the pull of her leaving, like a tide. I wait and wait, then lift each eyelid to a world without her, a world of floral and yellow-tinted surfaces, all familiarly strange. Nothing wants to move. The place has the thin resonance of a theatrical set awaiting the entrance of malicious characters. A murder scene an hour before the murder.

What connects me to Evelyn Moore? And why not someone else? I think of the people crowding sidewalks, entering cars, spilling out of elevators—every single one of them radiating a universe just as heartbreaking, just as eternal.

How can the world bear it?

She's closing in on me, June, from too many directions. At some point soon I'll talk to her. I can't imagine the words. Anything you say, there are ten other things waiting to be said that could shoot it full of holes.

And then there's Tarantula sitting, hunched over a corned-beef sandwich, patient, his ear to the grate.

✽ ✽ ✽ ✽ ✽

I used to think this: I am separate from what I see. My life is an unrelenting television screen. Light-years couldn't bring me to the closest person. I'm sterile, useless in the dark, watching.

Then I wondered, what about beyond this? What could it be that isn't on the screen? Back behind me somehow, I imagined my arms reaching. What's there?

It was hopeless. Like finding another television screen, another channel.

* * * * *

A few of us are standing around, talking. The subject is hallucinations. Eddie, William, Rye, and I. And a tall, quiet guy named Dennis Finn, who's supposed to leave tomorrow. A panel of experts.

Meanwhile Penobscot has gotten into the electronics of the soda machine, exhaling his way along the circuitry, experimenting with the switches. Every so often while we're talking, a stream of orange or root beer spurts out of the nozzle for no apparent reason. The first time it happens everyone looks, but nobody says anything. After that, nobody looks. Just once in awhile, during a pause in the talk, we hear the SHWSHHH of soda.

Eddie, bristling fearlessness, claims hallucinations don't bother him one bit. They're there, they're not there, what's the difference? Sure, he'd just as soon do without them, but no way is he afraid of them.

Dennis says that in church when he was little he could hear the votive candles whispering the sins of the congregation all during mass. The statues would move and speak to him. Ever since then, even though he's not a believer, he can't get rid of the feeling that his visions might be messages from God.

Eddie says, "Yeah, Jeez, stay away from churches."

A stream of orange soda hisses from the machine. A paper cup clatters into position, but no soda squirts into it. A second cup plops into the first. And a third. Then the machine is silent.

After a pause, poor Dennis Finn pulls himself out of the conversation and drifts off down the hall. William stares after him, then commences to nod, as if Dennis is carrying away some truth. William, not looking at anyone, says his own visions seem like communications too, but he's not sure what from. Usually what he sees terrifies him, but he's also fascinated. There's a part of him that would hate to give it up.

Rye pokes a finger in the air, enters the debate like a professor leading a class discussion. "Ah, the terrible beauty of raw experience! That fierce . . . nakedness of apprehension! If he remembers correctly, it was Julian Jaynes who observed that the schizophrenic's perception of reality is so potent because he fails to reduce the world through the filter of consciousness."

Rye's slippered feet rock from heel to toe with enthusiasm.

"Yeah?" Eddie says. "Who's Julia James?"

A Million-Dollar View

Wherein, in the history of the House, a pattern of sudden autumn death is revealed.

E︎THEL FOSTER, the nurse on duty with Amy, will be ready to retire at the end of next year. Grey, stick-like, she bends alongside the younger nurse like a parenthesis. Now, as Evelyn approaches, Ethel pushes her sweater sleeves above her elbows. Her cheeks are puffed with indignation.

"My God," Amy is saying, "you wouldn't think to look at her she'd be capable of something like that."

"That one?" Ethel exclaims over her shoulder. "Don't fool yourself."

Amy collapses into her swivel chair. "It sure goes to show." She looks at Evelyn.

Evelyn asks, "What happened?"

"Pfff!" Ethel's huff can't quite cover the flicker of a smile. "Little Miss Never Says Anything just walloped Frank over the head with his own folding chair. I'd say bloodied him up pretty good. They had to get an ambulance come and take him up the hospital."

"Oh no! *Who* did this?"

"Faye," Amy says, her voice all hushed significance. "Faye Morse."

"Oh." Evelyn directs her attention to the dayroom, where a few patients protrude like sculptures from the overstuffed furniture. Sophie Davenport is not among them.

Ethel shakes her head. "Working Forensics, he ought to know better than to leave a metal chair lying around like that."

Amy shakes her head too.

* * * * *

Then from Walter Rafferty she hears that, around the same time, a patient in D-ward tried pitching a sofa through a dayroom window.

"Little Rodney." Walter levels his palm about breast-high. "Maybe five-foot seven, wiry. Usually the guy's a sweetheart."

Evelyn, stopped dead in the hall, likes the feel of standing deep in her boots. "Where do they get the strength?" she says.

She isn't aware of having expressed anything else, but Walter steps closer, lays a large hand on her shoulder.

"You get outbreaks like this," he says. "Then it settles down."

He looks searchingly, almost tenderly at her.

* * * * *

Yes, she has known all along, but not in the way she knows now: the Hospital has a history. And the history has been recorded. The institution has maintained records for all of its ninety-six years of operation. "We keep everything," Marilyn Spellman, who oversees Hospital Records, told her. "Forever," she added. Marilyn Spellman's evanescent smile communicated a mixture of pride and forbearance. This was during the first-day tour, when Marilyn also showed her how recently things had changed.

"It all used to be paper. The material here in the Records Room went back twelve years. Books and books and books. Anything older than that they'd ship down to Archives, in Augusta. Until that filled up. Then they started using the empty space here. And there was plenty of it. We've been downsizing ever since the mid-sixties, even though we're housed in the same buildings. So we've inherited lots of places to store things. Anyway, that's all over with now. They've been scanning every last bit of it and putting it on CD-ROM. All the way back to 1932. They're having trouble with the older material. The paper falls apart."

Evelyn thinks 1932 is old enough for what she has in mind. She has been at her computer, exploring, mostly during those interminably empty nights when she's on call, acquainting herself with the Hospital history on CD-ROM. Patient charts. Annual Reports. Internal Reviews. Using keyword searches, experimenting with different combinations, limiting the fields. She is looking for ghost stories.

It isn't long before she finds one. Then another. And another.

On October 26, 1990, Dr. Marcus Einhorn fell, or was thrown, from a window. On November 29, 1957, Dr. R. Sydney Melton apparently hanged himself from one of the Hospital's steampipes with a length of electrical cord. And on November 17, 1935, Dr. Albert Spiegel broke his neck from a fall down a third-floor flight of stairs.

And earlier than 1932? If she were to pore over the remaining thirty years of records in Archives, would she find another one? Or two?

The recurrence of sudden autumn death. What is it about the place? After awhile at the computer screen, she gets up from her desk and walks along one corridor after another, trying to retrieve the thread in her thinking that for an instant seemed to have revealed itself and then vanished. But, Evelyn knows, the Hospital corridors work like morphine, and, sure enough, by the time she returns to her office she can barely recall her motivation for leaving.

* * * * *

Saturday morning dawns in fog. Richard is bent on visiting The Canning Plant again. This is how he speaks of it now, the proper name pointing the way toward the reality. He has been to the place already six or seven times, inspecting, planning, jotting notes on a clipboard. Today he's invited her along.

On the ride there, he tells her about the phone calls. Three this week. When he answers, there is silence, then the caller hangs up. If it happens one more time, he's getting an unlisted number. As he talks, she directs her gaze out the passenger window upon the particular stream of greyed and unsurprising images pressing at the roadside: mailboxes, guard rails, utility-poles and anchor cables, speed-limit signs, for-sale signs, mounds of bagged leaves, tree trunks—a profusion affecting her with a sensation like weightlessness. Almost out of Milbridge she hears the turn signal. The engine growls as her husband downshifts. He rounds the corner neatly, swoops to the curb, and stops dead in front of Anchor Realty. "Have to get the key," he says halfway out of the car. In response, she nestles into the warmth of her seat and through the window watches him bound up the steps of the realty office, which is what the grand old white-clapboard house on Rt. 1A has come to.

In the dirt lot of the Canning Plant, bordered thickly in weeds flecked with paper and polyethylene, she and Richard open their car doors to the comfortless white day. From their Sunday visit weeks ago, she recalls vaguely the locations of things buried now in mist. That occasion was quiet, the harbor just scenery, backdrop for a property that had stirred

Richard's speculative instincts. This morning, though, the fog is alive with the noises of gulls and boat engines, voices, and the on-again, off-again knock, knock, knock of hammers pounding nails down by the wharf.

The factory looming before them appears to account for the whole of visible space. Beginning flat on shore ledge, the blocky two-story structure continues onto pilings over the beach to suspend itself stupidly in fog. Low tide has disclosed the beach: a stony brown-green muck, that has become a graveyard for tires and muted artifacts of rust. A few of the pilings lean away from vertical. Crossmembers dangle or are missing altogether. But Richard dismisses these defects, and in any case he is hiring a professional to inspect the underpinnings.

Now she stands at the door with her husband, who has entrusted her with the two flashlights. He waves a hand at the factory wall. "You notice the finish on this siding?"

Teeming particles of fog drift and undulate against the building's dark exterior. This is what she notices.

"There are restaurateurs in Provincetown who'd sell their mothers for this look. You can't put it on like aluminum. Beautiful buildings are like fine wines—they take time."

She watches as he twists the key in the padlock and flicks open the hasp. He has a flair for this sort of activity, as though, never mind the BMW and the Pendleton plaid woolen shirt, he's been opening padlocks all his life.

"And the thing is, the age lowers the price." He chuckles. "Because people who buy buildings have Manneschevitz minds."

He pushes the door open. Dull light spills over a floor, a wall, a table leg, indeterminate boxes.

"Can I have one of those flashlights?"

She, too, certainly appreciates old things, the past's dusky reachings into the present. But what troubles her is this cosmetic interpretation: that what is acquired in age is essentially a "look."

Richard, entering, turns to her. "Watch your head, and look out where you step."

He has a routine. To keep the door from swinging closed, he props it open with a wooden crate. Then without a word he's off, like a museum tour guide, leading the way to another, much larger room jammed with rows and rows of packing tables.

Richard stops, plays his flashlight beam over the tables. "Reminds me of freshman chemistry lab."

Through the factory walls she can still hear gulls crying.

"I wonder what it would have been like," she says.

"What?"

"The women of this town—I imagine they spent a good part of their lives at these tables."

"Yeah." He shakes his head. "Cramming sardines into cans. Probably a couple dollars a day."

Down by the wharf, a carpenter's saw whines, and she is reminded that it is still foggy outside.

His flashlight beam jumps. "See?—kitchen in the middle, dining area around the sides, by the windows. Except for private parties and the lounge. They're upstairs."

He moves off down the length of the dining room. She follows. Perhaps in order to hold onto him, she asks a question. "Are you sure you can get a liquor license?"

"If not, I give up the whole idea. It'll never fly without a bar."

He stops abruptly. His light swims around her feet. "This'll need reflooring, but the joists are plenty solid."

"What about the walls?"

"The what? Oh, yeah. They're fine."

He ducks through a doorway.

She hears him say, "Look at this ceiling, will you."

In the next room, her flashlight beam catches an old rotary light switch. She reaches to try it.

He says, "The whole place'll have to be rewired."

Turning the switch until it clicks in her hand, she asks him about plumbing.

"No problem, the field across the road has soil-tested out O.K."

"Across the road?"

She looks, but Richard has disappeared up a stairwell.

She follows him up a winding flight of stairs to the second floor, a series of smaller rooms off a central hall. He has taken a tape measure from his pocket, and is laying it across doorways. She wanders ahead of him down the hall, directing her flashlight left and right into the dim rooms.

From the last room, all the way at the back of the building, directly over the water, the cry of gulls is suddenly louder. She pokes her head in and notices the upper sash of one of the windows leaning against the wall.

She goes to the window, peers through the slits between the boards, out at the bright fog. Now again she hears voices from across by the wharf, heavily muffled by the mist, voices consisting only of vowels and rhythms.

"You found the room with the million-dollar view." This voice is Richard's—distinct, apparently close, so that she turns, anticipating an encounter with his face. But he is squatting instead in the corner by the door, applying the tape measure to the threshhold, scanning its numbers with his flashlight.

He mutters, "What we're going to have to start thinking about up here is a fire escape."

Evelyn ignores the pool of light on the floor, contemplating instead the ruddy plaid anatomy of his back.

~S~

So HERE we are. Those silent banks of clouds have overtaken us, obscuring our former ways of being with something that looks like fog. Now people will complain they can't see anything. But what were they seeing before?

You'll hear it said that the fog rolls in. That is the way it looks from a distance. But once it has you locked inside, it's not like that at all. From inside, it's more like the forgotten condition of things. You open your eyes, and there you see what has been all along, inescapable now that the air has appeared like the wall of God, shutting out all that familiar, private noise.

Once, years ago in Gloucester, I went walking in a thick fog, exploring down along the harbor. I crossed over a jetty and wound up in a part of town I'd never seen before, though I thought I had wandered every inch of that town. A few days later, after the fog had lifted, I tried finding that part of the town again, and I couldn't. I tell you, I felt pretty excited after that.

But Aroostook insists *this* fog is nothing to fool with. The forgotten condition of things, after all, can be deadly, if you're hurtling toward it at the wrong angle, the wrong velocity. *One of these souls*, he says, matter-of-fact as the ticking of a clock, *will not make it through to the other side.*

I look around the dayroom, wondering who he means. *Not these,* he says. *One of the others.*

A Kind of Alchemy

Evelyn is surprised by the appearance of the Wild Child's mother and, late into the night, makes a study of elopements.

LATE MONDAY MORNING she runs into Walter Rafferty in the corridor. He seems surprised.

"I thought you'd be with Madeline Davenport," he says.

"Who?"

"Sophie's mother. She was meeting with them here at eleven o'clock. You didn't know about it?"

Evelyn, burning with a mixture of emotions she cannot name, snaps the pencil in her hand. "God! Nobody tells me anything around here!"

* * * * *

So she slips, unasked-for, into the conference room, seeing little against the stares, the heads swiveling after her progress along the wall to an empty chair at the far end of the table. A white lab frock, a crimson tie, unspecified sportcoated arms and shoulders, a ballpoint pen, Warren Griswold's spider-black eyebrows—all twist and wriggle under the stimulus of her entrance. A woman is speaking.

Settling in her chair, Evelyn feels already severed, reckless, even before she looks up into the gelid eyes of John Kilgallen. Those eyes hold on her just long enough before returning to the woman speaking, the woman in the veal-colored suit. Nothing else of John Kilgallen moves, only the eyes.

"I understand how it appears," the woman concedes from her place at the head of the conference table. This is Madeline Davenport. Sophie's mother. Her fingers reaching now to adjust an earring. She turns her earnest eyes on Paul Sun, even manages to touch the sleeve of his lab frock. "In the end, it all seems very much like my failure, doesn't it?"

John Kilgallen flexes his brow. "It's not our task here to assign blame."

"In and out of schools," she says. "Trouble with the police. Three o'clock in the morning the phone would ring. She went through I don't know how many counselors, therapists. You must understand my weariness with this sort of thing."

Evelyn has not yet connected with this constellation of human beings enclosed within the high, white walls of the conference room. The questioning of Madeline Davenport moves in no apparent direction. Giddy, anguished, fiery by turns—the woman manages to direct her answers never at the one who asks. Her talk strays from her daughter to her recent vacation, the climate on the Iberian peninsula, its blue-blue sky. Her silver-blonde hair and green-green earrings drape and swing with the list of her head as she speaks. Not once does she look at Evelyn. In fact, no one does. Meanwhile, Evelyn waits for some indication of what anyone here thinks about this performance.

"Of course, you know," Madeline says, "several years ago, she was admitted to this institution. I can't say it did her any good. Nothing, frankly, seems to have done her any good. I have lived a good part of my adult life in fear of the question—how much worse will it get with Sophie? How much worse *can* it get? And perhaps now, finally, I have the answer."

Her lips compress in a dimpled smile that suggests punctuation. Perhaps she is finished.

"Still," she continues, tilting her head at Paul Sun, "I have to say I was shocked."

Paul Sun sits back from the table, folds his arms, nods. His half-smile, that remarkably constant feature of his face, might mean almost anything.

Gary Benjamin, seated just to Madeline's right with his chin planted on his fist, his attention frozen on her, looks, in the unforgiving atmosphere of this conference room, like a statue of a man punching himself. Straightening now, he exchanges glances with John Kilgallen.

"So your daughter," Gary says, "didn't seem inclined to violence?"

Madeline Davenport draws herself in with a pensive breath, lifts her face ceilingward. "There were incidents—windows broken, fights with the girls at school. Then, when she got into this wilderness thing, there was the gun. But I never thought of her as violent, no. Never that she would shoot someone."

Warren Griswold's hands, hairy and quick, appear restless, jealous of space. One nudges his clipboard toward the center of the table, and the other drags it back again. "Mrs. Davenport," he says, "'this wilderness thing.' Can you describe what you mean by that? Mountaineering? Or what was it?"

"Oh, no." Madeline's eyes, on John Kilgallen now, are wide. "No, quite something else. She wanted to purge herself. She said that. Being civilized, you see, was something to be ashamed of. That's what she thought. So her solution was to live like an animal. In the woods."

"With a gun?" John Kilgallen says.

Paul Sun, leaning further back in his chair, crosses his legs, one ankle on the other thigh, an almost yogic posture.

"That's right," Madeline says, looking directly at Paul Sun. "It makes no sense. Of course, she got it all from books anyway. She always had her nose in some book."

Warren Griswold perks up. "What sort of books?"

"Oh!" Madeline exhales a little puff of amusement. "A lot of mysticism and anarchy. Novels with black covers. Far, far out religious books. I couldn't even begin to pronounce the author's names. Most of it I never caught sight of. I absolutely was not allowed in her room."

"What about her friends?"

"She had only one friend that I ever saw. In high school—a girl named June. Another 'free spirit.'"

"You didn't approve of her?" John Kilgallen asks.

"She and Sophie were wonderfully adept at feeding one another's fantasies. The two of them created their own little world together, and most of the time, I'd say, they were pretty well lost in it."

Warren Griswold has been turning the pages of Sophie's chart on his clipboard. "Did your daughter and . . . this June," he says, "have a particular fascination with the occult?"

Madeline Davenport gazes as though attending to some other, more distant question, one that, after some consideration, she answers by vaguely shaking her head.

Warren Griswold frowns at the page. "There's mention here . . . ."

She cuts him off. "I don't want misunderstanding. My daughter did experiment—foolishly, I believe—with a kind of . . . earth religion. And that's all I wish to say about it."

Evelyn looks down at the point of her pen, drying, not an inch above her blank yellow pad. She wonders. The past two weeks have been filled to overflowing with the silence of one woman, and now she has walked in on this, the talk of another. Where is the connection?

But her attention has wandered.

" . . . . Window Lake." Now it is John Kilgallen's voice, his well-formed mouth preoccupied with those consonants, his gaze angling down at his own notes. "This would have been April of 1992. You and Sophie had a confrontation there?"

Madeline addresses Gary Benjamin. "I'd never used the camp. So naturally I was advised to put it up for sale. That morning I drove up to give the agent a tour, check the rooms over, remove any personal things. Sophie, well, I hadn't seen her since the summer before. Please understand, I was never sure, during her disappearances, whether I'd ever see her again."

Gary Benjamin nods.

Madeline, taking a breath, proceeds as though suppressing nausea.

"Anyway, I'd let the agent in through the front. I was still on the porch latching the storm door, when I heard him say something. I went in and, there, I had the scare of my life. Standing over the kitchen stove, was this . . . creature, this . . . vagrant-looking character. Wearing animal skins of some kind. Absolutely absolutely filthy. I was terrified. Thank God, I thought, I have someone with me. And immediately I wished I hadn't. Because then, you see, came the real shock. Then came the shame of it. This was my daughter. My daughter. Looking as if she had just wriggled out from under a stump.

"She had some mess bubbling away on the stove in a stewing pot. The entire place just stank to high heaven. I cannot describe to you my rage, my shame. I could not speak. I went around opening windows, just shaking. The first time I'd seen the girl in over a year, and she looked as though she'd spent the time with . . . wolverines. I was physically sick."

John Kilgallen asks, "Then she'd been living in the lodge?"

"Oh no. She'd been living, if you could call it that, out in the woods somewhere. She had come in just to boil up this . . . God only knows what."

Madeline looks away toward the window, where there is nothing to see but fog.

"Ms. Davenport . . ." Paul Sun leans in, hooks a finger on the edge of the table. "You've seen your daughter this morning?"

"Yes. I have."

"What do you make of her silence? Did she say anything to you?"

"No, she did not."

"Do you think this might be willful on her part? Do you think she might be, say, malingering, to avoid standing trial?"

Madeline shakes her head. Her eyes glisten. From somewhere beside her chair she has produced a handkerchief. She simply holds it, her fingers giving it a squeeze. Her voice is flat.

"I don't know about that. For the past ten years, my daughter and I have had little to say to one another. My meeting with her this morning, aside from the venue, didn't strike me as terribly unusual. Talk with her accomplishes nothing. Somewhere along the line she's made her decision. She will not adjust. It's everyone else who's wrong. There isn't a grain of compromise in the girl. And whatever she chooses to despise had better stay out of her way."

Evelyn, pad and pen at the ready, crosses her booted legs and studies the woman. And then, suddenly, she hears her own voice. "And can you tell us what it is she's chosen to despise?"

Heads turn, and for the instant Evelyn is aware mainly that this voice of hers doesn't at all resemble John Kilgallen's or Paul Sun's. Perhaps she ought to have waited. Perhaps it wasn't the right moment for her voice to have inserted itself.

Madeline Davenport applies her gaze down the tunnel of Evelyn's dwindling focus—whether with the intention of answering or dismissing her, Evelyn can't tell.

"No," she says. "I'm afraid I can't. There have been times, of course, I've felt that it might be me."

"Why is that?" Evelyn asks.

Madeline's composure softens to not quite a smile. "Really, I think you'd have to ask her that. If you find out . . ." She tilts her chin, as if peering over obstruction. " . . . you'll let me know?"

Warren Griswold glances straight up, as though just seeing something flit through the air overhead.

Gary Benjamin shifts in his chair, looking as though his next remark might be conciliatory.

* * * * *

This night again she is back at her computer, having recovered the thought she had lost. Now it is escapes she's researching, which, in Records, are scrupulously tallied under the heading of "Elopements." Most are overstayed leaves, patients remaining off-grounds without authorization. And there are quite a few of these. But once every couple of years, someone under lock and key manages to actually break out. Usually they are found and returned to confinement, but not always. Some seem to disappear.

She learns all this in one night. She learns also that on November 20, 1935, three days after Dr. Spiegel's fall, a "young female inmate" in one of the locked wards escaped. As far as Hospital records show, she was never subsequently caught. And on December 4, 1957, five days after Dr. Melton hanged himself, a "young female patient" escaped, again from a locked ward.

In the first instance, there was either confusion or a change of opinion about the identity of the escapee, whose name has been neatly inked out, without an insertion. The name of the 1957 escapee was recorded as Clara Himmel. And the identity of the patient absconding after Dr. Einhorn's spectacular death, of course, she knows. Three deaths, three escapes.

On this night, after her research, Evelyn does not get up and walk the corridors, but instead wheels her chair over to the window, where she sits gazing for a long while at the nocturnal restlessness of the pines under the Hospital floodlights.

* * * * *

Little by little she has come to feel that she has set herself against an array of men none of whom she can say has actually done anything wrong. But it occurs to her also that this is one of the principal troubles of the world, the evil done by people who are neither evil nor incompetent, but rather who are acting in ways that are entirely defensible.

She continues hearing voices from the ventilation grate. Mostly they are muffled, too faint to understand. But now and then, as if by the removal of some barrier, the sounds become words.

One day this:
"There's nothing up there, it's all empty."
"Is that right?"
"They keep it locked."
"What for?"
"They don't want anyone up there."
"Why not?"

And then she has Gary Benjamin bursting into her office, his voice booming with false jocularity. Immediately the voices are silenced. After Gary leaves, she listens. But, unlike the voices of crickets in the grass, these don't start up again. She doesn't hear them for the rest of the afternoon.

* * * * *

Roland Rye says, "Listen. Here, in this medieval institution, there is a game they like to play. It is a kind of alchemy, and it works this way.

"First, they locate a life. For which, he needn't tell you, they have deployed the most sophisticated sensing devices. They capture this life, luring it, say, with fistfuls of tutti-frutti into a room such as this one. Then with deft waves of the hands . . . *mm* . . . the unfortunate life cowering, sweating before them, they transpose a couple of consonants, and what do think they come out with? Hm?

"A *file*. See? One moment 'life,' the next moment 'file.' Hah! Presto! They love it. They hold it up to the light between their fingers and opposed thumbs, or squirrel it away in one of those drawers. They can stuff a lot of them in there."

He leans in to whisper.

"Of course, they don't call them files anymore. 'Chart' is all the vogue now, which, if he can trust his sources, is rumored to be part of a 'database.' Ah, the sounds roll off the tongue. But of course you know perfectly well what they're up to. Securing the walls with legitimate science, fomenting the dumb impression of seamlessness. Charts! Farts! Every living soul here in custody knows exactly what they are."

In a sudden movement, he snaps his head to the side, fixes his gaze on the wastebasket. "Oh, what is it, poisoning him with this angst? Some pernicious chemical imbalance, left over from Original Sin? Who knows? Herr Doktor is awaiting the lab reports. Meanwhile, take two of these tiny pink ones. Thrice daily. They should make the discomfort less interesting."

She says, "I share your distrust of files and charts, Roland. But they have the advantage that they do hold still while you're looking at them." Then, "What is it, Roland? Is something the matter?"

He raises a finger as if for silence. His eyes, on her, flit back at intervals to the wastebasket. He remains like this for minutes, as if on alert.

* * * * *

It is late in the afternoon. Here, compressed into the bleary little Visitor's Room, she has spent the past half-hour trying to cut her way once again through Sophie's silence. Until finally her own talk seems to have caved in on her.

Now, as she stands, regarding the walls, her hand settles on the bony contour of Sophie's shoulder. "Where do you suppose we are headed, you and I?" she asks. And, through her fingertips, she feels the throb of Sophie's blood. It seems to her the nearest thing to communication that has passed between them.

~S~

FOR AWHILE Nurse Boil has left me alone and gone off to manage something else. I think she may have forgotten about me, which isn't like her. Normally she sticks like flypaper. I wonder what's gotten into her. I could imagine a man—older, red-cheeked, with a tweed jacket, knit cap, and a rat-tail. On Sundays he deals in comic books at flea markets. But he treats her nice. It doesn't go much further than that, but it's enough to make her forgetful.

So here I sit.

I'm practicing the art of being on the edge of my bed, experimenting with where I begin and end. Androscoggin urges me in these directions. Now that I have so much time. My position is good. I can see out the window without turning my head. The door is closed. The room has almost no substance. Outside, what there is to see is fog.

I begin with the idea that my weight is tireless, like Hubble's constant. It never rests. Before that moment long ago when I first blinked into consciousness, my weight was there already. And in the end it will outlast me, urging me with the force of dark music down into the grave. These are the laws of physics. I picture electrons and force fields, molecular clashes in blind space having nothing to do with me. I take all this into account while balancing nicely at the center, slack as an accident.

Then I let go.

Weight? I have no weight. Boundaries? There are no boundaries. The province of my body reaches down, expanding, taking in things I used to be separate from: the bedsprings, the walls, the creaking rhythm of this building. The air in the room shudders, a small involuntary spasm. Communicated from some distant event, it runs clear through me. Motionlessness acts like an antenna, receiving transmissions.

Outside, fog twists by the window. At the edge of the mattress, I am purified, almost a point of view. Almost out of here.

The door opens.

"I nearly forgot about you." It's Nurse Boil's voice, muttering. Her hands fasten on my arm, my shoulder.

Rye says we enter the House and after awhile the House enters us.

The patients, this slurry of fermenting souls—we don't look like much, hanging on, surviving the appearance and disappearance of our days. But we may be the ingredients of something dangerous, corrosive. We hardly have the courage ourselves to come together. Just look at the effort that's spent to contain us. Why?

In Motion

A doctor disappears, and Richard sees apparitions on the lawn at night.

WHILE DRIVING, she thinks about driving, this thing she does twice a day. What is it, aside from sitting in motion from one location to another? Half an hour speeding west, then half an hour back again, day after day—this must mean something. In the architecture of living, it must over the seasons and years sculpt out certain rooms, obstruct certain doorways.

* * * * *

A summer evening in Connecticut.

Heading home on I-86, as she had the evening before and the one before that, she felt an urge to slip out of herself. She seemed actually to drive into the urge, as one might drive into a swarm of bees or the odor of honeysuckle. It started, she recalls, with a tactile reawakening in her fingers, which had gone almost entirely slack around the steering wheel, piloting the missile that was her automobile along the designated pavement of its lane, through thinning traffic. And it was clear all at once that her life was exactly this, so elaborately had she loosened her control over it, that she was moving rapidly, in apparent stillness, toward something decided long ago out of frailty. From behind the glaze and tint of the windshield, over and over again, she had been making her way through the leaden inevitability of her days, settling into the lulling trajectory of her existence. Then what, all of a sudden, was this new sensation?—this ache and sparkle, like an abrupt failure of gravity. It had come without words, with an appetite only for the dark and unnameable, for a future about which nothing was known. It held as she drove and even as she pulled into the driveway, so that after she'd turned off the ignition she sat there with her hands wrapped over the steering wheel, seeing—it seemed, for the first time—the garage door. "What in the world is happening?" she asked herself out loud in a voice that was lovely to hear. In awhile the figure of Richard caught her eye, scouting from the diningroom window. She opened the car door then and, feigning distraction, gathered her things and headed for the house.

How could she have forgotten this until now?

* * * * *

Navigating by headlights and taillights through the dawn fog, she conjures these memories of herself driving not in fog. On the I-395 bridge, now suspended in cloud, the traffic crosses the river below, which can't be seen. This is the way the world runs, she realizes, according to patterns almost wholly obscure.

The fog does not enter the hospital with her but hangs back, dragging at her sleeves. She passes through the doorway of aluminum and glass, thinking that some steps propel one further than simply through time and space. In here there can be no fog. In here the atmosphere is another kind of grey.

In a side corridor, she spots the two as if in conference: Paul Sun and Warren Griswold. Neither turns his head to notice her. Warren Griswold, perhaps, has no need to turn his head. But before she passes out of earshot, she is surprised by the tone of Paul Sun's voice.

"I don't have to debate with you," he is saying. "All I have to do is pick up the phone."

* * * * *

This morning Walter Rafferty smells like something different. He smells like chocolate. And he seems talkative. Not that he's saying a lot. But in between the times when he does open his mouth there is a particular nervous energy about him, as though there is something he *wants* to say.

Meanwhile, she notices the lettering on his coffee mug: "I LOVE GRANDPA." As far as she knows, Walter has no children, much less grandchildren.

"Is that your mug?"

He tilts it to get a look. "Yeah." The skin ripples around his mouth, a smile mixed with something else. "Given to me by a friend."

It is a small answer, maybe leading to larger questions. "Oh."

They are in Evelyn's office, where Walter has stopped by for no declared reason. He sits against the window, half in wild silhouette. Evelyn, her chair rotated to face him, is taken again by the shaggy size of him.

He asks suddenly, "Is something bothering you?"

"Oh . . . I don't know." The idea hadn't occurred to her until he said it. And then of course it's obvious. "That meeting with Madeline Davenport. I feel completely out of the loop here. Gary treats me as if I'm a pain in the neck."

"Don't mind Gary, he's an administrator. From where he's sitting, everyone's a pain in the neck."

"It's more than that."

"Maybe they're just not used to you."

"Why? Because I'm a woman?"

Walter frowns into his mug. It seems the talk may be finished, but then he looks up. "O.K., here's a bit of information. Take it for what it's worth. Ethel says renovation of the Female Forensic Ward is about done."

"Ethel? How does *she* know?"

Walter shrugs, draws in his far-flung legs and looks out the window. There's nothing to see out there but a wall of fog, but he looks anyway.

But Ethel is not what interests her. Rather it is the grinding progress of this . . . something, which seems now to have advanced one click further.

"Well, there you go," she says. Whatever that is supposed to mean.

In the silence, her eyes travel the length of Walter, floor to fog. She mulls over the skew of his socks, the knot repairs in his laces. Despite her anger and her fear, she is sorry. She would like to say something to him. She thinks of asking him about his friend, the one who gave him the mug. But her lips find her own coffee mug, and this somehow gets in the way of the question.

* * * * *

Evelyn, Evelyn, Evelyn.

For awhile she persuaded herself that what fails to arouse the attention of others must really be unremarkable. But her own attention will not rest.

Her suspicions, of course, are vague. Do the deaths of three staff members on Hospital grounds over a period of sixty years amount to a pattern? And if each death were followed by the escape of a patient? Who can say? But statistical significance aside, she is herself a staff member, witnessing the return of one of the three escapees. And it is getting on into November. Yet she is not exactly afraid. She doesn't know the name of what she feels. But if she could put the feeling into words, the words would be these: who, or what, is Sophie Davenport?

It has reached this point. She has met with Sophie, watching that face for signs of something. She has looked, without distraction, long into those eyes. She has sat in mutual silence, then gotten up and navigated entirely around the woman's presence, as if to make sure of it. She has drawn in close enough to smell the hair, the skin, the breath. And this she knows, as thoroughly as she has ever known anything: there is no danger to her, not in this woman. The real danger, it seems, is to Sophie herself.

And what of those panic attacks? What of her looming disintegration? And the terror behind it. Is she moving well enough now? Somehow outrunning it? She doesn't have the answer to this. What she does have is a new feeling—as though her hands are finding a steering wheel.

* * * * *

It's a long shot, and she feels silly, but she is punching the number anyway, the Bangor phone book on her knee. Bernard Hanks—according to Records, the oldest surviving employee—retired in 1984. He should now be eighty-two years old. She hears it ringing.

"Hello," the voice answers, energetically enough. Though there is something about it belonging to another time.

She pretends she is compiling a directory of employees at the Hospital. She's calling to check his listing and make sure her information is correct. He sounds delighted to talk to her.

"So when were you hired?" she asks him.

"Right after the war. 1945. June the fifteenth."

No trouble with his memory.

They chat for awhile: what it was like back before antipsychotic drugs, what it's like now. She feels a bit guilty.

Then she says, "You must have been here when Dr. Melton died."

"Oh, yes. Just after Thanksgiving holiday."

"That must have been awful."

"Oh, yes. It was. A great shock. Awful."

She is afraid of arousing his suspicions, but Bernard Hanks never hesitates. He seems happy to tell her anything she wants to know.

She ventures, "Wasn't there a female inmate who escaped a few days later?"

"Yes, I believe you're right. I believe there was. That's right. We had police everywhere. That was a week turned upside down."

"But they never connected her with Dr. Melton's death."

"Oh no. No. That never came up. That was the way it was. Just every once in awhile someone would disappear. You couldn't keep a hundred percent. You just couldn't. It wasn't a prison."

"Young women, usually?"

"Escaped? Well, I suppose. We didn't keep such a tight grip on the women. Maybe we should have."

On a whim she asks, "Do you remember when Dr. Griswold arrived?"

"Dr. Griswold? Oh, no. No, he was there when I came."

"Dr. Griswold? I thought you started in 1945."

"Yuh. He came, I think, a few years before I did. And he was still there when I left. Retired by now, I'm sure."

Evelyn, with the record right in front of her—Warren Griswold, beginning date of employment, July 15, 1967—doesn't say anything.

Evidently Bernard Hanks is confused.

* * * * *

Mid-afternoon there is activity in the corridor, voices off and on.

Gary Benjamin sticks his head in her office. "You haven't seen Paul, have you?"

She thinks, shakes her head. "Not since this morning, in the hall. He was with Warren Griswold. What's up?"

"I don't know. He's not in his office. He hasn't been meeting his patients. Nobody's seen him since before noon."

"Maybe he's taking a long lunch."

"Paul?" He frowns. "Anyway his car's in the parking lot."

There follows an instant of silence, during which the situation seems contrarily familiar. Her *own* fingers now are suspended over the keyboard while Gary awaits a response from her.

"Hm!" she says.

It is enough to allow Gary to withdraw his head.

* * * * *

She keeps coming back to the interview with Madeline, exhuming questions she ought to have put to this woman in the veal-colored suit. She wonders about the source and the magnitude of her bitterness. Years of silence between mother and daughter—how would this be possible? Even she and Richard manage to say something, once in awhile send out some signal. The little flicker of words passing between— it almost doesn't matter what words they are—to keep it all from turning to ice. But utter silence. How would it begin? What would it feel like? What would one have to become in order to maintain it?

* * * * *

"I saw your mother yesterday."

Evelyn has been making more pointed use of silence, letting her questions and statements ring and hang on the air and dissolve into a thick nothingness of anticipation, which by the sheer pressure of her will she tries to imbue with hope.

It occurs to her that Sophie's defense is not an outer shell, not a wall, but a real form of self-abandonment. If you were to lunge for the girl, it seems, you would pass right through her.

"Your mother," Evelyn repeats, her voice trailing off. The words come back to her like returned letters. She could almost laugh at the thought that their separate hearts, again and again, turn up together in this room, which is like a yellowed state of being. Often her gaze has wandered the wall behind Sophie to a rectangular discoloration, where it seems a picture once was. And then there is the door, beyond which Frank's replacement stands, rocking on his heels, chewing gum.

* * * * *

Over dinner Richard is going on about the economy, the tourist industry. The Canning Plant. She keeps losing the thread. If there is one.

"All these downeast entrepreneurs." He chuckles. "A lot of goddamned accountants. Driving with their eyes on the rear-view mirror."

"What do you mean?"

"Backward. They're navigating backward." He holds his glass of Bordeaux, turning it, examining the rim, then sips.

"They think, 'The fishing industry's dead, what are you going to do with the place? It's an eyesore, a liability. Get rid of it.'"

"And what do you think?"

His eyes flare, taking her into the confidence of the wine. His arm holding the glass sweeps toward the window. "All this out there . . . the Great North Woods, the Rockbound Coast of Maine . . . ten, fifteen years from now, what do you see?"

His eyes hold on her. Apparently he expects an answer.

But her imagination, as if from the magnitude of some looming absurdity, is stunned. It is all she can do to return his stare.

"A playground," he says. "A playground. Here we are, smack on the edge of the last natural wonder on the East Coast, and people are moaning that there isn't any money here. There aren't any jobs. Incredibile. Another few years down the road, this place'll be shaping up like one big national park. And if you're already here, already set up, it'll be like inherited wealth. You won't even have to do anything for it."

"You don't think other people have thought of that?"

"Of course people have thought of it. But just thinking about it doesn't get you very far."

Richard sits bright-eyed, twirling his glass by the stem. After a moment he gets up for another bottle of wine.

He is at the counter, working at the cork, when the strain of a truck engine out on the highway seems to catch his attention. "Oh, yeah, I meant to ask . . . ." The cork squeaks, pops out of the bottle. ". . . have you seen anyone hanging around outside here?"

"What?"

"Before, when I pulled in the driveway, I thought I saw someone out there on the lawn. Right at the edge of the headlights, over by the maples. But, I don't know, when I got out of the car, there wasn't anyone."

"You mean this evening?"

"Yeah. Just after twilight."

"What did they look like?"

He shakes his head. "Like . . . no one. I don't know. Maybe I didn't see anyone. You know, it's hard in that light. Your eyes can play tricks."

It is as if now there are three people in the kitchen: she and Richard and the black square of window at her elbow.

"Anyway," he says, "I think it's good that we lock the door."

"Yes," she says.

A moment later Richard has returned to the table and is refilling their wine glasses. He sets the bottle down, smiles, and looks at her.

"This could be a classic case study," he says.

He appears almost giddy over the idea, whatever it is.

~S~

I WONDER what's happened to my rifle. Of course I can't ask anyone.

I mentioned it to Eddie. He says the firearms used in crimes are locked in rooms without windows. Every state police barracks has one. The weapons are tagged: Exhibit B, Case 04-006173. And so on. All this vicious hardware lying around for law enforcement officers to contemplate. Each trooper carries the key to a little museum of violence.

Contemplate this. Last year, I'm walking up along Disappearance Ridge. The beech have already given up their leaves. Grey trunks reach into grey sky. The air quivers with a light rain. And far below, hidden in softwood, the highway whines with the traffic of wet automobile tires. The sound comes at me all at once, ambushes me. I can't hear anything else. I lean into the bark of a dead balsam, unable to lift my eyes from the flood of crumpled leaves on the ground. I've been living in the woods now for half a year, without a human conversation. I'm beginning to succeed, or so I believe, in gaining back all my original sin. The cars are a problem. For a long time I stay there burning, brooding war against them.

The next day I descend the eastern slope at a run, switching back, skiing over wet leaves, carrying Dad's old Remington. I've decided on destroying one of them.

Lying on a boulder at the edge of the highway, I am out of breath. The boulder has been spray-painted with signatures in many colors. At night I've heard the cars stop, then voices. And in the morning, there's fresh paint over the old, still gummy to touch. As if there can never be enough of these signatures, this paint. Tomorrow they'll be smearing it on the trees. I'm lying there, and I'm thinking about this.

I'm keeping my head low while the first one or two cars go past. Then silence. Then the sound of another coming. I look up. There at the faraway bend in the road, it slides out of the trees. I'm looking at the thing head-on, the little chromium rectangle on stick tires, coming at me, sinking, disappearing where the road dips, then rising again out of the pavement, bigger. I'm sighting my rifle now, aiming at the windshield, where it seems this evil is, this noise, this hunger for spreading paint on rocks. It's then that I notice faces, ghost-like through the glass reflection of the sky. It confuses me. I hesitate, lower the barrel. The car sails past. Its faces, supported by high-speed thoughts, stare straight ahead. They haven't seen me, those faces. Through their windows, I wonder what it is they do see.

For awhile I lie there, in a daze, the sounds of cars zipping past hammering the idea home. I've forgotten about this, that there would be faces.

Who are these people anyway?

* * * * *

The contemplation of hardware. Automobiles are hunks of steel capable of killing. Evelyn Moore steers hers through fog in order to get here. She feels the urgency. She feels the mists closing in. Tatters of them cling to her purest intentions. They baffle her. The mists drive her inward, which is where she needs to be found.

Her automobile can be found out in the parking lot, precisely inside its quadrant of pavement marked by paint. The automobile is not supposed to have a mind of its own, but she doesn't remember putting it there. Its tires only pause before rolling again. Other lines of yellow paint, determined by a remote intelligence, govern the path of this machine on the highway.

    One-hundred-mile-an-hour head-on collisions avoided by Evelyn Moore's subliminal adherence to . . . what?

The Presence of Men

Evelyn achieves a breakthrough with the Wild Child.

SHE WONDERS about her failure to remember, which one psychiatrist likened to the blocking of pain during childbirth. She is inclined to believe that there was pain. But what, during those eighteen months, was she supposed to be giving birth to? And whatever became of it, this thing that, by all rights, should now be in blazing adolescence?

* * * * *

All the talk is about Paul Sun, who continues to be missing. In his office, next door to hers, the light is on. His briefcase stands open beside his desk. Phone calls to his home trigger the answering machine. The police have been notified. Meanwhile, his silver Saab Turbo sits in the parking lot like a mistaken delivery. Something that doesn't belong.

* * * * *

She is meeting with Sophie.

Amid the wash of high-pitched sounds that, in this building, passes for silence, she wanders onto the topic of mothers. She says, "Mothers are important to us, Sophie, even when we don't see eye to eye with them. We may end up loving who we are or hating who we are, simply because of things our mothers said or did to us, without them even being aware of it, without us even being aware of it."

Sophie sits, incidental as the brush-strokes of her hair. But Evelyn now can imagine seeing through this. She can imagine seeing movement in there, like the movement of a child stirring in sleep.

"Mothers generally mean well. But they are, after all, human beings. Sometimes it helps to imagine having a child of your own, to put yourself in the position of . . ." Evelyn's eyes wander the carpet, trying to navigate in advance of what she is saying. " . . . of having to grow apart from someone that close," she concludes. Her forehead resting in the cradle of her fingertips, she inhales a breath, reassured by the smell of her own skin.

"If you like, Sophie, I could tell you a little about my mother. We can start with that. I'll try . . . to forget that I'm a psychologist, and see if I can just ramble, not analyze. OK?" She sincerely intends this.

"Let's see . . . what can I tell you about my mother? Her name is Grace. She's fifty-nine years old. She still lives in Oneonta—that's in New York—the same house I grew up in. And . . . I think she has some talent musically, which I do not. She used to sing, in church and at weddings. And play the piano, when she was younger. And . . . let's see . . . she's a wonderful cook, which also I am not."

Silence presses in like fog on a lake. Direction is obscure. There is only the liquid surface, and whatever is beneath it.

"Hmm. What else can I say about my mother. I suppose a lot is hidden, where mothers are concerned."

If only the room had a window. Perhaps then she would see better, remember better.

"I wonder whether we can ever really separate mothers from ourselves. Whether we can ever judge them. But then . . . " Her voice trails off. "I'm not supposed to be analyzing." Her eyes rove the room.

"Mostly, I remember my mother at home. And in restaurants. She loved dining out. She loved dressing up and being waited on—more than Dad and I did, I think. Going out to eat, that was mostly her thing."

It is coming back to her. Without a thought to her next move. The words tumble into position.

"Dad was more the outdoor type. I seem to have mostly winter memories of him. He took me skiing a lot."

Remembering is like falling through a familiar twilight.

"He was an engineer. On the wall over his desk were photographs of bridges. All in black-and-white. Bridges strung across rivers, the cables big around as trees. Bridges wedged among city buildings, like pieces of the architecture. There were no people in any of the photographs. Really, they were photographs of geometry. His desk looked like a little altar to me. Everything on it was mysterious. He had a rivet the size of a baseball bat that he used as a paperweight. And there were tools he kept in a black leather case—protractors, compasses, slide rule. At night, I'd see him, silent and careful, working with these things, like sacred toys in the glow of his lamp. I guess that's another image I have of him, a chiaroscuro father.

"But . . . " She glances up at Sophie. And it doesn't register right away, her vision still immersed as it is in the glow of that desk lamp. "I was supposed to be talking about my mother."

Then of course she sees. Sophie is watching her.

She doesn't stop talking. "My mother . . . says I was a somber child. In the kitchen I'd help her, grating carrots, fetching spices, licking bowls. Nice, little girl jobs. But I knew even then, my mother's kitchen wasn't the world. Outside those cheery curtains and steamed-over windows, the autumn light was fading. Wild older boys moved into the neighborhood.

The dog next door would snarl on its chain. Men came in trucks and dug up the yard. Who knows what it was?

"Anyway, I couldn't be my mother. And I suppose mothers back then weren't very well-equipped to imagine the lives of their daughters. There was bound to be disappointment. And fear. Maybe a little envy."

She has been looking and looking into Sophie's eyes.

"Sophie, won't you speak to me?"

Again that urgent look, a shake of the head, and the angled glance, which Evelyn follows up the wall, past the ventilation grate, to the ceiling, where there is nothing.

* * * * *

Entering the house this evening in a nimbus of thrill and exhaustion, she walks right into the smell of Italian cooking. As she pushes the door closed, she can see Richard's desk is empty, the computer humming, screen black. She expects him in the kitchen, but not as she finds him, frozen in the middle of the floor, his head twisted toward her at a improbable angle, eyes skewed to the ceiling. No part of him moves, not even the eyes. In his hand she notices the fly swatter.

"What are you doing?" she says.

"What does it look like?"

"I'd hate to tell you."

"Shh."

Evelyn sets her bag on a chair.

"I can hear the damned thing," he says.

"Hear what?"

"Goddamned fly."

"I don't hear anything."

"Well you keep talking."

His brow wrinkles with the strain of listening.

She glances over at the stove. The oven is on.

"What are we having for dinner?"

"Scallopini. Breadsticks." He relaxes his stance, his eyes still scanning the room. "It pisses me off."

"What?"

"That fly has been dive-bombing, hit-and-run, in and out of here for the last hour. It bugs me."

"You've been hunting this fly for an hour?"

"It's one of these big stupid ones. Buzzing against the window, buzzing along the ceiling, buzzing into the lightbulb. Incredibly annoying."

Evelyn is cheerfully opening drawers and cabinets, setting the table. "Well, one thing about obsessive-compulsives, they may waste a lot of time, but they can still get dinner in the oven."

"Who's wasting time? You see this fly, you're going to wish I'd killed it." Richard is still surveying the ceiling. "By the way, before I forget, I've got a meeting tomorrow, in Boston."

"Oh?"

"Little fishing expedition."

"In Boston?"

Richard hangs the fly swatter on its hook over the sink. "For venture capital."

"Oh. The restaurant."

"Yeah. I talked to Darryl and Wayne last night. They may actually be interested. The three of us are meeting tomorrow over lunch. I doubt I'll be back in time for dinner."

As she works at putting together a salad, she hears the ring of glassware. Washing, draining the endive, she glances over at the figure of her husband contemplatively pouring wine, two glasses cradled in the palm of one hand, stems between the fingers. Richard, in the kitchen, but at the same time not in the kitchen.

"Sometime," she says, "I'd like to have a talk."

He looms, holding out her glass.

"What about?"

"Thanks. About what we're doing. You and I."

She sees, at closer than the usual range, the flicker around the eyes. Something in him getting ready.

He turns, sipping his wine, moves over and leans against the wall. "Sure," he says.

"You know, this isn't a battle you have to prepare for. I just think it would be good if we kept in touch with one another."

"Hey. I'm all for that."

Shaking her head over her salad fixing, she says, "I guess I'm wondering about this restaurant idea. At times you seem pretty excited by it. But then the other night you said you'd probably let go of it after a couple of years. I'd just like to know, do you have some long-range plan?"

Richard, crouching, looking into the oven, says nothing.

"You said, if we had enough money, we could do whatever we wanted. Well, what would that mean? Would you like to get out of this real estate thing you've been doing, go into something else?"

"Like what?"

"Well, I'm asking you. I don't know what your plans are. I can't read your mind, Richard. When we moved here, it seemed there was a spirit of change somehow."

"You're saying you want change?"

"I thought we both did."

"Well . . . " His arm sweeps toward the window. " . . . after all, this is not Connecticut."

"I'm not talking about our surroundings. I'm talking about us. For instance, you used to have an interest in anthropology."

Richard rearranges his face, simulating thought. "Ah, now I see where this is headed."

"Do you?" she says. "I wish I did."

She brings the salad plates to the table.

"I don't care, Richard, honestly, whether you're in graduate school or the garage, whether you have this degree or that degree or no degree. I'd just like to think that you've got something in mind other than how to turn a profit."

She pulls out her chair and sits down.

Richard chuckles. "That old academic prejudice does die hard."

"It isn't prejudice, it's appreciation, an interest in the ingredients of whole human beings." Touched by her own words, she smiles. "I come home, I look at you, and I wonder, 'What's going on with him? What does he think about?' Really, I'd like to hear it. It's important to me."

He sets his wine glass on the table and smiles back at her. He is good at smiling. "Sure," he says. "I'm all for communication."

These are Richard's words. He might just as easily have said others. It doesn't matter. It is the almost sing-song abstraction in his voice that convinces, that leaves her floating.

Richard—here, but at the same time not here.

* * * * *

It is late. Evelyn, standing before the bathroom mirror in her nightgown, has been brushing her hair, taking far longer than usual, watching her reflection. This is something new. She isn't willing to stop. Her own eyes, looking back at her, are relentless. She is trying to suspend the noise of her own thoughts, trying to come to something like objectivity. Richard, she isn't forgetting, has said that she has a pleasant face. But this image staring back at her—what does it have to do with her?

Is it like this for other people? Looking stupidly into mirrors, unable to recognize what they see?

The brush works the hair. She can see it in the mirror, feel it in her scalp. But she misses the connection, the assurance of continuity. And something more, the impression of being at the center.

Put it another way: who is looking at whom?

And before she knows it, she is laughing. Wonderfully, the feeling welling from within, no thought of control. She slumps, with the pleasure of it, against the towel rack. In the mirror, her hand coming up to cover her mouth. As though the two of them were enjoying it together.

And then the door in the mirror opens, allowing Richard's head to poke in. He looks at her, a look intended as a question.

But Evelyn isn't about to answer. Her eyes return to the eyes that a moment ago were strangers to her, and she is off again. She couldn't stop herself even if she wanted to.

"What's so funny?" he says finally.

She is shaking her head. And after a moment, "Oh, nothing. It's nothing. I just . . . amaze myself sometimes."

A little flip of the eyebrows, and Richard's head is gone.

Later as she slips into bed, still smiling, she is thankful for the dark.

~S~

FINALLY it happened.

She was there, talking about her own life, forgetting all about me. She was remembering the image of her mother growing smaller, receding under the low ceiling of some long-ago October. Those fearful skies that had loomed so close. Then she saw me looking at her, and for a minute the walls of that stale little room dissolved. She wanted me to speak. But I couldn't risk it. Not yet.

Meanwhile, inside the House, the lights are going out. Dr. Sun has vanished. Eddie saw him heading up the stairwell. Eddie said he had a look in his eye, like he was closing in on something. Now everyone is wondering whether maybe he got it. Or it got him.

* * * * *

Mothers generally mean well. That's what Evelyn Moore said, but I don't know about that. My own mother can suck the light out of the day. For years she's been out of the picture, inhabiting the dark places behind me. Always I carry around this possibility: that at any time, in a weak moment, she might just pop out and surprise me.

Like yesterday.

She came here to meet with them. Already when they were walking me down the hall, somehow I knew what it was for. They opened the door to one of those rooms, and there she sat, demure, erect. A lady's posture. Clutching a balled-up kleenex, hands in her lap. They plopped me down across from her and left us alone, my eyes bearing on the collar of her pinkish suit. I didn't blink. I stayed perfectly cool.

But I bet there was never any doubt in her mind.

After a long silence, she said, "Is this what you want, dear?" With that little twist of her lips.

On the wall to the left of my mother's chair was a painting of a yellow-slickered man in a small boat. Waves surrounded the boat like iron mountains. The man was hauling a rope out of the water. The painting was called "The Lobsterfisherman." And I noticed something. I could clearly see that the painting, which you could say had nothing at all to do with my mother, was in fact growing out of her life. I sat there staring at the space containing the two of them.

After a few minutes she stood up, dropped her kleenex in the wastebasket, and left the room. I kept staring, faithfully, right over the back of the empty chair. I could see, the painting now was empty too.

I tried, long ago, disconnecting her from the furniture, rescuing her from the world in the television. I tried simplifying her wardrobe, pouring her chemicals down the sink. She screamed at me until police actually broke through the front door. We all stood then in the swirl of indoor and outdoor airs, looking at one another. This was no good, I thought.

After that, Mother grew more distrustful, not only of me, but of being alive. She wouldn't venture outside. She'd come and go in Town Car, which waited gleaming in its garage, two steps down from the kitchen. How she got from Town Car to the supermarket I don't know. I never went with her.

I'd be upstairs crosslegged on my bedroom floor, my back against the wall. Half the day, trying to see through the pile carpet. This went on and on, it was even worse than it sounds. Till one night I knew it had gone far enough. I knew the room was ready to explode. Any minute. The air was going to rip open, you could feel it, letting in something. I didn't want to see what.

I climbed right out the window, skittered down the roof, hit the ground, and ran. Under a full moon. I ran, avoiding familiar roads. I was out of breath, but I kept on running. I was amazed at how long I could keep it up. The road ended in a field, and then the field ended. The night had no direction. I wasn't running anymore, I was stumbling, then just kneeling, my blood thundering in my ears. The dark felt different, all around crowded with shapes. The moonlight barely sifted in from overhead.

This was how I discovered our woods. By running right into them.

Long Ago

Finding herself plunged in darkness, Evelyn experiences the awakening of distant and troubled memories.

WHAT DO WE DO with pain?
Mostly we shut it away, in chambers fabricated of dream, where it can seeth and burn darkly, like a magma annealing our lives. We carry around, each of us, these mute, unknowable fires. They are our true engines of decision, moving us in unwanted directions, distracting us, spoiling our aim. She understands, she is no exception.

* * * * *

She knows something has changed even before unlocking her office. The door swings open onto darkness. She gropes, flips on the wall switch. In the flat-white light, her eyes jump immediately to the scab of plywood where her window used to look out on pines.
Yesterday afternoon on her way out, closing the door—now she recalls—she met the two workers just getting to her office. "We're taking your window," the older one boomed, fairly chipper about it.
"So I understand," she said.

"Won't be long, we'll have you a better one." He stopped, saluted her with a smile in which there seemed also something like a challenge. "Not so drafty."

So now she stands close by the doorway as if immobilized by this transformation, neither unreasonable nor entirely unexpected, that has been wrought on her office. She stands as if debating what to do, as if wondering whether to go on. And gradually it seems that she is, in this room, not exactly alone. There is a sound in the room with her: the semi-melodic rise and fall of a voice. A kind of sing-song chant, like a jump-rope rhyme. It is coming from the ventilation duct, whether a man's or a woman's voice she cannot tell. She moves closer, squats, and cocks an ear, and then she can make it out. The voice is counting by fives to a hundred, and then starting over again, on and on. She lowers one knee to the tile and listens—five, ten, fifteen, twenty, twenty-five, thirty—looking around her office at her filing cabinet, her wall calender, her Morisot print, her desk and chair. All these things look different, forever changed, now that she is kneeling on the floor, with no window.

* * * * *

Her memory arises out of indifferent rooms.

Pale walls, flickering people. Bloated, forgettable furniture.

Blinds ration the light.

It is morning.

The lighting is queerly diffuse, almost fuzzy, as if, in coming to this place, she has arrived on the other side of life.

Like it or not, the furniture prevails, giving definition to the people, who come and go like apparitions.

And, while she sometimes hears sounds, no one communicates a word to her.

Like one bordering on nausea, she learns to be careful where she directs her eyes.

At this point, it is detail that troubles her. The vinyl baseboard is coming unstuck. The blind cord hangs in a crimp. She can expect, at the sight of these complications, the intolerable heaviness that precedes the beginning of thought.

And, somehow, she knows that more awaits her. Virtually everywhere. She does not consider anything larger than this—where not to look. That is what it means being here. To fend, to shy away. It is as fundamental as breathing, not to evoke anything.

Once in a while (it is like hearing a knock on a door that is not her own) she is tugged or prodded, rearranged or conveyed to another room. And back again.

The water in the paper cup grows warm, forming little, tiresome bubbles. Her eyes move on. Or close.

It may be that she sleeps.

The air smells not like actual air, but like the tacit intention of this place. She inhales as though it is medicine.

After awhile—she can't help it—she notices things. The cords on the blinds, made of string, will not support her weight. The windows are screened from inside.

Her eyes veer.

A sudden presence in the shape of a nurse may take the cords in hand, manipulating the blinds. Perhaps phrasing a question. Not to her exactly. Rather as if addressing the window itself. Would she like a bit more light? Or less? Not waiting for an answer.

And when finally someone does sit down beside her, when finally someone talks to her, it is a relief. The words amount to nothing. Sentences crumble. The face is a curiosity, unconnected in any way to her situation. The lips move as he clicks and unclicks a pen. There is no need for her to do anything but close and then open her eyes.

Afterward, her breathing a miraculous calm, she can look even a little forward to the next time.

There is night.
And.
There is morning.
The nurse draws the plastic blinds, letting in the milky light.

It is a morning without resolution, stretching on into the distance like an endlessly repetitive corridor. Like a sleep that comes and goes.

At some point, she is simply beyond it. She doesn't know how. Holding tentative conversations with her doctor, her mother.

She walks on the lawns. She eats breakfast again. She discovers that it is summer.

* * * * *

Today the police are about. In the company of Gary Benjamin and two of the janitors, they are unlocking closed rooms and inspecting them, one after the other. Earlier, on her way in, she noticed them in the fog, hiking the perimeter of the grounds. All morning long they have been interviewing staff. The closest she gets to scrutiny is a couple of instances of eye contact from a Detective Matthews (she overhears the name). With him is another police investigator whose shoes she hears wheezing back and forth, emerging from and then vanishing into the alerted white silence of the corridors.

All this activity. It's as if the building has a new heartbeat, everyone awakened because after all it is a mystery: where could Paul Sun be? For one wild moment, she feels the circle of attention, the arena of surmises closing in on her, as though soon it might be she who is implicated. She has been aware of little else this morning, with her window gone. But for some reason, no one thrusts a head into her office, no one thinks to interview her.

And then: "What do you suppose Lizzie would have to say about it?"

At her desk, her back to the plywood, she hears someone say this. Someone in the hall? A voice from the grate? An inner voice? She has no idea. The fact is she may have been dozing.

She listens, but nothing follows.

* * * * *

Roland's eyes avoid the plywood, but it's plain to see he's bothered by it. His eyebrows stir. They seem to urge his gaze to the other side of the room. "What was it he recalls? You wished to talk . . . about art?"

"We can talk about whatever you like, Roland."

"Whatever he likes." His attention resorts to the backs of his hands. "Whatever he likes. Which seems itself an echo of the aesthetic question. He wouldn't know where to begin."

"Is it true that you used to paint?"

He takes a quick breath. "It is true. Ah, yes. He once possessed paints and brushes and a dream of practicing that art. Yes. But the dream proved a cruel absurdity. A little like arriving at the stadium after the game has been played. No, nothing is there, except sadness. In this democratic age, sadness and small-talk. And red-faced applause. Nothing more. The once-fertile ground, now perspiring toxins, sprouts *nouveau* varieties of art. Astonishing. Have you seen? Crinkly-bright transmogrifications, they take the breath away. Oh yes, a new era of . . . *mm* . . . liberation has dawned upon the realm of the aesthetic. Neon! Lasers! Technologic euphoria! The

Meditative Veneration of Hairspray Containers. Giftwrapping of the Oceans. Masturbation over the Worldwide Web. He has seen them all. He has seen the mall. Packets of snack food for Mammon. He would sooner attend an exhibition of thumbscrews. No, one day—this was quite a few years ago—he took his oils and his artist's brushes and painted a monumental bull's eye on the seat of his pants and stood eating french fries on the sidewalk outside the Museum of Modern Art. It was . . . his last show. Perhaps his finest hour and a half. Ever since then . . . *mm* . . . " His hand slopes toward the floor.

"And you've never thought of painting again?"

"Again? God, what a terrifying prospect—it would be like the xeroxing of anguish. No, no, it is all he can do now to keep to the path, one foot and then the next, and then the one and then the next, careful not to dislodge any of that other kind of thinking."

"What kind of thinking is that, Roland?"

"Oh, he doesn't even want to think about it." Roland's eyes have been making forays toward the boarded-up window but, so far, always stopping short of it. "Perhaps," he says, leaning forward, "the half-hour is up?"

Evelyn looks at the clock. "No, the half-hour is not up. You've been here barely ten minutes, Roland. Usually it seems you like talking to me. Is there something troubling you?"

"Hm?"

"Is it that the workmen have covered up my window?"

"The workmen." His eyes fix on her. "Oh, the workmen." He laughs. "No, no, not them. Not at all. He knows them quite well. He has often conversed . . . stopping by the tavern . . . and in hardware stores . . . no, no." He looks now at the plywood, as though assessing its quality.

"I should have my window back soon," she says. "So they tell me."

"Oh, no. Think nothing of it." He leans back. His entire aspect has brightened. "No, even on the best of days, he doesn't paint anymore."

The toes of his slippers lift alternately from the floor, manifesting some sprightly, noiseless rhythm.

"That was long, long ago," he says with a sigh. "Long ago."

* * * * *

Then one day, on that hospital terrace, a man out of nowhere sits down next to her. He asks permission first, his fingers grazing her arm. She can do little more than nod, smile. He is as tall as her father was. Only blonde.

He identifies himself: a graduate student from Cornell. Cultural anthropology. Managing this with a charming mixture of disparagement and pride.

An absolute stranger, he talks to her easily, inquiring after her welfare the way he might about a friend they both love. She is aware of a sensation, as of motion sickness.

What is he doing here? (It is he who asks the question.) "I'm interested," he says, clasping his hands, "in the way institutions affect human beings. Institutions . . . like this one." He glances away toward the line of trees bordering the lawn. He nods in her direction. "Human beings like this one." It would be a real help to him if she would take just a moment or two to look at his survey. Of course, she shouldn't feel any obligation to participate. "Only if you want to," he says.

He slides the three-page questionnaire and Number 2 pencil onto the table in front of her. She stares at it as she might at a chess move.

She looks up at him, this man with the quick teeth and the sage cologne. Her hesitation comes, not from doubt. She is unused to this forward velocity of time.

Perhaps to reassure her, he presses nearer to explain the questionaire. It doesn't need explaining. A child could fill it out.

She takes a breath and then hears herself offer, for no good reason, that in the semester before her illness she elected a course in anthropology. She enjoyed the course very much, she adds, looking down again at his questionaire.

His smile is mostly in the eyes. Seeing and apparently confiding something beyond the moment.

Her fingers play with the pencil. She moves her lips as she reads, a question about changes in eating habits. Probably he watches.

A question about clothing. A question about human contact.

She pauses over another question. 'How free have you felt in this institution to express your innermost self?—very free, free, somewhat free, somewhat inhibited, very inhibited.'

"'Your innermost self,'" she repeats out loud.

He laughs. "Be honest now."

Finishing, she feels a little flushed. She can remember none of her answers, barely a few of the questions. The day, pressing in on her from outside the boundary of her vision, is just too new. Her fingers relinquish the pencil.

He tucks the questionaire into a folder without looking at it. He seems all of a sudden at a loss for words.

It isn't long and her eyes are pursuing him across the terrace, past the other patients and the staff, he already recombining with the world from which, some while ago, he emerged.

And she is left with . . . what? It isn't easy to know. She feels physically as though she has been transported, away somewhere and back again, and is sitting even now under the influence of that motion, a little dizzy in the sloping light of afternoon, among these other hushed voices on the terrace. From the trees across the lawn, the fuss of birds subsides. And, moving into that pool of stillness, there is the flicker of shadow that tomorrow makes upon consciousness. All of this seems new.

She does see him again, and then a third time, always on the terrace, where, without really thinking about it, she waits for him. She asks him how his study is going. But it is never long before he would like to talk about something else.

He has different ways of watching her. Easily himself, he is anecdotal, a little elusive, glancing now and then for responses. But when she speaks, his features quietly align, eyes steady, taking her in until she wonders if there could be enough of her ever to satisfy him. She stops then, and he looks away and back again, as though there is continually something he is about to say. As though out in front of the hospital (she imagines) a little roadster might be parked for the two of them, and it is only a matter of his waiting through all these impatient and premature moments, so that it will finally be time to tell her. He frightens her, this slightly older man, seeing in her apparently something she knows nothing about, something beyond them both.

"Your face," he says at last.

He looks at her in silence, then shakes his head. "I just can't get over it."

A woman and a man, both patients, are ambling toward them, not speaking. Evelyn wishes he would wait until they pass, but, reckless, he seems not to notice.

"I have to tell you. On the wall at home, there is a painting . . ."

The eyes of the woman patient have taken her in.

"—well, actually a print. Morisot's *Young Girl by the Window*. Do you know it?"

She says that she does not. But really she is thinking about those patients moving within range, perhaps apprehending his words, perhaps preparing to carry them away. She wonders whether, in this, there might be some loss.

"The face of the girl in that painting," he says, "—it's your face. The first time I saw you, it hit me."

He does not say the face is beautiful. The hush of his voice suggests, if anything, something more.

He would like to show her the painting.

The air seems to stir.

She looks, and the patients have gone. And something else has gone, too. The outlines of things seem clearer.

During his afternoon visits they sit. The sun pours from behind her. He turns to gaze over his shoulder across the lawns, flaunting the line of his jaw. He holds this posture, unaccountably, as if by the leverage of his thoughts. Strands of his hair sway in the slow air. The seconds are like an immersion, from which they each take breaths.

Looking at her, he remarks on the lengths of her fingers, running one of his along one of hers. But as he says this he is watching her eyes.

She considers all of this. Even that some day it will end.

Back in her ward the nurses are playful with her. Judging from her complexion, they would bet she has seen Mr. Moore again today.

It is almost impossible not to smile, often.

Although day by day she feels the world opening up, she is able—as she pictures it—to remain still at the edge of the wood, peering into the brilliance of the meadow through the trees. She is able to ask herself, without ever resorting to the bluntness of the words, whether this is what it might be like to be in love.

She is released from the hospital, and the same day he calls her.

* * * * *

There has been that change: now Sophie is always watching. Whether Evelyn talks or sits or gets up and moves around. Those eyes hardly leave her.

She tells no one.

~S~

I DREAM about ravens—seven stocky black males working their way over a frozen cornfield. In between pecking the rows of hard earth, they talk at one another through glinting eyes, while graying mountains parade in the background. They talk in the manner of soldiers, about the drought, the deteriorating air, and the familiar barrenness of this cornfield. They are not exactly happy here where they are. They seem to be waiting for something better. They seem to be waiting for orders. I don't know why there aren't any female ravens. But these males don't seem to notice. Their attitudes seem fixed, resigned. They are tough ravens, used to severe conditions, and used to talking about them, though not in a complaining way. These ravens have flown here, have descended straight into this field some indefinite time ago. But taking off and flying someplace else does not, at this point, seem a possibility for them. It does not seem even to occur to them. They act just as if there is something to wait for, not a specific something, perhaps only direction, perhaps only an end to their forgetfulness.

For two nights I've dreamed about these ravens. I ask Androscoggin, what does it mean?

She won't tell me.

❊ ❊ ❊ ❊ ❊

I keep coming back to these windows. There's something about the idea that bothers me.

Humans contained in buildings hunger for what is not contained. They look outside. They want views. If what they see out their windows won't do, they hang pictures. In the end they hang lots of pictures because the views from most windows are like exhibits in a museum of sorrow. Insect voraciousness, exhilaration, and death, teased over the years to look like landscapes. Echoes of crimes centuries old have seeped into these hills, coated the grasses and the trees like soot. Our vision is hardened into a muted crust. Like paint dried on canvas.

Interview with a Witness

She travels through fog to hear of events that can't be described.

"AAAAAAAOOOOOOOOOOOOOHHH!!!"
She is there when it happens. She sees Mrs. Dibrizzi stop dead, reeling in the corridor, her hands gripped tightly to her walker. The old woman convulses, throws her head back, and then lets out that unimaginable sound. Though Evelyn hears it and sees the woman produce it, still somehow she cannot put the two together. It is as if poor Blanche Dibrizzi has become the conduit for a howl from another world.

As Evelyn moves to comfort the woman, two mental health workers come running, then Esther Boyle with a needle.

Blanche Dibrizzi seems hardly substantial enough to hold up her own clothes, but the two mental health workers have their hands full immobilizing her and bending her forward. Esther fills the syringe, and as the diaper drops, they all get a look at Mrs. Dibrizzi's shrunken buttocks. "No more of this," Esther says. "She's going right to B-Ward. Beds or no beds."

* * * * *

When she enters Walter Rafferty's office and plops herself down in a chair, he looks up but doesn't say anything.

Neither does she. She wouldn't know what to say, even if she *could* talk.

After a minute, he says, "You O.K.?"

She has her gaze averted. It seems she is on the edge of tears, but the very thought will prevent her from crying. She can depend on this—the abstraction of sorrow.

Although she is not looking at him, she can see Walter put down his work. He simply sits, apparently watching her.

He says, "Would you like some tea?"

* * * * *

She is back, over her lunch break, at the Bangor Public Library, thinking to satisfy her curiosity about Drs. Melton and Spiegel. The newspaper accounts and obituaries don't reveal a lot. Still, she comes away with the impression that the two men had lived, prior to their spectacular deaths in the Hospital, fairly unspectacular lives. Of any subsequent escapes from the Hospital, she finds no mention whatsoever.

As she is leaving, feeling the scrutiny of eyes, she glances over at one of the reading tables. And there, looking up from a newspaper, is Detective Matthews. Immediately he smiles, gives her a little two-fingered salute. She manages to nod, and then she is out the door and onto the sidewalk, hurrying into fog and the sound of traffic and the distant ruckus of crows, rehearsing in her memory the fact that she did return the microfilm reels to their places in the drawers.

* * * * *

Saturday evening seems in a way empty. And in a way full. Empty because Richard isn't home. Full because, now, neither is she. It is as if the evening has been shot so full of emptiness that the strain of it has set her in motion. Normally, at such an hour, she'd be home with a book. But here she is, as the light is failing, driving through the fog toward an obscure end.

The road winds and descends to Franklin. She steers by the centerline, seeing never enough of the road ahead to gain the impression of progress. It is rather as though the white ether of the world is rushing past her. As though this condition is, to her, intrinsic, definitive. Her tires hiss over wet pavement. The windshield wipers clear the glass with a rhythm slower than breathing. A rhythm perhaps slightly hypnotic. Then suddenly, out of the blank background, she spots the name on the mailbox. Unable to brake in time, she passes it, turns around and comes back.

Expectantly, she urges the car up the driveway, toward nothing visible, until first the lighted windows and then the gray farmhouse itself take form out of the mist. And then, as if evoked by the pressure of her foot on the brake pedal, there looms on her left something she isn't sure of, a complexity of shadow, beneath which she slows to a stop and parks. Through the windshield she looks up, and the dusky shape sorts itself into the multiple trunks and boughs of a pine. A moment later, standing in the resinous space underneath it, she can see the tree is immense, ancient.

At the top of the stoop, Lizzie Farnsworth stretches herself into the fog, holding the storm door open for her, then shutting it firmly after. At the brink of the livingroom, Evelyn hesitates, smelling wood smoke, cinnamon, cats. Lizzie Farnsworth takes her coat, motions her to the sofa, and offers her coffee, but does not smile. Evelyn accepts the coffee, although she hasn't an appetite for it.

Lizzie turns, and Evelyn watches her grey braid, which hangs almost to her waist, recede into the kitchen. A moment later, she returns unhurriedly, without speaking. As she bends over the woodstove, the braid creeps up her back. The woman works clankingly at the levers, and opens the stove door. Pushing up the sleeves of her cardigan, she pokes eruptions of sparks out of the fire, adds a stick of wood, and closes the door. Then she is back to the kitchen.

The works of the pendulum clock on the mantle spin through a preparatory grind and click, in readiness for striking the hour. The clock hands read five minutes to four. Evelyn's eyes consider the intricacies of the oriental carpet, the tassel and embroidery of the furniture. She wonders how there can be so much anger in one family.

Lizzie reenters carrying thick, steaming mugs. She hands one to Evelyn, then seats herself obliquely in a wingback chair. In order to look at Evelyn, she has to turn her head.

Evelyn sips the coffee, which is hot, weak.

"Ms. Farnsworth. I hope not to take up much of your time."

The works of the pendulum clock revolve, unwinding, striking four times.

Lizzie looks at her, taut-faced. "I've no shortage of time," she says.

"Since I've been seeing your niece, I thought I needed to talk to you."

Lizzie sips her coffee. "Are you her therapist then?"

"No. She has no therapist at present. She's been admitted only for evaluation. Whatever therapy she'd receive would come later, in the event we're charged to treat her. Except possibly for medication . . . if that seemed necessary."

Now Lizzie smiles, nods. "Things haven't changed a lot over there."

"You weren't happy with her treatment before."

She doesn't phrase it as a question, nor does Lizzie move to answer.

"Ms. Farnsworth, I should say right away I'm not on Sophie's evaluation team. I've come to you because . . . I've taken an interest in her. The others don't know I'm here."

Lizzie turns and this time holds her gaze.

Evelyn, on the sofa, tightens and relaxes her grip on the mug perched upon her knees. "She seems a very special young woman. I'm afraid, frankly, of what might happen to her . . . if things keep on as they are."

Lizzie purses her lips, then looks away toward the window. It isn't easy to guess her age. With her sharp eyes and weathered skin and long, long braid, she could be fifty-five, or seventy-five.

"What do you want?" she says, her voice softening.

"I'd like to understand her."

Lizzie laughs at this. "Naturally," she says. She sips her coffee.

"She appears to have had," Evelyn offers, "a troubled relationship with her mother."

Lizzie waits, as if for calmer air. "Madeline has always insisted on control," she says. "It's her way of compensating."

"For what?"

"The fact that the world scares her to death." Lizzie's eyes grow wide.

"Sophie lived with you for awhile."

"Yes, in a manner of speaking. She had a room here whenever she wanted it."

The wood burning in the stove pops, then settles.

"Ms. Farnsworth . . . ."

"Lizzie, please."

"Lizzie. The past two weeks . . . I've been meeting with Sophie. I talk to her. She sits there. I've never gotten an answer back. Not one word."

"Well, you can hardly blame her, can you."

"I want to help her."

"Giving somebody something she doesn't want — that might be helping, and it might not."

"And if she spends the rest of her life locked away in that institution?"

Lizzie pulls in her arms, rests her mug on her lap, and stares toward the slit of window left uncovered by the draw drapes. "She isn't like other people." Her eyes measure Evelyn for a moment. "She has something that people recognize. Something missing in themselves. They see it in her."

Lizzie peers into her coffee. Her sentences come spaced apart, like items remembered one at a time. "This probably won't make sense to you. But I've spent time with her here, in this house. What I have witnessed . . . I couldn't begin to describe to you."

Evelyn asks, in spite of herself, "What?"

Lizzie shakes her head. "Talk is impossible. It would sound to you like lunacy. I am neither a religious nor a superstitious woman. But I believe there are things your science can know nothing about. I picture her there in your hospital, with your . . . evaluation team, or whatever it is. And I don't wonder at all about her silence."

Evelyn shifts slightly on the couch, stirring the phenomena of her own existence. Forgotten muscles try one another. Her legs feel the fiber of her skirt. Her hands work the lukish porcelain of the coffee mug. From these boundary encounters, she recognizes herself. "No," she says, "on some level Sophie's silence has always seemed appropriate." She considers further. "But in the end it may also work against her. I said before that I'd like to help. I meant that."

A single chime from the mantle clock announces the half-hour.

Lizzie settles back into her chair, her eyes reflecting some unaccountable fluorescence, as if they might be nuggets of the vitrifying fog outside. "Be careful. She may not harbor a single ounce of malice. But God help the soul who loves her. Man or woman."

* * * * *

Her days seem defined by the steady trickle of loss. She doesn't know what it is she's losing, or even whether she wants it back. It seems that she is no longer Evelyn. She is instead someone riding the verge of existence, someone who hasn't been named, someone beyond the reach of worry because so far she hasn't said anything or done anything.

    That night, alone in her bedroom, she cracks open a window: there is the need to let something in. Attentively, she slips out of her nightgown and, for awhile in the dark, sits on the corner of her bed, feeling a new and significant pressure against her skin.

    What is it like? It is like the end of everything and the beginning of something else.

~S~

IN WHAT SEEMS the middle of the night, I rise from a dream more actual than life and begin walking. I don't think about it, but I know where I'm going. While my various doctors are shut in their houses, lying far-flung, insensible in their beds, I experiment with travel here at their place of employment, stealing along their corridors, my feet on cold floor. The nurse sits at her station, reading. I continue down the hall, the moments streaming against me with the weight of rivers. Up ahead is something large and vague, some form of annihilation disguised as architecture. All the same, I'm not afraid, aware of the immunity that goes with pointlessness.

Still, I wonder what it is that's moving me.

Beyond the locked stairwell door that opens with an exact wiggle of the knob, my feet find steps, first one, then the next. I climb in complete darkness, careful not to touch the walls. For all I know, there are no walls, only stairs going up and night falling away on either side. Ascending this way requires attention so deep that the first glint of light on the stairs confuses me. I step onto the fourth floor like someone else, someone in a story.

Through an open doorway is a large bright room. The brightness is from the floor, where moonlight glows in a row of skewed window shapes, each one cut into mosaic by the shadows of its steel mesh. In one of the glowing shapes is the blot of a larger shadow. William's. He is standing at a window, perfectly still, except for the rhythmic motion of his head and the continual slither of his cigarette smoke down along the window and across the floor. I begin to move closer, then stop to watch him.

William glances my way, dragging on his cigarette, then he's back to staring out the window. His head is moving, but I don't see that. What I see is the shadow of the mesh undulating, back and forth across his face.

He says, "You're wondering what I'm doing up here, right?"

I don't say anything. I think, maybe I'm still dreaming.

"See," he says, "I can't be sure. My life is not continuous. There are these . . . gaps. A moment ago I was here, and now I'm here, but I have this suspicion, there was a time sandwiched between when I wasn't here."

I expect him to go on, but he doesn't. A few more minutes of silence and it seems as if there's been no talk between us. Only anticipation.

He looks around now at the big room we're in. "The thing is, see, my grandmother . . . my grandmother was kept in a place like this. *Alot* like this," he adds, as if only now appreciating the magnitude of the similarity.

"Schizophrenic," he says. In his voice there is something like pride, something like an understanding of the end. "Same as me."

He takes another drag on his cigarette, exhales the smoke at the window. "I visited her once, when I was a kid. Actually it was a mistake, my being there. I wasn't supposed to. There was some mix-up. Anyway they didn't let us in . . . to where they kept her. They brought her out to us in a room across the hall. But there were like . . . a couple of seconds when the doors were open, and you could see in. You could see. It was like . . . I don't know . . . like a warehouse, for broken people. All these . . . bent bodies in rags, or naked. Like in storage. It was weird. There were these . . . bright lightbulbs, even though the place was dark. And the smell. I didn't know what was going on. I'd heard she was *sick*."

While I'm listening to William, I'm moving again now, one foot exactly in front of the other, keeping my distance from these walls. I'm taking in the pictures of his words, but I'm pacing, wearing a path in the dust over the floor. I don't feel right about these walls.

"But what got to me really," he says, "were the sounds. When they opened that door. I couldn't have . . . dreamed anything like it. Like . . . animal voices talking. Like . . . people barking and growling. To me, it was like the worst thing I could think of, that there was this possibility that a human being could slip into becoming an animal. How could that happen? What kind of world was this?

"And then, Jesus, there was my grandmother. They'd put a fresh gown on her, brought her out like a . . . dessert tray, like a . . . repaired television. So we could all look at her. My mom tried talking to her, but Grandma kept ducking her head away, like we were too many bright lights. And clicking her tongue. She kept making this sound with her tongue, as though . . . I don't know. It was the most scary part about her, that tongue click. Like . . . a reptile sound."

William's breathing is coming deep now and regular, as though he's paying attention to it. As though he's trying to keep himself alive. This fourth floor is like an appetite. I feel it, and I know he does too.

Lies

She contemplates her husband's suspicious behavior, her own erotic dreams, and the distressful imaginings of, indeed, Dr. Roland Rye.

IT IS ONE THING MORE coming loose. Richard is acting strangely. His venture capital expedition to Boston on Thursday lasted, not one day, but three and a half. She was supposed to content herself with the abstraction of his voice-mail: oblique but sunny reports on the home phone, always while she was at work. He never called at night.

Early Sunday afternoon his car pulled in the driveway. Evelyn, reading on the couch, stayed put. She heard the car door shut. Then, in the rectangle of the livingroom window—the stubble of hedgetops against fog—passed the profile of his head. She had the impression he was carrying something. But it was the jaunty vacancy of his expression, implying an easy preoccupation with the flagstone walk, that sent Evelyn's eyes immediately back to her book. He had not looked in.

She heard him fumbling with the front door, but made no effort to help, intent as she was on a particular sentence near the bottom of the page before her, though she could barely see it. Then the door banged closed, and the air around her swirled with cold and a sweet, exotic rancidity. She looked up from her book.

Richard was holding aloft, apparently with pride, two full-size grocery bags stained with—it looked like—grease.

"Brunch," he said, grinning ruggedly, steadfastly, as if, in all the world of her desires, he'd figured brunch was foremost.

She cocked her head.

"Chinese breakfast." He peered into the bags. "Here, Peking Ravioli, Rose Petal Pie, Melon Cakes, Roast Pork Bun."

"I've already eaten," she said.

"Look." He shifted the bags, pulled out a white cardboard carton. "Curry Pie, Sticky Rice with Lotus Leaf."

"I've already eaten."

He went ahead anyway, on into the kitchen, where she could hear him loading things into the microwave. Ice chips spewed like coins from the freezer into the ice bucket, a sound she hadn't heard in days. Then he was back bringing napkins and champagne glasses, setting them on the coffee table, smack in front of her. As he continued moving in and out of view, purposing his way back and forth from the kitchen with uncommunicative zest, she closed her book over her thumb and lifted her eyes to the window, through which, despite the fog, she could now see the spiny branches of the maples, where before she could not. There was something beautiful, even luminous, about the sight.

"Twigs in fog," she said softly.

"Hm?" Richard had pulled up a chair across from her. But he had poured the champagne and was right away back to talking, his hands busy over the cartons of Chinese take-out, packed assembly-line fashion around the lazy Susan. In intervals between plucking out the novel pastry shapes and poking them in sauces, he would flick a finger at her. "Go ahead, try some. The stuff is great."

She shook her head. She would not eat with him.

But she did listen.

The trip, according to Richard, had turned out well. Both Darryl and Wayne were intrigued by the idea of The Canning Plant. They hadn't exactly committed of course—

only a fool would have, based on so rough a prospectus. But what little they'd seen had impressed them. Darryl wanted more on demographics. How many subdivisions in the area? And what about zoning?—coastal properties these days could be dismally restrictive. Then they both wanted an updated appraisal. The one he'd showed them from the real estate office was four years old. And Wayne was insisting on a liquor licence up-front, which, Richard conceded, was one feature of the deal he hadn't thoroughly explored. He had his work cut out for him.

And then—oh, yeah—during that same luncheon, who should show up but another old friend from college—Gina Somebodyorother—who's become, to Richard's astonishment, a lawyer. And—would you believe it?—*she* was interested too. Evelyn thought of asking whether there were anyone left in Boston who *wasn't* interested. But, fearing the sarcasm might rupture her composure, she rather kept her silence, meeting and absorbing his enthusiasm head-on. She found within herself an unexpected reservoir of distance, which carried her through, quelling her skin, wrinkling her mouth for her at appropriate junctures, broadening her stare. All the while, bubbles continued boiling up the stem of her champagne glass. She didn't move to touch it.

Her husband talked on. From what she could gather, over the past three days he'd been to quite a few restaurants, looking over the layouts, picking up ideas. Richard—having a grand time and making it sound like business. You had to give the man his due: he had a talent for presentation.

He flared his palm over the lazy Susan. "I can't believe you're passing this up. I tell you, Shanghai makes the best Dim Sum east of San Fransisco."

By now her smile came readily, without effort. Legs tucked under her on the couch, the interrupted book resting in her lap, she was finding her mood transformed. She was enjoying herself.

"Honestly I'm not hungry. Maybe later."

That was Sunday. And now, Wednesday evening, Richard is in a fever. He's going to have to return to Boston. And there are so many things he needs to pull together to hold onto Darryl and Wayne. Not to mention this Gina, whatever her interest is.

But there is something more. In the midst of—even in spite of—his frenzy since returning, Richard has been undergoing little spasms of cheerfulness. The feeble puns, absentminded chuckles catch her off guard. The news, the weather, even the laundry gives rise to them. Honestly, she doesn't like the feel of all this. And now, into the bargain, he has taken up whistling—classical melodies, of forbiddingly complex orchestration, that strand him trailing off somewhere in mid-phrase, only to jump in again wherever the going is easy, sometimes a different musical piece altogether. It sounds to her, some of it, a little like Mozart. When in heaven's name has Richard ever listened to Mozart?

* * * * *

Roland appears increasingly edgy, in distress over something it seems he cannot communicate. So he seethes randomly. His outbursts, at least one per session now, arise and subside like waves in calm water. Today it begins this way:

"He can imagine what it is like for you. At day's end, for example, you're finished here. It has come to be, in the cant of the drudging masses, Five O'Clock. You close the door on this house of proselytization. You step out into the open air. It is a moment you look forward to. A bit like the experience of falling, hm? An event outside the domain of will. And coming a little too soon. Yes. You'd expected an interval of distance, but no, you are already entering the fuselage. That sleek and white-enameled state of mind that is for you each evening reconfirmed, like a familiar surprise, in the parking lot. Of course. The dark interior. The give and groan of the upholstery. The intimate fit of the seat. The bittersweet and complex aromas of hydrocarbons . . . *mm* . . . . All a seduction, is it not?

"The vehicle—oho!—moves like liquid. Pours through the parking-lot exit. And without a thought. Without ever actually marking a beginning, you find yourself in transmigration. Not yet home, and certainly no longer here. You experience—how shall he phrase it?—that light-headed precision of disconnectedness, of being Neither Here Nor There. As if falling, yes. As if suddenly exempt. There is nothing, nothing for you but to maneuver your automobile, your eyes at rest on an eternity of hiatus.

"The road curves and slides easily by. He can picture this! The broad perpendicularity of the river sweeping beneath you. As you progress through the obliterative drizzle of twilight, your mind a lonely traveling theater. In a little while, up ahead—uh oh—could it be construction? Traffic slows. The glow from the dash is steadily green. Your feet engage and disengage the pedals. Behind the construction barricades, you notice only machines. John Deere and his Caterpillars . . . *mm* . . . at rest. The men have gone home. In the gathering darkness, all that lies beyond the roadway seems perfectly still, and perhaps, in some nagging way, imperfectly understood. The car stops and waits, then rolls again. It does not stall or lurch or wander out of lane. There is no hesitation, no wasted movement. All is as it should be. The car seems to decide for you, to operate without you, and you without yourself, everything pulled along rather by requirement of things external. Highways of cleanliness. And quietude. Tire treads rubbing over asphalt like legions of Eberhards. Even now. Erasing all memory that anything has ever been. Could ever be. Otherwise."

Roland rises in his chair, electric. "Lies! See him bring his fist down into the palm of his hand! Watch his meek blood rage! The vessels bulging in his neck! Lies! You ask what upsets him? These false, false promises, leading to dyspassion and . . . *mm* . . . dysfortunate episode."

And just as suddenly, Roland is subdued, a note of sadness in his voice. "Suppose *he* were to drive . . . *mm* . . . Suppose *his* were the hands steadfastly gripping the wheel. Do you know what would happen? He has seen it. More than once. The painted lines themselves are erased. The pavement crumbles, turns to muck. Straight ahead, a black arrow points insanely into the woods. Of course, the automobile veers, who can blame it? With him at the controls."

Roland shakes his head. "No. For him, the driver's seat suggests far too many possibilities. He would feel the burden of choosing—he can feel it even now!—pressing him into the floorboards. He would, for the sake of terminating the experience, maneuver the gleaming machine straight into the first utility pole at hand. And that . . . *mm* . . . would be the end of it. Except, of course, that it never ends. Because then they would come, like white blood cells, descending on him with emergency vehicles. And nothing . . . *mm* . . . nothing would be clearer than that they had come to clean up his mess. Again. They would, amid flashes of red, amber, and blue, extract him from the wreckage and transport him over a bleary landscape of primal embarrassment for which he would decline to fully awaken. And later. Much later. As though the page had opened on a new chapter. He would find himself here. Where mercifully nothing is new."

His eyes have closed.

"Roland?" she says.

His eyes shut even tighter.

* * * * *

It seems she is at her desk, working at her computer when someone moves up behind her. For a moment she is frightened by the near feel and shadow, but then she recognizes the face as William's. And they are William's hands, also, which she can see-feel, in some combined way, until they are like her own hands navigating her surfaces down there underneath her clothes. Her understanding of this is like some new identity she has slipped into, but one rightly originating from the very beginning. Those hands that are her hands take her own hands in them, which is a wonderful sensation, a kind of dance they have entered, whirling very slowly, a dance approximating some new shape of the world. And they can see the world spinning away beneath them there, the towns and rivers and highways, and the sloping flanks of mountains, over which they veer like a pair of great, wingspread birds, the sun on their backs igniting the pleasure in their limbs, until they are the two of them nearly overcome with the blinding, annihilating thrill of it.

Afterward in the dark, while the wind moans around the eaves, she lies awake next to Richard, taut with erotic longings, not a single one of which concerns him.

~S~

THE FOURTH FLOOR survives as a museum of echoes. They funnel out of the past, from those erratic forms locked in the stink and the barking and whimpering. Did any one of those crushed souls ever imagine a future for this space? A future like now. This prolonged grey dusk of vacancy, of purgatorial quarantine, this future that William and I and the other patients break into now and then, irreverently, like schoolchildren.

    William and I, we're still up here, but the walls seem paler now, not as hungry. I think we're moving toward something, the two of us. I'm in a thin nightgown, which doesn't even belong to me. At any moment it could be removed.

    "What do you think, William?" I say.

    He doesn't answer right away. Moonlight is leaking across the floor like rectangles of slow tide, illuminating dust, particle by particle.

    "I'm a virgin," he says.

    "I know," I tell him. And it's true. "William," I tell him, "you're one of the best men I've ever met." And that's true, too.

    He nods, though I don't think it means he agrees with me. I think it means something else. What's coming next is between him and me. It's coming very slowly. But there's no getting around it.

"Do you ever wonder," he says, "how you do things?" He's looking away as if, in some far distance, he's found something to squint at. Maybe he's stalling, but I don't mind. This isn't a thing he's going to rush into.

He says, "Like, you know, getting up in the morning. What little . . . particle might tip the scale, see, in favor of staying in bed? What decides? I've tried it, lying there. I've watched, wondering when it comes, that . . . spark of decision. I can think consciously, 'Well, now I'll get up.' But that's not it. I'm still lying there. I haven't moved. But then somehow something happens, and I realize I've started to get up, and I don't know how. I don't know how. It's as much a mystery to me as it would be to anyone watching."

I don't say anything. I don't think there's anything to say.

He takes an annihilating drag on his fresh cigarette, exhales into moonlight, glances over at me. He says, "Are you sure about this?"

"I've never been surer about anything in my life."

It's the first time I've seen him smile. His smoke twists and tangles in the air by the window. The two of us are standing as if we're observing it.

"Get rid of that thing," I say.

He nods, extinguishes what's left of the cigarette, and flicks it into the hole in the wall. His arms, at his sides, look as if there is nothing left for them to do. I reach up and straighten his collar. Love begins with kindness, I tell him. His eyes seem to peer deep into this thought.

My hands move on, slow, inquisitive, appreciating his shapes. He stands perfectly still, taller than he looks coiled under those loose-fitting clothes. But there isn't a place on him I can't reach. My fingers veer for the buttons on his shirt. They undo one. Then another.

He doesn't budge. It's plain. There isn't a dishonest muscle in his body. What more could I ask for in a lover? I'm peeling him open, little by little. By the time I'm done, I've made a snow-melt of his clothes on the floor. Then I'm all over him. He fits so nicely. I'm laughing. There's so little gravity. We could fly right out of this place.

It's then I begin to feel the man, finding me, unwinding against me. We're down rolling in the dust along the floor, a slow-motion hurricane of dirt and love in the moonlight. I keep biting into him. I believe I could swallow him, make a full meal of him, tuck him away down inside me, carry him around. He's the other half of the world, this William. The half I'd forgotten about.

Our blood is electric. Obliterating. In the burn and glow of our love, the floor evaporates. Direction dissolves. We are floating here at the center, inside one skin. We go together, and the brilliance of it is like a window through time. We see things. The images flash and hold, like prolonged lightning:

A horizon of unquiet weather, glimpsed one morning from low along the bank of a dark river (something gliding beneath its surface).

More. A broad plain, where light beats down and ancestral grasses wait out epochs under a vaulting sky. All around range crowded mountains of fire and anthracite and snow. The grasses are tall enough to conceal whatever lives there.

In a clearing is a small white house, its windows open, its single table set. A red roof. It is afternoon.

Draperies that have long hung motionless now undulate in the sun.

Teacups vibrate on saucers.

The sky, for all its energy, is cloudless.

Time hasn't touched this place. For as long as anyone can remember, it has not been night here.

William and I stand along the edge of a path, looking into the mysterious distance. We don't question why we're here. Our eyes close, ready for explosions of light.

These things come, not from us, but from the memory of the world.

Six forty-five in the morning, Nurse Boil pokes her head in my room, and I hear her take a breath. She sees my nightgown, my skin, my hair, all smudged with the grime of the fourth floor. I haven't even tried to wipe it off.

"What in the name of God?" she says.

With stiff-armed roughness, she huffs and yanks until the nightgown's off, over my head.

Then she looks at me close. "So where've you been, Dearie, out riding a broomstick?" I can hear the anger in her breathing. "Doctor'll want to hear about this. Just you wait."

Opening

The fate of Dr. Sun is revealed, and Evelyn is visited by a long-awaited apparition.

D URING THE NIGHT the fog has lifted. And now at the crack of dawn Richard is leaving again. For Boston.

Last evening already he had his bags packed, and this morning he sweeps about the den, gathering and shuffling the contents of his briefcase. She watches him, fingertips to his brow, keep a running mumbled dialogue with himself.

" . . . and then . . . let's see . . . Statement of Intent to File . . . with this . . . no, no, wait . . . let's hold Zoning. That should come later . . . right, later." Switching, rearranging packets of documents, like cards in a bridge hand, he is a blur of last-minute thinking and hard-to-pin-down eyes. It is as if, slipping a step behind himself, he has become stuck in a continual dawn of quandary.

This hectic display, she understands, is intended for her. Otherwise, why would he bother with it? It is, in Richard's own way, a method of dialogue — maybe the most solid he has to offer.

This could explain why she does not withdraw but instead holds her ground at the kitchen door, watching him. It is, after all, her husband disappearing, the outline of him coming apart, turning to tatters like the edges of an old and well-used paper doll.

He glances over the table surfaces of the den. "O.K." He says this three times, with the rhythm and finality of a clock striking the hour. "O.K. . . . O.K." Then he's gathering his bags, looming up, pecking her on the cheek. "Give you a call," he says just above a whisper, "soon as I know what's up."

She says nothing. She doesn't even nod. Why should she? As it is, he's practically out the door. Behind her on the kitchen counter the coffeemaker gurgles and sputters. The door brushes the carpet and clicks closed. The coffemaker expires with a hiss. And then there is a terrific calm in which she is still taking in the space where, seconds ago, he was. Her eyes are wide. Her thinking is like an immersion.

* * * * *

All morning there is a commotion of ravens outside the plywood covering her window. Then, around eleven o'clock, she is staring at her computer screen, finishing up patient evaluations, when she hears the rumble of a truck engine, maybe two. There are voices, the clank of metal, and the sporadic squawk and rasp of two-way radio. It occurs to her, perhaps she's about to get her window back.

Some heavy machinery, like that of a crane, whines and strains, stopping and starting, and there are more voices, more radio. This goes on for awhile. She's had trouble enough this morning concentrating, without expecting any minute the intrusion of steel claws to pry away that slab of wood, letting in a flood of natural light.

But the plywood stays where it is. The light doesn't come. And now in the corridor there are sporadic, breathless words. A door closes. Footsteps head off somewhere. Evelyn, tired of the distraction, gets up and shuts her own door. After awhile, she hears a truck engine rumble away, then a second. But the annoying two-way radio hangs on intermittently.

She is just about to head down for lunch when there is a knock on her door. She opens it to see Walter Rafferty—taller, it seems, than ever, and now with some new look in his eyes. Immediately she has an urge to see beyond him, for she knows that something has changed.

He says, "Have you heard?"

"About what?"

"Paul. They just found him, right outside here." He adds, "Up in a tree."

"What do you mean?"

"Paul Sun. He's dead."

Her lips form in the shape of a question, but not knowing even which question to ask, she just shakes her head.

Walter says, "They don't know what happened. A couple of fire trucks were here. They took his body down out of one of those pines out front. Way the hell up in the top branches."

"Dead? I don't understand. How did he get up in a tree?"

"Who knows? It looked like he'd been up there for several days. I guess it would have been hard to spot him, if anybody'd even thought to look. This morning the ravens were making a ruckus. Billy Patterson went over to the tree, just out of curiosity, looked up and caught a glimpse of Paul's white lab coat. He called the police. They've got the whole area down there cordoned off. Forensics people crawling around the grass on their hands and knees."

"I just . . . can't believe this. They don't know what he died of? They don't have any idea what happened?"

Walter shakes his head. "The entire squad down there, firemen and all, looked as if they'd pretty well had the wind knocked out of them."

Yes. She can imagine that feeling, for it so nearly describes her own. Indeed, there seems at the moment to be too much feeling, too much suddenness, too much dissonance for her thinking to know where to begin.

On her way to the cafeteria, she detours out to the granite steps of the east entrance, from which she can view the pine, one among the ancient stand surrounding the hospital. The grass around the base of the tree has been fenced-in by a rectangle of yellow tape. Just outside the tape, Detective Matthews stands talking with a uniformed trooper. On the lawn near them, a police photographer moves, as if in a slow dance, snapping pictures. When the trooper takes a step back, craning his neck to peer up into the boughs of the pine, Detective Matthews' gaze sweeps across the lawn and locks on her. She offers him a little wave from the wrist, and he nods.

* * * * *

"I could talk about Richard," she says. "He's my husband." She is pacing, back and forth across the area of open carpet, as if to get rid of something, as if to distance herself.

Sophie follows with her eyes.

"I've been married to Richard for—what?—twelve years?" She speaks slowly, tentatively, testing the way. "It seems incredible, but I don't think I've ever talked about him to anyone. I don't know why."

Finding herself at the chair in front of Sophie, she sits down.

"What has it felt like, living with Richard? Well . . . let's see. Like a large, vacant house." She laughs. "I'm not even sure what I mean by that. Not our actual house, of course, but as if our life itself has been a sort of house, in which there have been . . . a certain number of rooms. It happens in stages. When you move into a place, the first thing you do is explore the rooms. They become familiar, then comfortable. After awhile they don't seem to be rooms anymore. At some point, without knowing why, you realize you've become like fluid, taking the shape of the thing you're in."

She shakes her head. "It isn't clear. It isn't clear to me at all. When I first met Richard . . . ."

She takes a breath.

"You see, there's something I need to tell you. About myself. Something important."

But then Esther Boyle appears at the door.

* * * * *

She can see the house in the dark, the livingroom and kitchen lights on, and for a moment it looks as if Richard is home. But she remembers then, the lights are automatic. And there is no car. It occurs to her that she may never see Richard's car again—as though it isn't Richard she misses, but his car, filling the emptiness of the driveway.

She turns in, and, as the headlights sweep the lawn, they reveal the bulk of something sinking away into the alders. Maybe an animal—but large. She brakes the car to an abrupt stop, leaves the engine running, her eyes straining into the dark at the border of the lawn. But the window's reflection of the dash light interferes with her vision.

So she is sitting inside this steel bubble, this envelope of darkness, itself inside a wilder darkness. It is as if, distracted, she has driven herself into some foreign and unreliable form of night. Out there, beyond the window, could be anything. She pulls the flashlight from the glove compartment, clicks it on to try it. With the engine running, she opens the car door, cuts the headlights, and, standing, plays the beam over the yard and adjacent field, the spooky light confirming lawn . . . weeds . . . alders. But what is it—there again!—she hears? Over the engine, it's difficult to tell.

Still with one foot on the floormat, she decides, reaches in, switches off the ignition. The noise of the engine caves in on itself, until there is left something like the sound that darkness makes. She listens, drawn into this, gradually recognizing overhead a passenger jet, traffic out on the highway, a distant owl. Her eyes adjust. Great wings of shadow, thrown by the rising moon behind her, reach away into the bath of chalky light. The puddle of her flashlight beam seeps over the lawn, accenting disconnected colors and shapes. Everything, everything appears suspect. She can not quite get ahold of herself, and she understands why. She knows that someone is watching.

The owl hoos, stops, hoos again.

Her life is so accustomed to lighted rooms. Beyond the car, for instance, is this house, which feels already (though she has only just moved in) more the house of her past than of her future. And, were she to return, following taillights along the highway, she would come eventually to the hospital, its windows luminescing on the hill, its corridors vacant now, like tunnels to something that has already taken place. But here, as Roland put it, she has fallen in between. She has lost all assurances with this chance of running into something here in the dark. She can feel it, the knife-edge of opportunity.

And again!—the snap of brush, the swish of grasses— the returning thread of this presence she has imagined in the alders. Eyes studying her. What does she look like, standing here?

She doesn't know what else to do. She removes the key from the ignition, shuts the car door, and walks herself to the side porch, not hurriedly, but once, twice glancing back to those alders and around the yard, as if deliberate, as if used to this. As if reason were in charge.

At the porch door, her back to the dark, she can see into the lighted kitchen through the glass. Her fingers recognize the key she wants. They fit it to the lock, and, as the door opens, it occurs to her that of course no one has been watching. The figure in the alders?—the play of shadow from moving light. The sound in the weeds?—a porcupine. She has taken to fabricating intimacies: in the void left by Richard, someone must be noticing her.

But no sooner has she shut the kitchen door and flicked on the porch light than she begins to doubt. It is perhaps that the silence here inside the house is purer, somehow louder than outside. There *is* someone. And for awhile, frozen, she simply listens. Yes, she is certain. There is someone.

She thinks even of calling Walter Rafferty, but realizes it would be pointless. He'd try to reassure her. She'd feel like a fool. And after goodbye, hanging up the phone, she'd be no better off than she is now.

She does move, however, closer to the telephone, into the corner among the cabinets, as far from the kitchen's three doors as she can be. On the counter her hand finds a wine bottle, picks it up, assessing its mass. She remembers a piece of advice from Richard, which seemed ridiculous at the time. "Hey," he said, in all seriousness, "if ever you're home and you need a weapon, boil a pot of water." So her life has come to this moment: she is backed into a corner of her own kitchen, contemplating weapons.

She reaches for a saucepan, turning back, and there, through the window, someone is staring at her. The eyes are first, under the porch light, then a brown solidity, draping limbs: the spirit of autumn in human form is what it looks like. Standing there, taking her in. It is—she knows immediately—someone she's never seen before. A woman.

Evelyn, on the instant, would not be able to name her feelings—fear, anger, relief? It is all she can do to set the saucepan down.

The woman, moving closer, appears young, in her twenties. She makes some gesture with her hand—that Evelyn, it seems, should come outside.

She moves to the door and half-opens it, but doesn't step out. "Can I help you?" As a thing to say, it seems too formal, almost mocking. She realizes, too, she is still holding the wine bottle—as if this is something she may need to explain.

"Is your husband home?"

It's not at all what she expected, that the figure in the alders—this woman—would be here for Richard. She shakes her head. "What do you want?"

"I need to know whether you're alone."

Evelyn peers at her. "Yes, I'm alone."

The woman relaxes at the knees, lets go a breath. "Could I talk to you for a minute?"

"Who are you?"

She doesn't answer right away, but glances off into the night, past Evelyn's car. Toward the road. Then turns, studying Evelyn.

"I'm a friend of Sophie Davenport's."

The words are sounds. Meaning comes in little bursts on the imagination. Sophie Davenport has a friend. In the dark. Out here in the woods.

She pulls the door open, wide. "Come in." And wider still.

The woman enters quickly, then inside seems immediately to slow down. In the thick light of the kitchen, her eyes are everywhere, circumspect, taking in the Waring, the Krups Caffé Bistro. As if she were shopping. She moves around, hands in the pockets of her oversize coat. She doesn't touch anything.

"I'm June," she says.

On the road outside, a vehicle passes: a neighbor's. Though she has no clear picture of it, Evelyn knows the rough-tread drone of its tires, the throaty growl of its exhaust. The sound twists June's attention vaguely in the direction of the door until it fades.

"Would you like something to drink? A glass of wine?" She has a hand on the door, which still is open. She nudges it closed.

"Sure. Thanks."

June's eyes go back to the counter, to the ceramic tiles of the floor. There is, Evelyn thinks, something extravagant, a little overrich about her clothing: the baggy russet sweater and corduroy pants under the tawny shell parka. The long scarf, wrapped once about the neck. Clothes to wear to a poetry reading: but worn, vaguely soiled.

"How is it you know Sophie?"

"Oh . . ." Right away she smiles, her hand grabbing for her hair at the back of her neck. "We're old friends, Sophie and me." She pulls the long, dirty-blonde hair outside her parka, tosses her head to shake it loose. "From high school."

Her determined eyes fix on Evelyn, who is pouring wine.

"I want to see her."

~S~

From this window, where the fly is beating itself senseless in the effort to reclaim its life, I have what some would call a view. A large rectangle of assumed distance. Often, I remain pressed against this.

In the window, daylight flares at dawn and dims at dusk, again and again, like an endless chain of gradual explosions. Speed it up and I can hear them.

Fffoom.

Fffoom.

Fffoom.

The view is deceptive. It doesn't tell the truth. It begins on the other side of the parking lot, among the pines, who've stood for more than a century witnessing the progress of this place. The pines say nothing about that. But along the driveway they stand apart enough to allow me to see into the valley, down to the river and across to the plum-colored hills beyond. The hills, too, remain inscrutable. As if the weight of the horizon has given them patience.

Day after day, I drill my stare into this view, this accidental slice of what is left, until it blurs over. Which doesn't take long. At some point dusk presses over the valley like a visible form of oblivion. The glass reflects more than it reveals. The outer world slips into dark. My eyes return to the lounge and, soon, to the intensity that is the wish not to move.

Until I feel the dull grip of the nurse upon my arm.

I know them by the pressure of their thumbs. This time it's Ethel, the kind-hearted one. She pulls me along, steers me to my cell. My attitude—stubborn, compliant—is supposed to make no sense. But it's begun to seem perfectly natural.

"Here, you have your room," she says. "And your bed." While undressing me, making me lie down, she lectures me. "It's seven o'clock. You can't be standing like a statue in the lounge all night." It is herself she is talking to, not me. I hear her pause at the door before pulling it closed.

I hold my breath.

"Good night," she says. The door clicks like punctuation.

Androscoggin replaces a dream.

She says, *This place is worse than a death house.*

"How do you mean?"

We have counted eight beautiful souls, much like yours, entombed on the Fourth Level.

I ask, "How can you entomb a soul?"

You don't want to know this.

Maybe not. I open my eyes to the ceiling. "Is there a way out?"

It takes a minute before she answers. *We are looking. But so much is hidden behind the lights. Didn't you escape from here before?*

"Seven years ago," I say. "But then he wasn't watching so closely." I turn my head to the door, whose tiny window onto the corridor glares like a rectangular sun. I could almost imagine having seen a face.

Some time later, I think I hear something.

June. Is that you?

I listen, but all I hear is traffic out on the highway, traffic down on Hamburger Avenue, traffic over the bridge. It's then I notice dawn bleeding through the curtains.

Wild Thoughts

Evelyn becomes acquainted with the history of the Wild Children.

THE WOMAN, June, speaks between bites from her fork, between sips of wine from her goblet. She keeps her husky voice down, as though she's afraid someone might overhear.

"I knew her from Gloucester, that was what?—ten, eleven years ago? We were close. All through high school. We studied together. Cut classes together. Got suspended together." She laughs. "We were inseparable. Till I moved away. David, the guy I was with . . . . well, let's just say he ran into some trouble. He took off for Canada, and I went with him. I couldn't even write her, David was so paranoid. And that was that. I lost track of her. One thing and another. Not that I didn't think about her. But there I was, with a whole new life. . . . I suppose it just swallowed me up. Two kids, one right after the other. We started the farm. Organic. Potatoes, blueberries. Maple syrup in the spring. We're . . . surviving. David works hard. We both do."

Evelyn, across from her, eats too. But mostly she listens.

June says, "This is good. What is this?"

"Stuffed chicken breast. It comes frozen."

June shakes her head. "If David knew I was eating this, microwaved frozen dinner, he'd flip. It's great, though, I love it."

She pauses, looking at Evelyn, as if requiring this moment of stillness. She says, "A couple of weeks ago I saw her picture in the paper. Front page. Even before I read the name, I knew it was her. It was weird, like all of a sudden running into a piece of my old self. And trying to assassinate the governor! I couldn't believe it. I thought *I* was an outlaw.

"I had to see her. I drove down here, what was it? — Friday. Tried first at the hospital, there at the front desk. They took one look, and they were all over me with questions. What was my relationship to the patient? What did I want to talk to her about? I didn't like the feel of it."

June is pushing bread around with her fork, mopping up every last stain on her plate.

Evelyn says, "So you've come here."

"I found out the names of the doctors in Admissions, saw one was a woman. I thought, what the heck, I'd give you a try."

Evelyn, in a rush of warmth, almost grabs her hand. But she says, "I'm glad you did."

"I came by a couple of times before, but your husband was here. It seemed to complicate things."

The woman takes Evelyn's breath away. So all-at-once and in reach, the connection to Sophie. The unexpected voice.

"Would you like some more? There's plenty in the freezer. It takes just a minute."

"Oh no. No thanks, this was great." June pushes herself a little away from the table.

Evelyn reaches for the bottle of Pinot blanc, angles it over June's nearly empty glass, watches the twist and tremble of the wine pouring.

"Thanks," June says. She directs her eyes on a slow inventory of the room.

Evelyn, in the chair normally reserved for Richard, watches. She can't think how to proceed. She has lost the certainty of what it is to be Evelyn. She could be waiting to see if something else slips into its place. Or she could simply be waiting. Outside, the night is an open sea, while here, inside, there is only the edge of the next moment.

Then, again, June's voice.

"The first time I saw her, this was high school, these three other girls had her up against a cafeteria wall, one about to smack her with a food tray. I stepped in and broke it up. Sophie, she could have had straight A's. But she was always in trouble. I mean, a lot of us at times have wild thoughts, but with her, they didn't stop at thoughts. Like the day in class she called the pope a gangster. I said, Jesus, Sophie, you've got to watch what you say. She was driving people crazy.

"It was no place for her, high school—no place for me either, for that matter. Sit in rows. Tuck your shirt in. Do this. Don't do that. After school we'd go off and study by ourselves. Far-out topics. Sufism. Gaia. That kind of thing. We got to be little experts in subjects our teachers hadn't even heard about. Which is a powerful feeling for a fifteen-year-old."

June sips her wine, flinging her gaze after some remembrance. Then she is up, walking the kitchen floor, with no apparent aim but to move.

"Music," she says. "We'd take records out of the library, weird stuff. Balinese folk songs, Chinese opera—I mean some of it was pretty awful, really. But we'd sit on the floor—usually my room, to avoid her mother—we'd load the air with incense and sit soaking ourselves in these . . . strange vibrations." She laughs. "Sophie thought, if you could enter into something that different, that disturbing, then you'd come out of it somehow larger. You could carry the knowledge of these sounds around inside you, like a kind of inner strength."

Evelyn asks, "What was her mother like?"

June takes a breath. "I don't know, she and Sophie were always at odds. I guess Sophie was an embarrassment to her. Not to mention the other way around. The woman was forever holding a cup or a glass of something. About noon she'd switch from coffee to vodka. Not that I ever saw her blitzed. But Sophie and I swore we'd never touch alcohol."

June lifts her wine glass. "So much for youthful ideals. I don't know, I don't like to be too critical. I guess we made a lot of people uncomfortable. Sophie was on a *mission*, I think, to make people uncomfortable. She thought it was her duty, to wake them up."

At the ice machine on the fridge, June pauses, her hand coming out of her pants pocket to touch the control lever. But then she glances over her shoulder, toward the porch door. "Is it alright if I open that?"

Evelyn nods. "Go ahead." Sitting here in Richard's place, she likes the idea of opening things up.

June turns the knob, pushes the door wide. "It's O.K.?"

Staring into the black aperture of the doorway, she nods.

June resumes pacing, diagonally across the glistening kitchen tiles. Her voice swells. "Sophie said, 'Don't take the life they give you. Make your own.' So we did. We lived in our heads, made up lives beyond our lives in homeroom, our lives in gym class. Faraway lives on sloping meadows, in log huts open to the wind. We slept on goatskins on the floorboards. We rode our horses up onto the high prairies, looking for forgotten ways of knowledge. We camped in snow high under the stars. We drank horribly bitter restorative teas, talked long into the night. Down below, humanity was waiting exhausted, depending on us. We were carving the world out of something entirely new. All of it—all made up. A couple of misfit kids leaving our bodies behind."

June's eyes narrow almost to a squint, as if to resolve an improbability.

"I remember, very clearly, taking a trip to some . . . oriental mountain village. I don't know what else to call it. Sleeping on platforms, some kind of droning chant in the background. Eating wild nutmeats and rice out of bowls with our fingers. There were ingredients, certain unusual spices producing . . . little tingling sparks in our mouths that were like a higher form of nourishment, lasting days after we'd eaten. The inhabitants wore robes and communicated without speaking. I remember we meditated with them, beside a pond. The lilypads were black, like holes in the reflecting moon." As she glances up at Evelyn, June's eyes are glistening. She moves to the open door, facing the night. Evelyn can barely hear her when she says, "I'm sure we never went anyplace like that. But it's what I remember. It's what I remember."

The kitchen seems too bright. Evelyn flicks the wall switch for the overhead table lamp, leaving herself in shadow except for the glow from the counter light. June's hand then reaches for the porch-light switch, and, as that bulb darkens too, it looks outside as if June has switched on the silver landscape of her memory. Evelyn's eyes travel the lawn, the alders, the evergreens, the meadow—all framed in the doorway and washed in moonlight.

Hearing June sniffle, she rises from Richard's chair and moves up behind her. She reaches across the woman's back, gives her a firm hug.

June is shaking her head. "I look back, and I know, in some ways, that was the best I'll ever be. I mean, I love my kids, I love David. We have a good life. But the way it was with Sophie . . . it was a real mistake, my leaving her like that."

Evelyn says, "Sophie seems that kind of person, to make people look into their own lives. That seems to be her gift."

The two of them stand together facing the night outside, which, under the platinum light of the moon, looks like something other than night. She can hear the rhythm of June's breathing.

June stirs. "How can I see her?"

She doesn't answer right away. "I don't know," she says finally. But she has the beginning of an idea. "Where have you been staying?"

"Saturday night I got a motel room. Since then mostly I've been sleeping in the car."

"Tonight you can stay here."

June shrugs. "Gee. You sure? Your husband won't mind?"

"No." The question brings a smile. "He won't mind."

* * * * *

All the talk this morning simmers around Paul Sun's death. The sheer horror of it seems to have galvanized the social instincts of the staff, drawing them to gather in offices and corridors, as though, if mixed together, the ingredients of their separate opinions might actually amount to something.

The autopsy established apparent cause of death as asphyxiation. No obvious instrument was found. The various theories under discussion—a former patient, an underworld connection, traffick in prescription drugs—all run out of steam in the face of a single bare fact: that the man was found seventy feet off the ground in the top branches of a tree. What emerges finally is the sense—which, for all its vagueness, seems in the minds of the staff to have a certain explanatory power—that Paul Sun was an inscrutable man, a man with secrets who worked in a mental hospital.

And Evelyn, with already too many secrets of her own, now has another one to add to the list: Paul Sun's argument with Warren Griswold just before he disappeared. She has not yet, in her own mind, fully re-examined that scene. Rather she has been circling, approaching gradually, as if something might still be lurking there, requiring caution.

For refuge she has fled to Walter Rafferty's office, whether to discuss anything else or nothing at all, she couldn't say. Walter, fortunately, seems to have his mind on other matters. With his fingernail, he is scraping a speck from his sweater, perhaps some bit of congealed food. "This girl Sophie," he says, "what goes on between you?"

She leans at her place against his window. She's happy to talk about this. "I tell her things."

"And....?"

"She listens. So far, that's about it."

"Whose therapy is this?"

She makes a sour face at him.

He says, "No, I'm joking. But how do you know she's listening? O.K., you talk, what does she give back to you?"

"Her eyes."

"She looks at you? Really? Have you told anyone?"

She shakes her head. "That would seem to me, under the circumstances, a breach of confidence"

Walter peers at her. "She hasn't spoken?"

"No, but I think she will. I'm getting close, I know I am. But I feel as though . . . I've been working against this place."

Walter chuckles. "Welcome to the field of mental health." He glances down at his sweater. "So what do you talk about?"

"Oh . . . about me mostly, my history, the shape of my life."

She allows her eyes to play over the man.

"So what do you think?" she says. "Am I more interested in her than I ought to be?"

Walter shrugs. "What kind of a system are we a part of, if you have to ask me a question like that?"

Evelyn nods. "Thanks."

* * * * *

She arrives at the impression that it is no longer autumn, but winter. Oddly enough, when she has this thought, she is sitting at her computer with her back to the window, and the room is warm, warmer than it needs to be. Her impression isn't a matter of sensory input, but rather like a question, mulled over unconsciously for weeks, suddenly answered.

* * * * *

Near the end of the session, she decides to mention it. "I've talked with June."

Sophie's head turns, her eyes entirely unguarded.

"She wants to see you."

Sophie's laugh is immediate, like an unforeseen burst of melody. Like a photograph sprung to life.

And right away the door opens. It is Esther Boyle, without even the courtesy of a knock. She stands like a chess piece with a jutting wrist, her hand joined to the doorknob.

"What's going on here?" Esther's glare moves from her to Sophie.

"I beg your pardon?" Evelyn directs some inner fire into her own eyes, and the nurse seems to shrink. "Will you wait outside? I'm meeting with this patient."

Esther hesitates. "Dr. Griswold needs to see her. He said right away."

Evelyn holds the nurse in her gaze, fixing her there for the moment, then nods.

Esther Boyle hoists Sophie out of her sitting position, the girl slack, effortless. Her laugh is already irretrievable, dispersing now into the vapor that was their time together. But as Sophie is shepherded past her, their eyes failing to connect, Evelyn feels a hand press hers, then let go.

~S~

JUNE, I don't know what I'm seeing anymore. Outside this window, I believe snow is falling. But then I wonder, with the window separating me from the snow, what is it I'm really seeing? A censored version of snow, a picture stripped by the glass of everything but the residue of light and shadow.

Anyway, I seem to require this: standing here, shutting out the lounge, tuning in to whatever it is that filters through the pane. And somehow, as if from other sources, the knowledge comes to me—like a call in the middle of the night from you.

Snow.

But it won't go beyond that. I can hold this knowledge, turn it over in my hand, but not spend it. That's the idea here. Most of what you can think of you can't do. The world shrinks to the horizon, then shrinks again. I stare out through veils of impossibility.

The afternoon sun seeps across the floor of the lounge. That sound somewhere in the belly of the building switches on. A shift of my weight rearranges the pain in my knees. My skin itches. I occupy myself wondering whether a certain doorknob will yield if I try it. The sound switches off. These are the crumbs my brain has to gnaw on.

Outside, I suppose, it *has* to be snowing. Otherwise, June, where would it lead? Another week, and my mind would be all glassed in.

Mrs. Dibrizzi never looks out the window. It could be that she has her own. It could be that this is what's left of her mind, a solitary window on her life. From the expression on her face, I'd say the window is dirty.

* * * * *

Snow. Evening. I'd shoot right out the front door, snow closing around my mother's voice even before the door slammed, the flakes fuzzing over her silhouette at the window as I turned around and around again over the yard to Oak Place and then on, swaggering, skipping, kicking powder, arms spread in pirouettes, all the way to Ridge Road and across the golf course, drifts pulling at my legs, unbalancing me.

Mother, hating snow, would stay trapped inside, awaiting some instruction. She'd move from the window to the TV, trying to put the two together. She liked receiving messages from screens. Once, in the mousy brown light of an open winter, I heard her reminisce about the beauty of snow. I stared at her then. She pretended not to notice.

But here I was with my collar up and no time for anything other than the night air, spun thick with snow falling like granular light, tumbling, reversing, slanting on the wind into my breath, into my eyelashes. I reached the woods, threaded my way to the river. I was a fox with intentions on the ice. I was watchful. Every few steps I'd stop and listen. The tide at the edge seemed exactly still—the water black with a thirst for snowflakes, a thirst for sound. An eternity of snow ending in flat blackness.

I held my head observant in the falling swirl, until the river and the ice seemed to be ascending with me. I was watching, June, for you especially. Trying to make your shifting shape emerge from the confusion of snow. You, out roaming like some snow leopard. Like some awakened gray being. But you didn't come.

On my way back, the woods were like a wall, giving up nothing. The only way to see anything was out of the corner of my eye. I tried whirling around, surprising my own thinking, but the trees were ancient, imperturbable. I felt like some discrepancy flickering around their ankles. I was delirious with incomprehension. I wanted to take it all in, coax it all into a thought I could carry back. I was afraid of the same old conclusion: me in my room, Mother on the other side of the door. Why that door?—when what I really wanted was for her to know.

Snow kept on falling, as if it might fall forever. Everything seemed to be lying low, out of the way of my questions. From hole to sudden hole, little claws and heartbeats skittered always out of sight. The snow was recording these, and then erasing them. It was burying everything, all the wreckage and digestion—branches and bones, leaves and undergrowth—all the complexity of the forest was being covered over, simplified. Made blank.

It wasn't something that fit into a thought. But it was what I had. I turned and left. By the time I got home, Mother'd gone to bed.

Autumn 1

Recollections continue: first, the meaning of wet leaves and, later, a nice seduction.

WET LEAVES.
    In bed she props herself on one elbow, feeling in two places at once. But the dream quickly dissolves, except for that single image. She knows where it comes from. Even after so many years.
    It was, her mother said, what the state police sergeant had told her, the event thus coming so indirectly that it seemed hardly to have occurred. But after a pause of minutes or days she was left with the knowledge that it had, brought on by the intervention of wet leaves. On that night after the storm, reported the sergeant, the curve in the road had been covered with them.
    In this way, her father, like some majestic process with a logic disconnected from her own, came to an end. Her father, builder of bridges, had understood highways. He'd appreciated mechanical design. Confident, exact in his driving, he'd enjoyed pushing tire against pavement until he gauged the friction had reached its limit. But he hadn't calculated on wet leaves. It was the sort of thing to escape calculation, the sort of thing to spring up in silence and ambush one's life. And with the end of her father, Evelyn knows, came the beginning of something else, which has not ended.

She took an absence from school to stay with her mother. There, in the declivity of the house she thought she'd left, she waited for the awful finality of it to swallow her. She did not expect to have to wait so long. After the funeral, the days blurred by like fenceposts, interspersed with night. She sat with her mother, at first the two of them barely speaking, then only of little things. They communicated in questions. Wouldn't it be better tomorrow to bring chrysanthemums? Had she noticed? — the backdoor lock was sticking. Who should they get to look at it? And what did she suppose had gotten into the trash last night? — lifting that bag out neatly and setting it aside to get at the chicken bones. At times her mother would rise in a burst from her chair, walk as though with purpose from the room, and return seconds later without visible effect.

Whether this were a period of mourning, Evelyn could not have said. Living receded into a regimen of hours, during which she and her mother navigated through unwelcome possibilities by maintaining an approximate stillness. Everything seemed suspended. Keeping her mother company, she was plausibly escorting her into the terminal inertia of her being. Like railway travel at night, it was a course free of friction or horizons.

On and on it went. Evelyn felt herself more and more indefinitely entangled, spellbound by the enigma of sorrow. She decided grief was private in the case of her mother, who, except for the loss of her smile, seemed only a little tired, a little depleted. There were instances of tears, but always without words, so that Evelyn did not know what to see, what to hold before her. She wanted something sufficient. She wanted her father's presence, in order to know his absence — her father at the lake, her father in the snow, the quiet engine of his breathing, the flicker of his mirth. His plaid shirts, the smell of outdoors on him.

Outdoors. He would not wear a hat, squinted in the sun, pampered the trees in the yard while scorning lawn. He was always driving off someplace.

Memories were themselves like leaves: flecks of the very substance of life, now scattered, promiscuous, subject to decay. Whatever she was looking for wouldn't be found in memories. Her father hadn't so much died as dissolved. Evelyn herself had driven off—to college. Already in the months before his death, she'd seen so little of him that he seemed to her now hardly more dead than alive. She remembered him as if through glass.

One morning in December they packed his things into boxes. They worked together, her mother particular in the removal of each clothes hanger, the folding of each pair of pants, as if laying out vestments for solemn High Mass. Evelyn knelt on the floor with a roll of tape and a felt pen, shutting the flaps on the boxes, locking away their contents, rescuing only the slide rule in its leather sheath as a keepsake, at which her mother paused and nodded with—in that moment—something near a smile. What had been her parents' bedroom had become now her mother's bedroom, a simple fact that Evelyn felt short of comprehending. On the window behind where her mother stood, extravagant patterns of frost flickered with twig shadows thrown by a weak sun. Through an unfrosted corner pane, Evelyn saw ragged cotton-ball clouds hurrying east. By early afternoon she and her mother had erected, in one of the spare rooms, a wall of cardboard boxes, each a little casket of her father's effects sealed in with his smell.

Time became a stranger. Searching for a photograph, opening a closet door, cleaning out a desk—incidental tasks like these could expand and fill entire days. Her mother allowed her the shopping. Evelyn, avoiding the car, walked the entire distance under various and heavy December skies to the store, two miles away in a little mall on Route 7. She bought only a few items at a time, as many as she could carry back, making sometimes two trips a day. The traffic noise on the highway bore down on her and bore down on her again, and still she walked, without ever coming to know what she was doing, what her place in all of this was. Storm-force winds from tractor-trailers flattened the weeds by the road and tore at her hair and blew her thoughts beyond reach. And on the crest of a hill, one grinning driver blasted her with a horn so up-close and loud that she seemed to lose everything, her walk tottering in little circles, and then she did come near to crying, and would have, if the idea of it hadn't gotten to her first and put an end to it.

All of this was preliminary, all of it falling on the other edge of what she doesn't remember. At some point time was moving again, ratcheting her toward spring semester. It was assumed she would return to school. On that day, backing the car out of the driveway, she heard her mother intone through the rolled-down window, "Drive carefully." In fact Evelyn conveyed herself over the two-hour ride to campus in something like a trance.

There is a pause, and she isn't sure what she remembers, or whether, if she digs deeper, more will emerge. Next, perhaps, was the door clicking closed and her standing in the residual dusk of what had been her dorm room. The room seemed apart from any other space. She could have stood there forever, before making any move. Beyond the windows, the world she had just driven through, the world she had just stepped from, was brilliant with sun and snow. But where was that world? She knew she could not have found her way back there. Her vision was deteriorating, darkening from the corners. First the air had been sucked from her life, now the light. She heard the chatter of students passing on the grounds below, and it terrified her. The sound might have come from almost anywhere. She stood, numb, as if she and her body were no longer connected.

After that, or perhaps before, she is walking the streets of a city, looking for something. She is riding a train. Ever in shadow. Experience approaches her in shapes, backlit, in silhouette. She seems to have been among animals. She has heard their movement, smelled their distress—primates and snakes and dark, muscular cats—confined in some aging building behind bars and walls of glass.

Are these dreams? Memories?

* * * * *

Arriving at her office this morning, she finds her door slightly ajar, when it is supposed to be closed, locked. She shoves the door open wide and switches on the light. She moves about the office slowly, even stealthily, alert for signs that he's been here. Who else could it be? Over by her plywood window she stops. There. Unmistakable. The scent of his musk cologne. She backs up a step and simply stands, not wanting to touch anything in this office that is no longer her own.

Later from Walter Rafferty, who has heard it from Mark Zieglitz, she learns that Warren Griswold has called a meeting for tomorrow. This is the way her information comes: second- and third-hand. Assessment team members only, the meeting is supposed to be an occasion for final input. The report is due next week. Everyone agrees on the need for closure.

Everyone?

She can feel time running out. The metaphor has become tactile. Time has become like sand. Like water, leaking between fingers. But what is she to do about it? How can she enter an equation that forever insists on excluding her? Perhaps even now, meetings are taking place, opinions are being traded face-to-face—all in that shadowy realm beyond the boundaries of what her eyes can see and her ears can hear. How would she know?

But one thing she does know. Among the phantoms of that other world, Sophie's future is being decided.

* * * * *

William's condition today seems worse. Whatever is coming, he says, is close now. They've left her office and gone outside so that he can have a smoke. She tries to get him to talk about it.

"Well . . . It's not like I have details. It's more . . . you know when you dream? and it's all so . . . tangled and impossible, your thoughts can't get a hold of it? But what you do have . . . it's like . . . a memorable location, like a feeling where your dream happened. You can't talk about it, it wouldn't make any sense. But in your mind, it's crystal."

He talks anyway. But he seems overwhelmed with multiplicity.

"I think I might give up cigarettes," he says. "I think I might . . . grow a garden. I think I might . . . fly off the handle. See, what does that mean?—fly off the handle. And where does it all come from, anyway, those strings of words? It's . . . like I contain some other person. I open my mouth, and words come out. Because, see . . . if it were up to me, I don't think I'd talk at all."

"Why not?"

"Because, see, there are . . . too many . . . possibilities."

"Possibilities."

"Yeah, like . . . spores. Like little black pinpoints, like little black . . . avenues that open up into worlds we can't even imagine. See, or . . . like events. There are too many. The way it is, I can't tell the difference . . . between one event and the next. Between event A and event B. It's true, say like I'll be out here on the lawn, having a cigarette, and that door will open, and I'll see some guy come out of the building and down those steps and walk to his car. Some guy, right? I've never seen him before. And then a moment later, I'll see *exactly* the same guy do exactly the same thing. *Exactly.* And . . . I mean, sometimes I really feel like I've gone beyond the walls of physics. Like beyond even the Immaculate Conception, any of that. I can feel it on my skin. Like the winds of outer space. And the scientists, they don't know. See, they'd just laugh, the scientists. I'd have to have . . . like numbers coming out of my mouth.

You know, they're not seeing colors like this. I mean, they're not . . . ."

With his mouth open in mid sentence, William falls silent. And he stays that way. She walks him slowly over the grass and the parking lot, back toward the building. In the distance, she can see the yellow cordoned area around Paul Sun's pine tree. William finishes his cigarette, shivering. He has refused to button his jacket, and the air is a biting cold, but the shivering seems to come from within.

* * * * *

The building feels crowded, hectic. All afternoon she is tied up with meetings. In between, in the corridors, she can hardly turn around without bumping into a policeman. And now in the stairwell, she passes the carpenters wrestling a large slab-shaped cardboard box over the railing. "No, let it rest on the edge," the older one barks. "On the edge." She glances their way, but, immersed in their own bickering, they ignore her.

Opening her office door, she sees first a flood of brightness, then the new window. And immediately something else. Outside those double sheets of glass, snow is falling. Large slow flakes. For a moment she stands immobilized, as if by a memory she doesn't want to startle.

* * * * *

"Before Richard, actually, there weren't very many. My first was a lacrosse player, freshman year, I forget his name. He had a sweet smile, but no more idea how to please a woman than how to solve a differential equation. We lasted . . . I can't remember . . . a couple of weeks? maybe a month?

"Then, let's see . . . James was an architecture major and, I guess, not much of a lover either, though for awhile I was slightly crazy about him. James had a habit, whenever he talked, of beginning with his eyes closed, then opening them to look at you. As if his words were coming from somewhere maybe a little outside the world. Like a lot of what he did. I don't think he ever once combed his hair.

"And then, oh . . . though maybe this doesn't count. In fact, I don't know if I can tell you this."

But looking up into Sophie's eyes, she sees that she certainly can.

"It was maybe a year after James. I was practically celibate, and very lonely. So, you see, I have an excuse. Anyway, I was in my dorm room on a Saturday morning. Most everyone else had gone for the weekend The dorm was just about empty. And all of a sudden there was . . . some guy at my door. A kind of a lazy look to him, frizzy hair and torn jeans. I'd never seen him before. He mentioned a name, someone he was looking for. Someone I hadn't heard of. Did I know where he could find this person? His eyes ran off down the hall and then back to me. And something shot from those eyes, and I knew right away what he was after. I told him . . . I told him he probably had the wrong dorm. That was what I said. But it wasn't what I meant, and he knew it. I turned and went to my window. Try Seneca Hall, I said, pointing across campus. We get a lot of people here, looking for someone in Seneca. I think I even laughed then at what I was saying. Because it sounded so stupid. I kept facing out the window, until I turned and our eyes connected. And the next thing, he was inside my room, closing the door. I thought, how easily these messages pass without words. And then I didn't look at him anymore. I wanted it that way, not to be responsible. It sounds awful, I know, but I wanted something done to me, something I had no choice in. Of course it was dangerous. I remember looking out across those empty lawns, thinking, maybe this is it. Maybe this is the mistake I shouldn't have made. Then I caught the smell of him. He was right behind me. I felt his hand travel down my neck, and still I didn't move. And as his fingers worked down the front of my blouse, flicking the buttons open one by one, and I took in each new breath, I felt myself opening, like a flower that had been waiting for this. And it was my holding still that made it this way. I felt my skirt loosening, falling to the floor. And then I had one more stupid thing to say. I said, 'Please, be nice.' He laughed then and said, 'Not too nice.'

"After that morning I never saw him again. I was lucky. He could have been anybody, some psychotic. But he wasn't. He was just someone who happened to fit nicely into that moment. Just some easy and experienced guy who took over. I didn't have to do anything or say anything.

"I suppose I could say the same about Richard. Except that this guy, who I knew absolutely nothing about, dropped in on me for one living instant and then vanished. I wonder what my memory of Richard would be if, after rescuing me from my depression, he'd just disappeared? Just smiled and driven off. Actually, he seems to be disappearing now. But I can't say I'm sorry to see him go. I do feel a lot of sadness, but I think it has to do with something else. I think it's like the sadness of leaving a house you've lived in, even if your life in that house wasn't so wonderful."

She finds her vision is blurring.

"Things go by, even foolish things. All somehow made precious by the fact that life moves always one way, never the other way."

Evelyn, sitting, looks up to where Sophie is leaning now against the wall, hands behind her back, watching her.

Somewhere down the corridor a door slams.

"I don't know," Sophie says. "Life moves in more ways than I can keep track of."

Evelyn's eyes veer a little away from her and then back again. The two of them, she can see, are still enclosed within this room. But nothing is the same. It is as if a fresh light is pouring into the world.

~S~

EVELYN MOORE sits me down and tells me of her lovers. Tarantula can't hear us. He's away in committee. On the defensive now. Evelyn Moore tells me of her illness. She tells me of her great mistakes. Especially her husband. I think she has never told anyone else these things. She sits here in front of me, near trembling in her shades of grey, her necklace, and her boots, allowing this all to pour out. I look at her, and I think of this husband, this man whose jaw I'd like to wire shut, and I am numb over the ravenousness of the heartless.

I listen to her sentences—sentences I could never say. They are like brush strokes painting another world. All my life I've been avoiding her, it seems. And here she is. Shining like the morning through her grey cloth. What more could a woman be than what she is? Her days carry her along, like boats drifting on dead water. Mornings, she rises from bed, leaving behind this Richard. She hurries here. Her thinking slips into the building even ahead of her, laying a trail to follow along the corridor tile. In her office, she switches on the computer before removing her coat. She prepares, studying our documents until her reading has scrubbed the pages clean. And then? Her attention suddenly freezes. What is that she hears? Her world has been like a river. She has just climbed onto the bank and is adjusting her eyes.

She doesn't tell me these things. They fall to me through the cracks in her sentences.

All these other doctors, except for Tarantula, I believe have about had enough of me. Day after day they've been hurling themselves against my skull, trying to get a peek at what's inside. I don't think they've been enjoying it much. I suppose I haven't been a very good hostess.

And now they've brought me into the jaws of this conference room, encircling me like a tentative inquisition. I can see that my time is up. They've given me long enough, they've decided. Any longer and it will look bad. Besides, now there are complications. Ever since what happened to Dr. Sun, these others have been spurred to wondering, what sort of a world is this? Something they should have wondered long ago. None of this is expressed, but the air is thick with it.

Two of them are trying to distract me, speculating back and forth about the severity of my future, while the others watch my face, my hands, in case I show some sign of paying attention. But why should I? My presence already fills this room. I overflow my face and hands. I miss nothing. It's their moment, not mine. They're the ones at the threshold. They're prepared for inertia and deceit in me, but not for this. They sit in their usual positions, their shoe soles meeting the resistance of what they believe is the floor. Time is streaming forward, they are reassured. Here on the gameboard of this carpet, within the illusion of these walls, they find themselves gathered with a particular momentum.

And now . . . just a minute . . . . What *was* that subtle sensation each of them felt? Just then. Like a puff of air inside the bones. No more than that. What was it? A moment ago it seemed they had clarity. But now it's as if they've forgotten something. As if the five of them have awakened in the middle of five distinct train rides. They can't recall exactly what is beyond the door, or what, really, is their connection with these other people. A simple pause in their talk yawns into a silence so profound that their eyes let go of me.

Like startled herd animals, they hold still, heads raised. They stop clicking their pens. Instincts stir them to shifts in their postures, but it doesn't do any good. Not one of them utters a word, but each of them knows: something new has infiltrated this space, something unwanted, something none of them has counted on.

The one on my left rises, goes to the door, and pauses. He opens it, pushes his head out into the corridor as if to inhale the familiarity of what is there. He remains that way a long time. Minutes. But finally he straightens, eases the door shut, turns his head to the others, and says something.

The sounds that come from his mouth are not human sounds. If reptiles wearing clothes were to gather around tables and address one another, I believe they would produce consonants and vowels like these. But the others, seated as if on the edge of annihilation, don't seem to notice.

All of them over the years, including the one at the door, have given too much of themselves away. They are not together. They are separate atoms of dread and discontent, organized to look like a team. And now the fear of nothing in particular is beginning to seep in, dissolving their sympathies for one another, prying them apart, opening rifts between them. They are pretty much interchangeable, these people, but this fact is hidden from them. Each one of them alone feels he's been found out. It is abrupt and terrifying, this free-fall of thinking they're used to observing in others.

They are nothing to worry about now: five little verdicts of isolation, five reprimands, five banishments. They feel their substances sucked away, as if the air in the room has turned inside out. They no longer resort to straightening their ties, tugging on their belt loops, examining their shirt cuffs, all of which they realize are pointlessly intact. They have, in fact, all but forgotten me.

Now Androscoggin appears, hovering over the dreary congregation of them. And for a moment there is a pulse of brightening throughout her loveliness—what a smile might look like on someone without a face.

Fresh Light

The Wild Child doesn't waste words, Evelyn hears an actual voice, and winter finally arrives.

W HEN SHE AWAKENS, her eyes open immediately. Something has changed.

Arising, wrapping herself in greencotton, she hesitates, then parts the bedroom curtain, and all at once sees nothing. Or rather, her vision collides with an abrupt and stony whiteness, which for the instant transfixes her. Then her eyes adjust, and she brings her hand out of the pocket of her robe to scrape at the tangle of frost on the windowpane. Tiny clots of ice melt beneath her fingernails as she enlarges a ragged opening, through which she peers.

Outside, last evening's snowstorm has buried the world. The morning air is glass. In the dim light of dawn she has the impression of viewing a magnificent brightness under darkened circumstances. Everything familiar lies muffled away. The front field, yesterday the texture of meadow, is now the rumpled white of hospital bedding. On the hummocks, spikes of grasses stick out like hairs. The hemlock and spruce at the field's edge have drawn inward, heavy-limbed, haggard with snow. And, close by the house, the dimples of her own filled-in footprints trail between the car and the porch, so that even she herself feels covered over.

* * * * *

First thing in the morning, Detective Matthews stops by her office. Her initial impression: it is written all over his face that he wishes to question her. But he doesn't ask anything. He stands in the doorway and squints out her window as though contemplating the very pine bough that, several days ago, bore Paul Sun's decomposing corpse.

"Always a shock," he says.

Not knowing how to answer, she pivots in her chair to glance out the window into the brilliance of the reflecting landscape.

"First snow," he says. "Seems I'm never ready for it."

"It's beautiful," she says, feeling in some way awakened by this simple observation.

He chuckles. "I wish, just once, it'd give me time to get my snowtires on."

He slaps the wall playfully. "Oh, well . . . ." As if on the verge of leaving, he half-withdraws from her doorway. But his hand, wrapped around the jamb, pulls him back.

"Any headway with the Davenport girl?"

She shakes her head. "You're asking the wrong person. I wasn't assigned to her team."

"But you have been seeing her."

"They keep her here in Admissions. When I have time, yes, I have been sitting down with her."

"Any progress?"

"It's difficult to assess, this early on."

"Early?" The detective's eyebrows jump. "It's been almost a month."

"When you're working to build a patient's trust, that isn't a lot of time. But she hasn't spoken to me, if that's what you mean."

"I'll tell you why I asked." Detective Matthews' eyes seem to look at many things, but not precisely at her. "Dr. Sun was supposed to have had several sessions with Ms. Davenport. But her chart contains no notes regarding those meetings. We've looked at his dictaphone tape. It's blank."

"No notes? That doesn't seem possible."

"Well, it'd be more correct to say we didn't find any. It does seem unlikely, doesn't it? Anyway, the matter of their relationship is material at this point."

"Relationship?"

"Well, say, doctor to patient. Or patient to doctor. However you want to look at it."

"Have you checked with Dr. Griswold?"

"Yes. Yes, we have." He pauses, watching her. "Just thought we'd check with you."

"I'm afraid neither Dr. Griswold nor Dr. Sun ever discussed her case with me."

"Well. There you go, then." Detective Matthews smiles. "You're just as much in the dark as we are."

* * * * *

She can feel her worry quickening regarding Sophie's incarceration. She has contemplated, for weeks now, the effects accruing from location within these walls. As if by some geometric chemistry. It isn't the matter of locks and bars and wire mesh. It isn't the medication. No. It is the thinking, the matter of where one can be led. And in this, the doctors are as susceptible as the patients. They can be dragged down just as easily, perhaps even more so, out of unguardedness. She can herself feel the suction. The image of quicksand comes to mind.

What would be permissible in pursuit of another's freedom? Short of criminal behavior.

Then a fresh surprise, an audible thought:

The soul cannot be held motionless; it is always either ascending or descending.

Speaking close to her ear—a voice, but not a voice. The absurdity reassures her, though she likes the idea. Then she hears it again:

Suppose they were not escapes.

* * * * *

The morning seems to have hurled her out in advance of itself. Everything is taking her by surprise.

Now Roland looks directly at her. His eyes are calm, but they won't let go of her. "He passes through these phases," he says. "The phases are like rooms . . . *mm* . . . without walls. Do you have any idea what it is like?"

The question is certainly ambiguous. But she says, truthfully enough, "Not a very good idea, no."

"Listen. Imagine he is your eyes. He will tell you what he sees."

She nods.

"He is standing alone. That is the first thing, the most important thing. He is alone. It is something like a place, where he stands. But it is also like something else. You see: 'something like,' but also 'like something.' Already the tremble of hesitation. Already . . . *mm* . . . ingredients of doubt."

His eyes now are focused on nothing in the room.

She prompts, "What is it like?"

"Where he stands?" His tone is vacant. "It is endless, featureless, flat. A virtual pebbled hardpan. He feels, bearing down on everything, a certain . . . *mm* . . . inevitability, as if what has happened before is there, waiting to happen again. A great light, perhaps. How else to describe it? Though it has weight. Insisting down and in on everything. With the intensity of impending suns. But even under the press of this light, enough to weld the eyelids shut. Even in spite of this! He is aware that shadows move. Somehow slow. Unexplained. And, also, there is a sound. It is not quite the trill of insects, despite what one might expect, despite the ravaged emptiness and ... *mm* ... no sky. No. Nothing but vibration and this bright, pernicious dust. Here in the obliterative heat he waits, his feet perspiring into his shoes, his hair follicles ringing with anticipation. He feels himself positively charged with an urgency to act. And then it happens. The moment is ripped open with the force of the explosion. Events flood in. And he is supposed ... *mm* ... he is supposed to do something. It is all up to him. Everything. Everything is riding on his expeditiousness. The terms of his existence have never been clearer."

"What do you do then?"

"What?"

"What do you do, when events come flooding in?"

"Oh, he watches. Yes. There is nothing for him but to watch, rooted to the spot, while the events thunder over him, like a panoramic hysteria of wildebeests, grinding him into the dirt. This has happened, he can't tell you how many times."

* * * * *

Suppose they weren't escapes.

Well, what else then? She has seen the records: three female inmates over the years have disappeared. Of course, it occurs to her, in an institution such as this one, people disappearing may not necessarily be leaving. But what then?

* * * * *

Now whenever they meet they talk, in spurts separated by lucid pauses. Evelyn feels continually on the verge of laughter.

Sophie says, "I wondered how it would be when I talked to you."

She wondered also. Now, closing her eyes, she knows. Sophie says, "I don't want to waste words."

Evelyn smiles. "I don't think you need to worry about that."

"I kept silent. Even though I knew you, right from the beginning. I could see you balanced on the edge. You needed to take your own steps." Then, "Aren't you going to ask me whether I tried to shoot the Governor?"

Evelyn's eyes run over her like a sister's eyes. "You don't look to me like an assassin."

~S~

ALL MORNING William is suffering, navigating some incommunicable horror. Whatever it is must be profound. The spirits won't go near him. *He has fallen through all seven layers of consciousness,* Aroostook tells me, *all seven veils of separation. Don't touch him.* I kneel by William anyway, holding his hand, as he compresses himself into a corner of the floor behind the dayroom sofa, out of sight of the nurses, trying to reduce his vulnerable surface to an area roughly triangular. His eyes are gem stones of terror. He endures all of this in silence.

Then, I don't know what happens, I feel an electricity. A shadow spirals through the air. From deeper in the building, something predatory screams. William's body relaxes. His eyes focus on me and, weakly, he smiles.

* * * * *

Aroostook admits that he and the others are fading, cut off from their principal source of strength, which is the forest. Actually, not the forest so much as what is hidden there:

A sudden, chance twist of air, and a two-hundred-year-old spruce lets go, its branches singing with the wind of the fall, its trunk exploding smaller trees like firecrackers.

One liquid night, a slice of moon succumbs to the black horizon. A porcupine halfway up a hackmatack wails.

Daylight. Something that looks like a mountain lion walks a sun-smeared ledge, where it is believed there are no mountain lions. The morning light warms and brightens. The figure on the ledge has vanished into the shadows of the pines.

Frost settles in, inflating the ground, then leaves, and the ground subsides again, an undulation that over time seems like breathing.

Meanwhile, Aroostook tells me, people burrow deeper into their own private dramas, outside of which they've lost the ability to recognize things. There are worlds of sounds that no one hears, sights that no one sees, goings-on that no one will ever imagine. Beyond the flashlight beam of human attention, lie the origins of spiritual strength. Those aren't his exact words, but they're close enough.

Sometimes I feel misplaced in my human body.

The Question of What to Do

Amidst reports of a strange meeting, Evelyn disposes of her aforementioned husband, and none other than Dr. Roland Rye proposes a solution.

Sophie says, "I read once about the structure of atoms. They're practically all empty space—just a few lonely particles knocking around, sticking together, repelling each other. That's what my life has been like when it comes to friends—a few beebees in a football stadium. It's a wonder we ever find one another."

"I don't know." To Evelyn, this sounds wrong. "For weeks I was doing all the talking. You weren't telling me anything. And still I felt I knew you, as if we had some common origin. As if we *had* to come together."

* * * * *

Just outside the stock room she encounters Walter Rafferty, whose hands are full of rumpled paper towels. His eyes, caught up in some urgency, seem startled by her. He says, "Do you have a minute?" She follows him to his office, a short distance down the corridor.

Inside the office, Walter attends immediately to his desk, on which a dark pool of coffee has spread, soaking into papers, books, manila folders. His Grandpa mug, spattered and empty, sits on the window sill.

She helps him remove things from the desk, blotting them dry with paper towels.

"This is embarrassing," he says.

"I'm assuming it wasn't why you asked me here."

He sponges the last of the coffee and uses the wet paper towel to mop the bare desk-top until it gleams.

She says, "Now your desk looks like John Kilgallen's."

He makes a face.

She glances out the window, where the day is heavily gray and white and still, as if something necessary to the progress of the world might be missing. When her gaze returns to the room, Walter is looking at her.

"You didn't happen to see Jeremy yesterday afternoon," he says.

"No. Why?"

Walter is slow to answer. "I saw him. On his way out of the conference room, just after the Sophie Davenport meeting. He looked like hell. He looked like someone you wouldn't want to get too close to. He went home early, said he had a headache. This morning he called in sick."

She can recall Jeremy, last week, talking about his migraines. She is on the verge of mentioning this when she realizes Walter is leading her somewhere else.

Walter says, "I wanted to talk to him, but I never got the chance. I was curious about that meeting, especially Warren's diagnosis." He adds, "I thought you might be interested. You didn't hear anything, did you?"

"I heard that there *was* a meeting. Period."

Walter nods but is silent, mulling something over.

"I don't know," he says finally.

"You don't know what?"

"I don't know." He shrugs. "You see, I've reached that exalted level of wisdom: I don't even know anymore what it is I don't know."

"Walter, this kind of conversation I can have with my patients. From you, I look for something a little more concrete."

"Alright. It's as if something happened at that meeting. The people who were there ... none of them want to talk about it. Listen, I asked Gary how it went. You want to know what he had to say? After a couple of minutes, staring at the floor, hugging his elbows, he says, 'I don't know, Walter. There are occasions when the theoretical complexion of things appears so tangled as to be irrelevant. One is left, then, with the simple question of what to do.'"

"Come again?"

"Yeah, exactly. Except ... you'd have to have been there. There was something about it. The guy seemed a little dazed, almost disoriented. This was our Chief Psychologist. I tell you, I was touched."

"So what are you saying?"

Walter shakes his head. "Just ask around about that meeting. I'd be interested to hear what kind of response you get."

* * * * *

So she does. She asks John Kilgallen.

John Kilgallen stares at her. He seems a bit flustered. He turns finally and pokes at his coffee machine. She can see him measuring out the non-dairy creamer, pouring himself another mug of decaffeinated coffee. His back is to her when she hears his voice: "You know, the police are coming for her on Monday."

"No," she manages to say, "I didn't know that." She takes a breath. "I suppose I haven't worked here long enough for people to tell me things."

John Kilgallen turns his handsome profile on her and ignores the remark. "We've done all we can here," he says. Gazing at a chart on the wall, he pushes his glasses up into his hair and holds them there, as if he might, by some alien talent, be examining a spot on the ceiling.

"No," she says out loud a minute later, making her way back through the corridor. "We've done all *you* can here."

* * * * *

She has come home early, taken the rest of the afternoon off. And now her anger at John Kilgallen is like a trailing vapor, dispersed along the highway, diffused into the stillness of the house. Each day, it happens to her. While at the hospital, she forgets about Richard's absence, awaiting her here like a new name. Like a space she hasn't yet penetrated.

At the kitchen counter, she is preparing a salad, rereading the note June left her yesterday, when she looks up at the phone and immediately it rings. She removes her plate of casserole from the microwave, sets it and the salad on the table, letting the phone ring four times before picking it up.

It is Richard.

She brings the phone to the table and sits.

"Wow, Ev, I'm glad I caught you." His voice sounds surprised.

"Yes," she says, "I'm home early today."

"Anything wrong?"

"No. I just needed a little quiet time."

"Boy." There is the familiar chuckle. "I could use a little of that myself. It's been unbelievable, unbelievable down here. I feel like I'm caught in a whirlwind."

"That sounds awfully exciting."

"Yeah. The thing of it is, there's good news and there's bad news. The bad news is . . . The Canning Plant is kaput. Dead in the water. Darryl and Wayne have pulled out."

"Oh." Evelyn is pouring wine into her glass. Darryl and Wayne, Darryl and Wayne. "Hey," she says, "guess what I'm doing."

"But . . . the reason *why* they pulled out—that's the good news."

"Richard, guess what I'm doing."

"Huh? Gee, I don't know, what?"

"Sitting in your chair."

For a moment Richard's voice is silent.

Then he says, "Yeah? What chair is that?"

"At the kitchen table. Where you usually sit. I like the view better."

"Yeah? . . . Great. . . ." His voice hesitates. "Anyway, see, the thing is, Ev, the deal has changed. Actually for the better. We've run across an opportunity, over in Salem, that makes the Canning Plant look like a House of Pizza. It was Gina's discovery. And the guys are in, Darryl and Wayne. But we need to move fast. I'm going to have to stay down here for a few days, until things are worked out. It's complicated, we're talking about a four-way partnership. Anyway, I should be back up in about ten days. Two weeks, tops."

"No, Richard?" Her fingers take hold of the stem of her wine glass. "Don't come back."

"What? Hey, Ev , wait . . . ."

"Don't come back, Richard."

"Look, Ev, don't be angry. Things are nuts down here right now."

"I'm not angry. Honest. Just don't come back."

"Ev, just hold it a second."

"What I would do, Richard, if I were you, is get myself a lawyer. Stay there in Boston, buy your restaurant, and get yourself a lawyer. But don't come back."

"It's not a restaurant. It's going to be an emporium. Right smack on the old waterfront."

"It does sound intriguing, Richard. Hey, wait a minute! Now that I think of it, isn't Gina a lawyer?"

* * * * *

The next day she asks, "O.K., what *were* you doing with that gun?"

"My rifle? I was aiming for the cooling line on that timber-harvester they're so proud of. I slipped, though. Missed by a mile."

"Sabotage."

"Call it what you want. Tearing out those pines for a *golf course*."

"Why didn't you just tell them that's what you were up to?"

"Oh, Evelyn Moore." Sophie shakes her head. "These people are not what you think. Really. You cannot tell them the truth. You cannot give them your thoughts, ever. They'll record your words, and they'll turn you into whatever they want. You won't know yourself. The spirits are right: they are without hearts."

"Spirits?"

"Oh." Sophie glances into the corner. "We'd better not get into that."

* * * * *

Some featureless hour. The afternoon seems to stick to them.

"Why are we in this room?" she says. "This mean, dirty little space." She gets up and paces, Sophie watching her.

The head of a passing nurse appears and disappears in the square of the observation window. It is not Esther Boyle, but Evelyn checks her watch. She wonders whether they've talked too long.

"Sophie, we haven't much time."

"For what?"

"Listen, today is Thursday. The police are coming Monday morning. The assessment team will issue its report, which is sure to be adverse. Dr. Griswold, it seems, wants you locked away in his Forensic Ward."

"Of course he does. Just like last time. I think he wants to add me to his collection."

"His what?"

"The others he has up there. The spirits have seen them . . . or not 'seen' exactly."

"What are you talking about?"

"The souls of eight women. Somewhere on the fourth floor. I don't know what he does with them. And I don't want to find out."

Evelyn is speechless. How is she to respond? It seems all the confusion of her days boils down to this: a choice between this dear patient's entirely fantastic truths and this institution's certain-to-be-reasonable lies.

It takes her no time at all to decide. She closes her eyes. "We have to get you away from here." Then opens them. "I know where you could go, but it doesn't do us much good. I'd never be able to get you out of this place."

* * * * *

She stops by to visit William, whose session with her this morning was cancelled. He is resting in his clothes, curled up on his bed, facing the wall, acquainting himself with John Kilgallen's 20 mg of Stelazine. She can't see whether William's eyes are open, so she nudges the door on its squeaky hinge and waits. He doesn't move. She slips from the doorway then, but in the corridor allows her bootheels to sound against the tile, giving her away.

* * * * *

She feels she doesn't have the strength for Roland today, but here he is anyway, going on and on about God-knows-what.

"Oh! Perdition, thy name is Consciousness!" He actually stands, then sits down again. "Ah, what's the point of raising one's voice under such lackluster circumstances?" His hands won't keep still. They wiggle and flick about the arms of his chair, demanding even *his* attention. It has the look of a consultation. He shifts his eyes from one hand to the other, as if conferring, as if receiving reports.

"Here in this . . . this . . . ." He squints at a vibration in one index finger. "The mediocrity of this purgatory could bore a social worker. If it weren't for the feeding tubes, he'd blow the place sky-high. This . . . this . . . finishing school! Whose distinguished faculty, sad to say, subscribe to the Ptolemaic laws of human behavior. And damn this wallpaper!"

She shakes her head.

Hands on the arm of his chair, he raises a finger like a little cannon. "And that!" he says. "Precisely. Is the danger. One is lulled too easily into derision. He is as guilty as the next. The question: can an establishment this ridiculous plausibly be worth worrying about? It is, alas, the Fatal Absurdity. Listen. There is a contest raging here. One that has been joined before. Souls hang in the balance. Yours. . . *mm* . . . and hers."

"Roland, listen . . . ."

"NO! YOU LISTEN! YOU'VE NOT BEEN PAYING ATTENTION! She must not remain here! The very architecture is intent on devouring her."

It isn't his voice that convinces her, but his eyes. She sits back. "All right, Roland, but I don't know what I can do. I can't get her out of here."

Roland leans forward, whispers, "Ah, but *he* can. Remember, his expertise. Yes. He knows a way."

~S~

THE GEOMETRY of this place rains down on us and down on us, simulating a world. Stone and brick and mortar and steel—exactly the materials someone would use who was trying to construct inertia. The place could be a monastery, a fortress, a museum. But it isn't any of these. We who are in here know what it is: a compound administered by the Bureau for the Correction of Errors. They have to keep the mistakes somewhere. Life is confusing enough without a lot of bad examples running around, tangling our wires, short-circuiting things. Creating sparks the size of Volkswagens.

Here in this forever box-shaped geography, the walls are too much like our parents. We sit with our elbows pulled in, contemplating our Jell-O, worrying over the length and complexity of the corridors, wary of churning into one another like so many bugs in a jar. Somewhere removed, the specialists on human defects stand with their arms folded, observing. One scratches an eyebrow. Another purses his lips. Afterward they'll have coffee together. We're stuck in the middle of nowhere, but not them. They can fall back on deliberation and caution. They can fall back on the fact that we're in here to begin with, which must count for something. Whatever mistakes they make won't be enough to land them in where we are.

✳ ✳ ✳ ✳ ✳

Time is a curtain. One can look through it.

The river at the foot of this hill flows slippery and dark. Winds from unexpected directions provoke its thick surface. Particles of gravel dribble from the banks. Boulders seem frozen in a moment of collapse. There would be nothing to hold onto. Everything seems to want to fall, cascade into the river. The heavy liquid doesn't reflect light. The river allows things to slip in, and then keeps them.

Holding my breath, I listen for a sparrow, a cricket, a leaf. All the landscape glints like dull metal. No one, nothing walks there. Still, I feel something has its eye on me. Vapors arise like whispers spiraling from the river. I keep my attention low. There is no such thing as sky.

This is where everything is headed.

I don't ask, where are the people? In a place like this there is only one question. Up here on the hill we all feel the danger of sliding, tumbling into that river. The spirits tell me it is not a dream.

It is time to leave here. Androscoggin says.

A Way

Evelyn learns about spirits and, in the company of the Wild Child, undertakes a daring adventure.

It MAY BE her imagination, but the room seems to have lost something. Perhaps a measure of its dinginess. She could more easily envision spaces beyond these walls.

She and Sophie have been sitting, enjoying the pauses that enter their talk like an infiltration of breeze.

"Sophie, can you tell me about your spirits?"

"Maybe they're not spirits. I don't know what else to call them."

"They speak to you?"

"Sure. Well . . . not exactly. The way it seems is . . . they allow me to hear the way their minds are moving."

"How many of them are there?"

"I know only four, but I have the feeling there are others. I have the feeling, when they're there, I'm holding right onto the edge of another world."

"And you can see them?"

Sophie hesitates.

"Sort of."

"What do they look like?"

The girl takes a breath and stares into the near distance.

"I've thought about it, how to describe them. It's a little like . . . . Think of a forest floor, where pools of water have gathered. And you can see right through these pools to the dead leaves on the bottom, so that from a distance the water's invisible. You can't tell it's there.

"Then imagine water dripping from the trees into the pools. And as each drop hits the surface, silver ripples blossom. The ripples travel outward, interfere with one another, and disappear, making beautiful, mysterious patterns. You're seeing these ripples, not knowing the pools are there, and trying to figure out what they are. You're fascinated, a little frightened.

"Now imagine seeing the same thing in the air in front of your face. In your bedroom at night, staring into the black ceiling. In bright sunlight on a crowded street. Anywhere. The first thing you feel is what you've known all along—that you really are separate from everybody else."

"Is that what you think?"

Sophie's dark eyes fix on her. "And sometimes," she says, "when they're by a window, they leave a breath on the glass."

* * * * *

The hospital seems extra quiet, as if in the aftermath of some bad news. People hold still as statues, or move over the floor tiles at the rate of slow liquids. The nurses' station is empty, except for Ethel, who is bent over the desk there, thumbing through page after page on a clipboard. Walter Rafferty's Office door is closed. Gary Benjamin stands and stands at the soda machine, as though studying the choices. Nowhere can she find eye contact. The pace of things seems intolerable to her. It is as if everything is awaiting the arrival of a cold northwest wind.

* * * * *

The plan is mostly Evelyn's.

Her part in it is simple enough. She is to leave along with the others, making sure that she is seen She is to take the front road out, as always. Then drive to the airport and rent, they agreed, a drab car. One hour later, at six o'clock, she'll return through the service entrance. An immediate left will bring her onto the connecting drive between the service road and the front road. The drive, hardly ever used, runs hidden among the trees and at one point swings close to the hospital, west of the North Wing. Somehow—Roland wouldn't elaborate—Sophie will be waiting for her. "He gives you his most solemn word," he said. "She will be there."

At exactly six, Evelyn is bringing the blue Taurus cautiously along the drive, her eyes alternating between the rearview mirror and the road ahead, when suddenly at the same instant every lighted window in the hospital goes dark. The impact of so much light extinguished at one time is almost audible.

"My God," she says, staring into the blackness beyond the windshield, where the hospital used to be. Her first instinct is to step on the brake. She has had the car stopped for only a few minutes when something appears in her headlights. It is Sophie giant-stepping through the snow, her feet in oversize men's shoes. The snow, only a few inches deep, has lightly crusted over. Her great, crunching steps are sprightly, elfish, blurring Evelyn's initiation into felony with play.

Evelyn turns off her headlights, rolls down the passenger window and calls softly, "Please hurry!"

With Sophie in and the car moving again, Evelyn switches the lights on. "Did anyone see you? How did Roland get you out of there?"

"It was so dark, I couldn't tell. My feet seemed to barely touch the floor."

Evelyn has to smile. "Where did you come up with those shoes?"

"Aren't they something? They're William's. He said he didn't want them back unless I returned them in person."

Within minutes the Taurus has left the deserted front road and turned onto State Street. Sophie flips the glove compartment open, and then closed. "Gee, what a perfectly spotless car!" She presses her palms against the roof upholstery. "Let's drive it off a cliff."

Evelyn glances at her.

"Oh!" Sophie sits on her hands, rocks back and forth. "It feels so good to move again!"

In no time they are on U.S. Rt. 9, what is called "the Airline," heading east. It is the first time Evelyn has driven the road.

* * * * *

She says, "Tell me about your father."

"My father." Sophie stares at the dashboard. "My father." She says nothing more. But a moment later Evelyn hears her voice. "He was six feet tall. He was the only person I knew who could seem both calm and restless at the same time. He could sit in a chair and look at me, and I'd settle right down. As long as his eyes were on me I guess I was satisfied. Otherwise, I know, I was a troublesome kid.

"He wore blue shirts, tie or no tie. Sleeves rolled up. He worked as an architect. I guess he did O.K., but the job took a lot out of him. He said to me once, 'Do you want to know what I do for a living? I design stupid houses for stupid people.' Although that wasn't the only thing in his life that was killing him. I'm not going to say what the other thing was."

Evelyn's eyes are wide open on the headlight-blanched highway rushing at them, shadowy at the edges. On either side, the walls of forest can not quite be seen. She thinks maybe Sophie is finished. Then she hears her voice again.

"The day his car went into the river, the whole world became an echo. Just like that, the life went out of everything. I looked. Inside his closet, there was this collection of blue shirts. No point in them, they were just hanging there like in a museum. I kept looking, everywhere. I had this hunger. Not for food, but for *something*. But there wasn't anything. It was all gone. Then the fear started, eating its way inside. It seemed like a fundamental law of the universe had been revealed. That things were, by nature, heading down. It didn't matter how you struggled. A person could live for a minute or a hundred years, it was all decided. All over before it began."

"What did you do?"

"Not a thing. I couldn't. I think in the end something else took over. Something inside me that wasn't me got up and dragged me along with it. Hitchhiked to the camp and jumped into the lake."

"Window Lake?"

"Yeah, the water was cold. It was night, and when I got into that water everything changed. The lake woke me up. And I knew something I hadn't known before. I knew that lake—this will sound nuts—but I knew that lake was there to take over for my father. I knew that I could ask for no better friend than that cold, absolute water. It wasn't going anywhere. I could feel it pressing in on every inch of my skin, supporting me. I wasn't headed down any more. I was just floating solid there in the night, blinking up at the stars. Like a little planet."

* * * * *

Entering Calais, she tells Sophie, "It would probably be safer for you to scrunch out of sight."

Sophie laughs, ducks down.

At the Irving station she pulls in to use the pay phone. "I'll be right back," she says. "If anyone peeks in, just pretend you're asleep."

Placing the call to Canada seems far worse than it actually is. The Irving is brightly lit. And her entrance interrupts the talk of the handful of people standing there, all of whom have nothing better to do than watch her as she picks out a small bottle of juice, lays a five-dollar bill on the counter, and asks for change. But the girl at the register is pleasant, and the others go right back to talking.

She takes a breath, carefully punches in the numbers, and waits through a sequence of anticipatory clicks and buzzes. It rings five times before someone answers. A woman's voice.

* * * * *

What is their purpose in visiting Canada? What is their destination? How long will they be staying? These are easy questions to answer, if not truthfully. The uniformed Customs and Immigration agent slumps low enough in his booth to catch a glimpse of Sophie peering back at him. Apparently satisfied, he waves them on.

Following the signs, they head out of St. Stephen on Rte. 1, toward St. Andrew and St. George. "Saint, Saint, Saint," Evelyn says.

There are not many cars on the highway. It has been years since she's driven this far at night. The road seems measured in movements of thought rather than miles of pavement. She reflects on the dynamics of opposing night traffic—that for awhile, conscious of approaching headlights, one guides on the centerline. But at a certain point, as the lights come nearer, their brilliance obscures the centerline, and unconsciously one switches to those headlights as the guide. And if one assumes that the other driver is doing the same, then for a giddy instant, the two vehicles are moving oblivious to the road, locked rather on one another, as in a dance.

A while later, in the dark of the car, she feels Sophie suddenly turn and look at her.

"We should stop soon," Evelyn says.

Just outside of St. John, she pulls into a motel and registers. They leave the car, walk down the highway to a truck stop, and buy a bottle of wine and groceries. They stay up half the night talking.

* * * * *

A car pulls up out front. Two doors slam. Footsteps, then a key opening the room next to theirs. Sophie, sipping wine from the bottle, listens intently. "In some ways," she says, "this place isn't that different from the hospital. Except here the staff leaves you alone."

The two of them are sitting barefoot and crosslegged and wrapped in blankets on the motel carpet, the room half-dark, a sheet draped over the table lamp by the bed. Sophie has opened the window, so they still hear an occasional truck on the highway. From time to time, Evelyn's eyes are drawn back to the sight of her empty boots resting beside William's shoes in front of the television cart.

She shakes her head, searching for a voice for what she's thinking.

"This . . . rift between you and your mother," she says finally. "I have to ask you this. It doesn't bother you? The other day, your mother spoke of your intense power to despise a thing. When I asked her what it was you despised, she said she didn't know. She thought it might be her."

Sophie smiles. "Just melodrama." She sets the bottle of wine down. "She said, once, our trouble was we both loved the same man."

"That's no excuse. She and your father should have loved the same daughter."

Sophie's eyes cast about. "I don't know, maybe she tried. We were always out of synch. We'd be, say, together in the car, and all of a sudden she'd ask, 'What makes you say that?' And I'd say, 'What makes me say what?' And she'd swear up and down that I'd just made some remark, about the weather or the price of bluejeans, things I didn't even have in my mind at the time. So I don't know who was crazy. It was like something perverse was warping the time between us. Maybe my comment about the weather was a comment I'd made two years ago, and it had just gotten to her. You know, like a lost postcard."

Sophie's legs uncoil, and she is on her feet. She appears restless.

Evelyn says, "She wasn't quite what I'd expected. Seeing her there under interrogation . . . I almost felt sorry for her."

"Hey," Sophie says, "let's get out of this room, go for a walk."

* * * * *

The next morning, between St. John and Sussex, there is a long silence. The highway keeps to the slope above the Kennebecasis River, running parallel. Somewhere off to their right, a weak sun strains to lift free of the wooded hills. They pass farm after farm.

Evelyn says, "Talk to me." And when Sophie turns instead and watches her, Evelyn says, "We have to keep in touch, you and I."

A few minutes later she hears Sophie's voice. "By the way, I'm pregnant."

The horizon ahead comes into sudden and sharp focus. It feels to Evelyn, at the wheel, as if she has been driving the two of them in some unexpected direction.

"Are you sure?"

"I'm sure."

She scrutinizes a roadsign, the traffic, the median strip, none of which makes any sense.

"William?"

"Yup."

She glances over at Sophie, and Sophie smiles. And then—she can't help it—she feels her own smile, spreading like a form of actual warmth.

"Well. Congratulations."

"Thanks."

"Now I'm *really* glad we got you out of there."

* * * * *

After Hampton, Evelyn is watching the road signs. She feels her blood quickening. "When you were last in the Hospital," she asks suddenly, "do you remember a Dr. Einhorn?"

"Yeah." There is no hesitation.

Evelyn, it seems, can't get to the next question, whatever it is. She turns back to watching the highway. But she can feel Sophie's eyes on her.

Finally Sophie says, "The same thing happened to him that happened to Sun."

"But why?"

"They both found out."

"And Dr. Melton in 1957? And Dr. Spiegel in 1935?"

"I don't know anything about them."

"They died. Did he kill them too? And others before them? Do you understand what I'm saying? Dr. Warren Griswold. Who is this man, that he can prowl this hospital for over sixty years?"

Sophie gives her a look. "He *is* the hospital. You didn't know that?"

* * * * *

They pull into the tiny memorial park on the Kennebecasis River. And there they see the car already waiting, an aging copper-colored compact, rust blending into its paint. She waves to June, who shakes her head, staring and staring at Sophie through the window. Then doors swing open, and it's all confusion.

Sophie, with a quick laugh, bursting from the front seat. June, barely halfway out of her car, overwhelmed to intoxication. Their meeting is like a flood, Sophie nearly knocking her over. June's same long scarf and same brown jacket all tangled and mixing with Sophie's thin flannel, two heads welded together. Then June turns to her and she's drawn in too, the three bodies together in a knot, until she thinks her ribs will break. The smell of Sophie, the smell of June's hair. The sky whirling with the full intensity of it.

June, her hand over her eyes, repeating, "Sophie. Sophie. Sophie." The three of them standing there between the two cars, laughing or crying, who could tell which? Failing to find even the beginning of something to say. And then again, like the return of a tide, they're back in another long, sure embrace. She hears June's whisper, "And this time, I won't let go."

It has not snowed here. The November day feels almost warm. The sun still hangs low above the blue hills, glinting hazily off the hay fields and the barns. The air, as if there were no such thing as winter, is full of the memory of September, August. The river, though, is dark and quiet.

Finally Sophie turns and just looks at her. Evelyn removes her jacket, slips it over Sophie's shoulders. "Hey," June says, "now *you'll* be cold." And gives her the long scarf. They both insist she come along and stay for awhile. But she declines. The fact is she has to be going. Later there will be time to visit. Though she does have a small favor to ask: that they wait until after she goes before driving away. She doesn't want to be left.

    The rest of the morning and all afternoon, the sun is in her eyes as it moves across her windshield from left to right. Perfectly appropriate, it seems to her, that she can't see where she is going. And then she turns off I-95 and is heading again straight into the sun as it sets. Walls of trees bordering the road unravel in her peripheral vision. But her journey isn't finished. Driving west in her dark sunglasses and wrapped in June's scarf, she feels like someone entirely new. She drives through town after town after town, not stopping until Gorham, New Hampshire, where she pulls in at the first motel she sees and registers, recording—for anyone who might care to know—her license plate number. And then, lying flat out on the bed in her room, staring at the stucco ceiling, she feels truly at rest.
    Later, waking, she is drawn to wander out by the perimeter of the parking lot, and then further, along the edge of the road. Down to her right, among the sloping woods, she can hear a stream running. Now and again, as she walks, she burrows her nose into the wild wool of June's scarf, which she has wound around her neck and shoulders and which smells of woodsmoke. She walks until she can no longer see the motel lights, and then she walks even a little further. Until she is wholly alone. Immersed in a darkness alleviated only by the tincture of starlight. And she looks up. The black limbs of massive trees arch high over the road. The highway is old, she guesses, the trees even older, and the stream running at the bottom of the ravine older still. All of these, she feels, are a measure of herself. Her aloneness seems an essential thing, a beginning.

Epilogue

In which Evelyn discovers that there is an afterlife, and the ubiquitous Doctor himself attempts to put things in perspective.

MONDAY MORNING, stepping out of her car, she is startled by something sailing over the roof of the hospital: what looks like the largest bird she has ever seen. But then she looks again and finds that it is actually a flock of tiny birds, sparrows maybe, angling off to the southwest above the pines. For a moment she is caught, frozen by this event, which has drawn her into three-dimensional sky. She is struck by the wisdom these birds possess, knowing their way, their place in the vast and complex geography of things.

And then inside the hospital.

John Kilgallen and Mark Zieglitz stroll side-by-side in the hall, passing while—it seems to her—pretending not to see her. Mark ransacking his pockets as he walks, John attending with a frozen expression. They might be about to trade phone numbers. In some fundamental way, they appear lost.

* * * * *

She and Walter Rafferty, holding paper cups of coke, linger at a table in the canteen, the first time they've seen each other since Friday. Evelyn's tongue works an ice nugget into positions inside her mouth where her teeth try tentative bites.

Walter says, "Gary was all upset, trying to reach you."

"I know. I talked to him this morning. I went to New Hampshire for the weekend."

"New Hampshire."

"That's right." She looks directly into his eyes.

Walter says, "How was it?"

"Liberating."

Walter's face comes close to a grin as, tilting his cup, he inspects the disposition of its ice.

"Is that what you told Gary?"

"No. But I certainly didn't pretend I was sorry."

"How'd he react?"

"The way he generally reacts to things—he looked worried. Though I got the impression he wasn't that sorry either. Just worried."

"Well, it's what he's paid for. God help him. He's got plenty of cause now. It took them till Sunday morning to get the power back on in here. They're lucky more of them didn't run off. Someone like Morgan Fontaine, the guy could have set fire to the place on his way out the front door."

And now behind Walter she spots William, approaching the soda machine in his socks, looking like a man who has awakened from a sleep of several days. Which he is. When he glances her way sheepishly, she smiles.

Walter peers toward the corridor, shifts in his chair. "Have the police talked to you yet?"

"For around an hour. They were very interested in New Hampshire. And why I rented a car."

"Why did you?"

"I wouldn't trust my car for a trip like that."

Walter's eyes flare. His fingers maraud through his hair. "Yeah," he says. "I don't blame you."

* * * * *

Roland Rye is playful again, philosophical, collusive.

"You needn't relate to him all the details. But, tell him, might he one day receive a postcard? Perhaps, from some Caribbean hideaway?"

"Perhaps."

"Hah!" He slaps his knee. "He thought so. He will apply his attention daily to his mailbox. Which, come to mention it, has not been dusted in ages."

"I wouldn't expect one right away."

"Oh. Certainly. Certainly not. He is prepared to be unprepared. Absolutely."

He subsides immediately into calm. When his voice resumes, it is so soft it startles her.

"You know, he dreams of one day, too, cutting himself loose. He dreams of one day, before his timely death, contemplating first-hand the bittersweet mysteries of actual existence."

* * * * *

For the next few days and weeks and beyond, not much is seen of Warren Griswold. He seems to have retreated like a spider back into the dinge of his Forensic Ward, where perhaps even now he waits for a fresh opportunity. Evelyn, stationed in Admissions, resolves to keep an eye on him.

Just now, alone in her office, she looks up to her brand new window, where for the past several minutes a fly has been buzzing against the glass.

"You don't want to go out there," she says. "It's winter."

But it's no use. The fly continues exhausting itself.

She gets up, opens the window, and shoos the poor thing outside. For a moment she stands there, the window open, letting the cold run over her.

Afterward, sitting again, she glances back at the window and sees, quick on the glass, an apparition. A little phantom of steam.

※ ※ ※ ※

"Once upon . . . *mm* . . . a time—back in the days when dreams for him were still possible—he dreamed it was after the end. He opened his eyes, and there he was, still . . . wherever he was. Very much as he is now. After everything else had finished, and before . . . *mm* . . . nothing else was likely to begin. Why? the exhausted observer might be moved to ask.

"He spills his words indiscriminately. It's enough to give his audience an identity crisis. Is it you, his therapist, he's addressing? Or you, the fire extinguisher? Ah, whoever you are, the truth is this. You inhabit a world of shadows, over which is laid a bright and lively picture show. You think you know this picture show quite well. Even as you move among the shadows.

"But let us say. Just for the sake of discussion. Let us say Wisdom were to enter a place such as this. The Goddess one has been on one's knees, praying for. That visitation of Perfect Thunder. Listen! Do you think She might be well received? Do you think they might celebrate Her? Oh no, not here in the House. Not these nincompoops, clutching their tinker-toy souls. No. Here, when She arrives, they want to lock Her into a file drawer. They want to cast Her in irons. Crucify Her!

"Oh! The rest is . . . . well, you know what it is. Indeed. Were he ever to found a religion, which, rest assured, he would not. But just for the sake of idle speculation, were he either to found *or* to find a religion—he is sincere in this—its sacraments would focus attention on regions of darkness within the human mind. Those pitch-black spaces, lying just outside what one imagines one knows, let us say somewhere in the mental cavity. How vast and substantial are those unexplored realms? He has often wondered. More than that. He has . . . *mm* . . . entertained the hope that somewhere within those spaces, which really become one space, God resides.

"Think of it! Bringing oneself face-to-face with the annihilation of all one knows. . . . *mm* . . . Staring at the vapor of one's life with eyes accustomed to the night. It might be enough to nudge one in the direction of insanity. Whatever *that* is."

Mafic
9

WITHDRAWN